Justin now s... ...se eyes were glazed wit... ...of her mouth revealed ...

Bending, Just... ...fallen soda can, then finding a roll of paper towels, he wiped up the spill. Tossing the towels into the trash, he washed his hands at the sink, wiped them dry, and then under Davia's watchful eye, he sat in a chair and got comfortable. He was prepared to be as stubborn as she was.

"So, you're not going to talk to me. Am I being punished because you think that I'm from a different world and that I would be shocked by what you have to tell me? Perhaps I'm more aware of the world than you think I am. After all, I am a full grown man. I know that our lives have been different . . ."

"Very different," Davia corrected, "and I'm not punishing you."

Justin's mouth lifted into a small smile. "It certainly feels like it. You've taken pains to tell me practically nothing about yourself. It's evident that you were a teenage mother and that you've been deeply hurt by a man." Justin rose and walked over to stand before her. "But, Davia, I'm not the man who harmed you. I'm the man who wants to ease your pain. That is, if you'll let me." He reached out to caress her cheek and she didn't move away.

Justin's whispered promises summoned Davia's every need and desire. She was tired of holding onto a past where love was nonexistent. She wanted desperately to throw aside the shackles of distrust which had bound her for so long. Here was a man who was offering her a different reality, one that she had never dreamed could exist for her.

Davia's silence led Justin to wonder if he had blown it. Would she continue to reject his plea or should he remain hopeful? He was persistent.

"I don't know where a relationship between us will lead, Davia, but I'm asking you to give it a chance. I'm crazy about you and all I ask is that you allow us to get to know each other better."

The room vibrated with the silence between them as trust struggled to make its presence known. Then, without a word, Davia started walking toward the door. Hope dimmed for Justin. He had gambled and lost. Steeling himself for her departure, Justin closed his eyes and signed deeply as he listened for her exit. Instead, he heard a click. His eyes flew open. Having locked the door, Davia walked back across the room and stopped in front of him. Taking an uncertain breath, she forced herself to take the boldest step of her life—a step into the future.

SMALL SENSATIONS

CRYSTAL V. RHODES

Genesis Press, Inc.

INDIGO LOVE STORIES

An imprint of Genesis Press, Inc.
Publishing Company

Genesis Press, Inc.
P.O. Box 101
Columbus, MS 39703

Copyright © 2010 Crystal V. Rhodes

ISBN: 13 DIGIT : 978-1-58571-376-9
ISBN: 10 DIGIT : 1-58571-376-7
Manufactured in the United States of America

First Edition

Visit us at www.genesis-press.com
or call at 1-888-Indigo-1-4-0

DEDICATION

This book is dedicated to all of those readers who have helped make this writing journey possible. Thank you.

ACKNOWLEDGMENTS

Here we go again with another thank you to Joni and Eunice. You may think that what you do to help me out is minor, but it's major to me.

Thanks to Sidney Rickman for her editing. Your suggestions were good ones and helped a lot.

PROLOGUE

Luxury automobiles weaving along the deserted streets in this well-appointed neighborhood were not unusual, but there were no witnesses at this early morning hour as one jumped the curb. It narrowly missed a couple of garbage cans as it came to an abrupt stop. The driver's door swung open and Davia Maxwell tumbled from its interior. Sinking to her knees, she knelt in the dew-dampened grass and vomited.

Spent, she rose shakily and turned, intending to get back into the car, but her legs betrayed her as she reached for the door handle. She slowly slid to the ground and leaned against the vehicle. Silent tears streamed down her face.

How had it happened? How had it come to this? She had always feared that her past and present might someday collide, but never had she imagined that it would do so with such deadly consequence.

How old had she been when it all began? Twelve? So long ago, and yet at times it seemed like yesterday.

She and her cousin Phyllis had been living in one of the many seedy hotels that they had occupied over the years. Since she hadn't seen Phyllis for two days, she knew that her cousin must be on a binge. Still, she wished that she were home. That way she would know that she was safe. Phyllis was her only living relative, and if anything happened to her, she would be a child alone in the world.

Finishing the hamburger that she had bought for dinner, she was putting the kettle on the hot plate to heat water for coffee when she heard the key click in the lock. Despite her feelings of relief, she frowned, crossed her arms and waited for her cousin to enter. But the face that greeted her was unfamiliar. It was a man's face—*his* face—long, angular and fixed with a look of surprise.

Explaining his presence, he told her that Phyllis had given him the key and asked him to wait upstairs, that she would be up shortly. With a shrug of her thin shoulders, she had resumed her duties.

She didn't fear him at first. When the water was hot, she made herself a cup of instant coffee; when he requested one, she obliged. Her plan had been to leave the room and retreat to the top of the stairs to her favorite place by the door leading to the roof. There she would draw pictures and wait until Phyllis had completed her business transaction. She was used to the routine. She had done it plenty of times.

As she measured out the coffee and made a second cup, the man sat on the bed looking out the window, seemingly oblivious to her. But there was something about him, something that made her uneasy. She was a child of the streets—a survivor. Every sense she possessed was alert. Cautiously, she handed him the steaming cup, then turned to leave. That was when he made a move to grab her. He was swift, but she proved swifter. She ran to the door, grabbed the doorknob and pulled. It was locked. He grinned triumphantly as he slowly approached. She clawed frantically at the door, fear dominating her action. Suddenly the door opened and Phyllis appeared, catching both man and child off guard. Recovering quickly, the child darted past her, unfazed by the string of profanity that followed her as she scurried down the littered hallway.

Still trembling from the narrow escape, she descended the stairs into the dark, dank basement that offered more security than the daylight above. There she opened the door of an abandoned closet. Long ago she had placed a blanket there for her comfort, and now she arranged it neatly with the fastidiousness of any twelve-year-old. Giving a final nod of approval to the pallet she had created, she shut the closet door firmly. She was safe—for now.

It was a few days later that all sense of security for her proved to be an illusion. She was at her post as usual, keeping an eye out for the cops on behalf of the neighborhood drug dealer. It was winter, and the afternoon chill penetrated the thin jacket that she was wearing. She owned no hat or gloves and the harsh November wind was relentless. She rubbed her hands together to generate heat. Her shift would end at seven o'clock, and today was payday. The money was badly needed. Friday was rent day, food was running low, and she needed to buy a heavy coat.

Jumping up and down, then around in circles, she was so preoccupied with keeping warm that she didn't see her cousin coming. Without a word Phyllis jerked her from her post and dragged her around the corner into the alley so quickly that she didn't have time to resist.

A car was parked at the end of the alleyway. The tinted glass looked ominous. Slowly the back window came down and a face appeared. She was confused at first. Then fear took over as recognition dawned. It was *him*! She was being taken to *him*. She pulled back, her instinct for survival taking control. She fought, but it proved useless. As the struggle ended, she knew that from that moment on this man would haunt her nightmares.

CHAPTER 1

The middle of the work week was always hectic for Davia Maxwell, and this day proved to be no different. The hour-long morning meeting scheduled with her chief financial officer had turned into a three-hour session. It was rapidly approaching noon and all she could think about was getting through the luncheon meeting scheduled with the company's division heads so that she could go home and relax. She was drained.

Returning to her penthouse office, she dropped into the chair behind her oversized redwood desk and kicked off her shoes. With a sigh of relief, she wiggled her toes, enjoying the solitude of the moment. It didn't last long.

There was a short rap on her office door and CeCe—dressed as her alter ego, Charlotte Charmain Green, attorney—swept into the room without an invitation, which wasn't unusual. CeCe was the only person in the building who would have the nerve to enter Davia's office uninvited.

"Hey, girl!" Her greeting was light, familiar and full of her trademark brass and sass.

"Hey!" A tired smile lifted the corners of Davia's mouth. CeCe always made her smile.

The two women had met a dozen years ago at a college coffee shop. At the time Davia was a struggling business student and CeCe a struggling law student. Times were hard for both of them then, but times had changed. They were no longer struggling.

Davia was a successful businesswoman, the founder and owner of Small Sensations, one of the largest manufacturers of children's clothing in the nation, while CeCe headed a thriving law firm, Green & Associates, which specialized in corporate law. Small Sensations was one of the names among her firm's roster of impressive clients. CeCe's law firm was located on the second floor of the Small Sensations building, and, despite their busy schedules, the two friends made it a point to see each other often.

Davia watched as her friend settled in one of the two wingback chairs across from her desk and kicked off her three-inch heels. Barely five feet two in her stocking feet, CeCe regarded the many pairs of heels that she owned as necessities. They gave her the height she needed when doing battle with the "big boys" in court. Cute, pert, a deep dark brown, with soft brown eyes and a dimpled smile, CeCe resembled a miniature doll as she curled her feet beneath her and settled comfortably in the chair. With her petite frame, she looked fragile, but she was as tough as nails when she needed to be. Opponents who had faced her in court could attest to that, yet to her friends she was warm, generous and loyal. She and Davia were as close as sisters.

CeCe smiled back at Davia, noting the tired lines around her eyes. "Are you sure you're going to make it tonight?"

Davia looked at her in confusion. "Tonight? What's happening tonight?"

CeCe looked incredulous. "Our little munchkin's open house at school? How could you forget that?"

Davia wanted to laugh at the look of disbelief on CeCe's face. Her friend took her duties as Gabby's godmother seriously, viewing each event in the child's life as major. As far as CeCe was concerned, Gabby walked on water. The woman had more pictures and videos of the four-year-old's life than Davia had, and that was saying something. They both prided themselves on keeping up with the child's activities. There hadn't been many events in which Gabby participated that either of them had missed. Usually, Davia was on top of each and every activity pertaining to Gabby. Somehow, this one had slipped her mind. She didn't remember seeing anything about it on the school bulletin board or in the many announcements that Gabby brought home. She tried to recall hearing anything about the open house and drew a blank.

"Well? You are going, aren't you?" CeCe prompted.

Mentally, Davia reviewed her schedule for the evening. There was nothing that couldn't be done at a later date. She'd made a promise to herself when Gabby was born that she would always be there for her, no matter what. It was a promise she never planned on breaking. "Yes, of course I'm going."

A smile returned to CeCe's lips. "Okay, then I'll meet you at the school at seven. I can't wait to see our baby's artwork on display. I know it's the best in the class."

Davia laughed. CeCe's kitchen wall was plastered with the colorful "artwork" a proud Gabby had bestowed on her beloved Aunt C. CeCe had even had some of the art framed and hailed the drawings and paintings as the work of a creative genius. She was convinced that Gabby was an undiscovered prodigy and had actively sought an art critic to evaluate the work until Reba, Davia's housekeeper and Gabby's nanny, intervened. She had informed the fanatical godmother that the "artwork" looked suspiciously like the finger paintings of a normal four-year-old to her. Heatedly disagreeing with that assessment, CeCe didn't speak to Reba for a week.

"I'm sure she did well, CeCe. Gabby always does."

She shook her head in agreement. "Yep! That's our girl. She's going to be the best attorney in Atlanta."

"Oh yeah? Before or after she takes over Small Sensations?"

Davia chuckled as CeCe stuck out her tongue. Their plans for Gabby's future were an ongoing issue, with each declaring that she would do better in her particular field. The child was the center of Davia's universe, and was loved with almost as much devotion by CeCe. Gabby Maxwell was strong-willed and independent, just like the two of them. Whatever the child chose to do with her life, it was certain that she would be successful.

"After the open house you ought to take Gabby home and go out with me for a night on the town. I can see that you need to unwind."

"Girl! It is not the weekend. I can't go out and about any day, any time, like you do."

"Weekend, weekday, it's all the same. Letting your hair down for an hour or two won't kill you." Agitated, CeCe glared at her friend. "I swear, Davia, you're worse than some old woman! When we went out last weekend you dragged me off the dance floor as if I were a misbehaving child. If I've told you once, I've told you a thousand times, just because you're a—"

"Don't go there, CeCe." Davia's eyes narrowed, but her friend ignored the threat.

"You are so pathetic. I am sick and tired of trying to help you. I've never heard of anybody who never dates! Girl, you've got to go see a shrink or somebody about this aversion to men. You are young, beautiful, intelligent . . ." CeCe sputtered in frustration. "I . . . I . . . just don't understand it! Men knock down my door trying to get me to talk to you on their behalf, and what do you do . . ."

Davia sat back and watched CeCe, totally unaffected by her tirade. She was used to it. Between CeCe and Reba she was lectured at least a half dozen times a month on their two favorite topics—her overindulgence of Gabby and Davia's constant rejection of men. The former had CeCe and Reba at odds in their opinions, but on the latter subject they both agreed. Davia's self-imposed hermit status was detrimental to her healthy emotions. At least that was the way Reba explained it. Both women were determined to do something about it. Unfortunately, after years of trying neither of them had succeeded.

"The only man you have anything to do with," huffed CeCe, "is old Leroy, and you know good and well that everybody thinks that you're his mistress instead of his boss. You need to deaden that rumor."

Davia's eyes met CeCe's and they broke into a fit of laughter. The speculation about Leroy and her was another private joke between them. The reality was so very different.

Davia had met Leroy Platten eight years ago when her small business was on the verge of becoming a success. He was a friend of CeCe's parents. When he and Davia met, he had recently been dismissed from the manufacturing company for which he had worked twenty-five years. In his early fifties, he suspected age discrimination and was seeking legal advice. Davia had been visiting CeCe that day, and she and Leroy struck up a conversation that eventually resulted in a business arrangement. That day became one of the luckiest ones in her life. Leroy's misfortune became Davia's salvation. Her skill in business and as a designer, coupled with his knowledge of manufacturing, had helped Small Sensations become what it was today.

Leroy served as president of the company. Davia held the title of vice president. Few knew that she was the actual owner of the company because it was he who was thrust into the public eye as the chief executive. It was his life that was scrutinized and examined, which was exactly what Davia wanted. The fact that her life was a closed book was more than likely the reason for the rumors in the corporate community about their relationship. The truth was that Leroy and his wife, Ernestine, had been happily married for over forty years. Theirs was a solid marriage.

Leroy and Ernestine Platten were childless. They were like family to Davia and surrogate grandparents to Gabby. Often the three adults would have a good laugh at the persistent rumor, just like she and CeCe.

Recovering from their laughter, CeCe sobered. "No, really, Davia, you need to give yourself a break. You need to date. I was talking to Kevin Tyler the other day and . . ."

"I've got to go. I've got a meeting." Rising from her chair, Davia slipped into her shoes. She knew where this conversation was leading and she didn't want to go there. Her friend had been trying to play matchmaker for years. Davia hadn't been interested in her efforts in the past, and she still wasn't interested.

CeCe pressed on. "Okay. I'll give up on Kevin, but I'm not giving up on you and you know it."

"How well I do." Davia groaned. "When you're on one of your crusades, you're relentless."

"You got that right." CeCe sighed in frustration. "And you know that I am not one of those dizzy females who believes that a woman can't be happy without a man. We've talked about this before, and I've said a thousand times that there's nothing wrong with men and women enjoying each other's company. If you would give men a chance you might learn to welcome their perspective, treasure their advice and respect their point of view. I want my best friend to enjoy that experience."

CeCe's words seemed to fall on deaf ears as Davia continued to get ready for her next meeting. Under other circumstances and with someone else, CeCe would have been insulted, but this scene was all too familiar.

In all the years that she had known her, Davia had never expressed much interest in men. CeCe was fairly certain that Davia's aversion to the opposite sex was related to her past experience with her daughter's father. As close as she was to Davia, she was still in the dark as to the name of the child's father. CeCe had brought it up only once. Davia had made it clear that this was an area of her life that was a closed subject. CeCe had never brought it up again.

Right now CeCe was getting the message that she was being dismissed. With a disgusted sigh she slipped from her chair and into her shoes.

"You're hopeless." She rolled her eyes to emphasize her point.

Davia scoffed at CeCe's dramatics. "I thought you said you weren't going to give up on me."

Her friend sniffed. "Later for you, Davia. I'm outta here." She slammed the office door behind her to the sound of her friend's laughter and a pleasant, "See you tonight."

Davia had gathered her things and was heading out of the office when the ring of the telephone stopped her. The call was on her private line, which meant that it was either from home or from Gabby's school. She picked up on the second ring.

"Davia Maxwell speaking."

"Ms. Maxwell, this is Mrs. Alexander, the director of Playful Tots Preschool."

The director? David's heartbeat quickened. "Yes? Is something wrong?"

Mrs. Alexander gave a heavy sigh. "Well, Ms. Maxwell, I'm afraid there's a little problem with Gabrielle."

CHAPTER 2

As Davia stood looking out her second-story bedroom window at the dark blue Mercedes sedan parking in front of her house, she got angry all over again. She was sure that the car belonged to the man she had spoken to about an hour ago. What a jerk! He had been arrogant and defensive when she said what she had to say about his niece Bianca Thomas, and she didn't care whether he liked it or not. She wasn't one to be intimidated. After all, it wasn't her Gabby who had bitten his niece, but vice versa.

The call from the preschool informing her that Gabby had been bitten had prompted Davia to leave her office immediately and hurry to the school. There she found her four-year-old in tears, with bite marks marring her smooth chocolate brown arm. Davia had been outraged, and after expressing those sentiments to Mrs. Alexander, she demanded that her name and number be given to the parents of the bully who had attacked her baby. She wanted to hear from them immediately regarding this incident. Then she had hustled Gabby off to Dr. Goodall, the child's pediatrician, where Gabby had received a tetanus shot to prevent infection, a Mickey Mouse Band-Aid to cover the bite marks, and a sucker to stop the tears. Gabby left the doctor's office happily licking what for her was a rare treat.

Now, settled in her room playing with her dolls, Gabby had all but forgotten the incident, but Davia hadn't. When the uncle called, she had demanded that she speak to the little girl's parents. He had explained to her that Bianca's mother was out of town and that he was acting as surrogate parent. He had suggested that he bring Bianca to Davia's house so that all accusations about the biting incident could be resolved.

Davia hadn't liked the way he'd said "so that all accusations about this biting incident can be resolved." There was an unspoken implication that all wasn't as it seemed. Yet the evidence was clear. Gabby was the innocent victim here and an apology was expected, as well as a check for the doctor's bill. And there should be no question that his niece would be reprimanded in some way. Yes, indeed, the "biting incident" would be resolved, *today!*

As Justin Miles stood on the front porch of the Maxwell house waiting for a response to the doorbell, he tried to remain calm. He was a man on a mission. This woman had accused *his* niece of biting her child, and he wasn't having it.

Justin's gray-green eyes glanced down at the four-year-old standing beside him, her tiny hand holding his so trustingly. He could feel the anger he had been repressing resurface as she looked up at him. She looked so much like his sister, Vanessa, who was eight years his junior. He had adored his baby sister from the moment she was born, and her daughter, Bianca, was no less adored. Her pretty face was honey brown and her eyes the same soft brown as Vanessa's. Her auburn hair held the same mass of waves and curls, and her smile was just as engaging. Bianca was his heart. There was no way in hell that some crazy woman was going to put the rap for this on his girl. He pinched her soft cheek and gave her a confident wink.

Who was this woman anyway? She had to be some busybody with nothing else to do but pick on little kids. He rang the doorbell once more and then turned to survey the neighborhood.

The Maxwell house was a two-story, red brick contemporary structure. A white wraparound porch to the left of the etched glass front door was draped in a canopy of red and yellow roses. Colorful flowers of every assortment were intermingled with well-trimmed shrubbery in the large front yard and lined the delicate curve of the winding walkway leading from the porch to the sidewalk. The house fit well into this neighborhood of costly, custom-built homes.

The subdivision in which the house was located was known as Ashland Heights, an enclave of upwardly mobile professionals, or, as his mother snobbishly referred to them, the "nouveau rich wannabe crowd." BMW, Lexus and Mercedes Benz were the cars to own in this neighborhood, where lawns were professionally landscaped and gardeners were hired to tend to them. This Mrs. Maxwell was probably an older woman with way too much time on her hands. Well, he was a busy man, and the sooner this nonsense was settled, the better.

With renewed determination he was about to ring the doorbell again when a feminine voice on the other side of the door inquired, "Who is it?"

Justin recognized the voice as the same one he had heard earlier on the telephone. "It's Justin Miles, Mrs. Maxwell, Bianca's uncle. You were expecting me."

He could hear the locks on the door being disengaged—there were at least two of them—and then the front door slowly opened.

Justin blinked once, twice, then blinked again. This couldn't be who he had been talking to over the telephone. She didn't look anything like what he imagined. The woman standing before him had a flawless complexion the color of burnt almonds. Her dark eyes were luminous. Her eyelashes were long, thick and luxurious. Her eyebrows were perfectly arched. High, sharp cheekbones gave her oval face an exotic appearance, and her lips spoke of the drums of Africa. They were large, pouty and perfect. The jet-black hair that framed her oval-shaped face was cut close to her head in sculptured waves of velvet. Dainty gold hoop earrings dangled from her ears. She stood about five feet, five inches to his six feet, three inches, and every inch of her was stacked. If this was the caustic Mrs. Maxwell, she was beautiful, and every hormone in Justin's body was acutely aware of it. His mouth went dry as he tried to speak.

"Oh, hi." The sound was more like a croak than a greeting. He gave it another try.

"Uh, I . . . I . . ." What was wrong with him? He was stammering like an idiot! Justin swallowed, took a breath and tried again. "I'm Justin Miles, I called earlier. Are you Mrs. Maxwell?"

There, he'd finally got the words out. He had to remember he was here for Bianca no matter what this woman looked like. Reeling in his spiraling hormones, he regained his self-control.

"I'm *Ms.* Maxwell."

She stood patiently, arms folded under her breasts. Her stance was assertive, as if she was ready and waiting to lock horns. Okay, he was ready, too. He hadn't come here to play games and he didn't care how pretty she was, he was going to take care of business and she wasn't going to distract him.

Justin looked down into the face of his little niece, who looked from one adult to the other, trying to make sense of what was happening. He squeezed her hand, reassuring her that everything was all right.

Not knowing what else to do to recover from this debacle, Justin gently nudged his little one forward. "This is Bianca, Mrs. Maxwell, my niece."

A smile tugged at those pouty lips that had Justin in a daze and Davia bent down to the child's level and stuck out her hand.

"Hello, Bianca. I've seen you at the school. It's very nice meeting you."

Bianca shook Davia's hand and answered with a shy hello. Davia rose and turned her attention back to Justin.

"And as I said, the name is *Ms.* Maxwell, not Mrs."
Each syllable was pronounced slowly and distinctly, as if
he were incapable of comprehending.

The warm feelings he held toward this woman a
second ago instantly vanished. Justin raised a brow. Oh,
so it was like that, was it? The lady wanted to show a little
attitude. All right, he could deal with that. "Well, Ms.
Maxwell about this biting incident that occurred at the
preschool today—"

"Davia, who was at the door?"

A female voice came from inside the house and Justin
glanced over the woman's shoulder in the doorway to see
another attractive woman in her late forties or early fifties
approaching the door. Bouncing down the stairway was a
chocolate brown child, about Bianca's age. Her hair was
braided in cornrows and she wore round, wire-framed
glasses. The woman reached the doorway first and stared
up at him curiously.

Justin gave her his most ingratiating smile. "Hello,
I'm Justin Miles . . ."

"Bianca!"

The delightful squeal of the little girl who had
squeezed her small body between the two women in the
doorway interrupted his introduction. He looked down
to see the girl greeting his niece like a long-lost relative.
Obviously, this child wasn't the little psychopath who
had accused his Bianca of biting her.

"Gabby!" Bianca's childish voice rang out in equal
excitement, quickly squashing that theory.

"Did you come over to play with me?" Gabby gushed, excited by the prospect.

Bianca nodded her head vigorously. "Uh-huh."

Needing no further prompting, Gabby tried to pull Bianca past the front door and into the house. Justin resisted the effort, tightening his hold on Bianca's hand. Both children looked up at him as if he were the enemy.

The older woman broke the mounting tension and extended her hand. "I'm Reba Fray, housekeeper, nanny, jack of all trades."

"I'm Justin Miles." He shook her hand firmly, slightly unnerved by the fact that she was looking at him as if he were this evening's dessert. Her eyes slowly raked over his body, taking careful note of the wide shoulders draped in a tailored sports coat. She noted the knit shirt that was molded to the lines of his broad chest and the finely creased jeans that fit his narrow waist and hips. Her eyes returned to his face, obviously pleased with what she saw.

Justin cleared his throat, ignoring her perusal as his attention turned back to his hostess. "Uh, Ms. Maxwell, I'm—"

"Come in, Mr. Miles," Davia interrupted him, somewhat unnerved by the startling gray-green eyes set in his cinnamon brown face.

"Yes, *do* come in," Reba said suggestively as they both stepped aside to let him enter.

Reba's manner was too flirtatious for Davia, and she gave her a warning look, which her employee pointedly ignored. The woman had no shame. It had taken all of Davia's willpower not to elbow the brazen flirt. She was openly devouring the man. Reba might not care if some child took a bite out of Gabby, but she did, and this was the culprit's uncle. This was no time to fraternize with the enemy. Silently, she led the man and his niece through the house to the family room.

As they walked across the buffed parquet flooring of the foyer, Justin noted that Mrs. Fray turned to the left and, tossing a parting smile his way, disappeared into what was likely her bedroom. Meanwhile, Justin and Bianca continued behind Gabby and Ms. Maxwell. Every step he took tested the strength of his willpower as he tried to ignore the gentle sway of the lady's curvaceous hips.

She was dressed in yellow knit leggings and a matching sweater. The outfit was becoming, but not provocative, yet it was difficult to camouflage her body's firm, rounded curves, which called to him with every movement. Justin inhaled. What he was thinking in regard to *Ms.* Maxwell was less than gentlemanly. He had to remember that he was here on serious business. Now, if he concentrated real hard, he might be able to keep his eyes from straying.

He turned his attention to his surroundings. As they walked through the foyer toward the back of the house, he noted a large dining area to the right of the entranceway. A glass table dominated the room, surrounded by numerous dining chairs upholstered in pale yellow silk. Past the stairway—which Gabby and Bianca tried to take before the two adults stopped them—the quartet stepped down into a breathtaking family room with a cathedral ceiling that extended to the second floor.

Light streamed into the room from skylights above. A stained glass rose was etched into each skylight. A set of French doors looked out onto a patio and beyond to a garden filled with an array of flowers.

The room they were in was decorated in shades of mint green, accented with yellow. Justin took a seat on a floral love seat as directed and wondered if Ms. Maxwell had done the decorating. It appeared to have been done with a careful eye for detail. It made him wonder if she put such care into everything that she did. Realizing that his thoughts were drifting back to the delectable Ms. Maxwell, he forced himself to remember his goal—clearing his niece's name.

Davia watched with interest as Justin squared his shoulders. She read the move as an indication of his resolve to defend his niece's actions. She chose to ignore the look of male interest in his eyes. If he thought that charm would sway her from getting justice for Gabby, he was sadly mistaken. It was true that Mr. Justin Miles, with his wavy brown hair, gray-green eyes and neatly trimmed goatee was a handsome man. But good-looking men were a dime a dozen. She knew what they wanted. Mr. Miles didn't stir her interest at all.

Davia sat on the love seat opposite Justin and restrained Gabby, who wanted to join Bianca, who sat next to her uncle. As the four of them faced each other, it was clear that the adults had drawn an invisible battle line.

"May I offer you and Bianca something to drink, Mr. Miles?" Davia's manner was formal. She was determined to be civil.

"No, thank you." Justin was just as formal. "I think that we should get to the matter at hand."

"You mean Bianca biting Gabby."

"I mean Gabby accusing Bianca of biting her."

Davia's eyebrows shot up. "Oh, is she denying it?"

Justin's eyebrows knitted together. "Most certainly."

Davia's face hardened. "Then it looks as if you have two problems on your hands."

Justin's nostrils flared. "No, I don't think so."

Davia snorted. "Then I guess that you're suggesting that Gabby bit herself, *twice.*"

Justin grunted. "You said it, I didn't."

All attempts at civility were rapidly disappearing. Davia's jaws tightened.

"I assure you, Mr. Miles, that although you might have had the experience with your niece, my Gabby is not in the habit of self-mutilation."

Justin's eye's flashed. "And I assure you, Ms. Maxwell, that my niece has not acquired that habit either, nor has she taken up the habit of cannibalism."

The two adults stared at each other with mounting hostility, while the two confused children looked from one adult to the other in growing alarm. Wanting to escape the escalating tension, Gabby broke the momentary silence.

"You want to go to my room and play, Bianca? We don't have to play vampires this time. We can play with my dolls."

Bianca's hopeful "okay" came a split second before Gabby's words became apparent to both Davia and Justin.

"Vampires?"

The girls jumped, startled at the simultaneous reactions. The wide-eyed looks of both girls as they glanced first at each other then back at the adults made it clear. There was much more to the story of the teeth marks on Gabby's arm than met the eye.

CHAPTER 3

Davia watched Justin Miles and his niece drive away from her house, then closed the front door behind them. How in the world did she get herself into these situations? She'd had to eat crow after the girls' revelation, and it didn't taste good at all, but thank goodness she didn't have to eat it alone. Mr. Justin Miles had his mouth full of crow as well.

With a disgusted sigh, she pulled herself away from the door and watched as a contrite Gabby made an attempt to scurry up the stairs before she could be stopped. She didn't quite make it.

"Gabrielle!"

Davia's tone of censure halted her in midstride. It also brought Reba out of her room, but Gabby was the last thing on her mind.

"Girl! Was that not a *hunk* of man?"

Davia ignored her. Reba's hormones were always raging, but she didn't have time to address them at the moment. "Gabrielle Stephanie Maxwell, come here right now!"

"Uh-oh." Reba glanced at the child dragging reluctantly toward the stern-faced adult. Gabby knew that being addressed by her whole name by either one of the two women before her meant big trouble.

The child walked as if she were approaching the gallows. With each step, the quivering lips became more pronounced. By the time she stood in front of Davia, she was ready to erupt into full-blown crying. She hung her head and threw in a loud sniff to evoke as much sympathy as possible. It didn't work. Davia lifted Gabby's chin, urging the little girl to look at her.

"Do you want to explain why you didn't tell me the truth?"

Reba gasped. "You mean she lied to you about the girl biting her?"

Gabby dropped her eyes, unable to look at either adult. Usually she could find an ally in Ms. Reba, but not today. She had lied. Or at least, she hadn't told the whole truth. The three of them had made a pinkie promise that in this household they would always tell each other the truth. A tear of shame slid down her round cheek.

"Do you want to tell Ms. Reba how you got those bite marks?" Davia's voice was firm.

Gabby shook her head. "No, Grommy," she answered, using the nickname that she had been calling Davia since the little girl learned to talk.

"Why not?"

Gabby sniffed and the trickle of tears became a flow. "Because I didn't tell the whole truth, and I don't want Ms. Reba to know that I broke our promise to each other."

"So you know that you were wrong in letting Grommy believe that Bianca was the only one who bit you."

"Uh-huh."

"And what do you have to say to me, and to Ms. Reba? She's upset about this, too."

"I'm sorry."

The dam burst as Gabby began to sob, throwing her arms around Davia's legs in total submission. Davia fought the urge to pick her up and cuddle her. She hated to see Gabby cry, but she couldn't give in this time. Stressing the value of honesty was much too important. Truth was paramount in any relationship, and it was a lesson that Gabby must learn.

Bending down to the child's level, she kissed her tear-stained cheek. "I accept your apology, baby, and you know I'll always love you, but I want you to go up to your room and think about what you did. I'll tell you when you can come out."

With a nod Gabby retreated to her room, still crying, while Reba followed Davia through the house into the family room.

"Okay, are you going to tell me what happened, or am I supposed to guess?"

With a sigh that indicated her distress, Davia recounted the story that the two little girls had revealed. At its end Reba sat on the love seat doubled over with laughter, which was not the reaction Davia wanted.

"You mean to tell me that the kid bit herself trying to draw blood, and then let Bianca bite her, too?" Reba could hardly get the last words out before breaking into another fit of laughter.

Davia was indignant. "I don't see what's so funny. Gabby lied about what happened. You know how I feel about liars!"

Composing herself, Reba wiped tears of mirth from her eyes. "Oh, give it a break, girl, you're trying to judge a child's reasoning with adult logic. It all makes sense to the kids. They wanted to play vampires and a vampire's bite draws blood. When Gabby couldn't draw blood with her bite, Bianca stepped in to help her out. Like the kids said, vampires don't bite themselves to draw blood, they bite others." Reba giggled. "Shoot, it makes sense to me. Anyway, the kid didn't tell you a lie. You asked Gabby who bit her and she said Bianca. She just didn't tell you that she told her to do it. It was you, the teacher, and the school's director who jumped to conclusions."

Although Davia knew that what Reba said was true, she still wanted to be annoyed at the whole situation. "I don't care, Gabby could have explained it before all of this mess happened."

Reba sat up, more alert to what wasn't being said than to what had just been said.

"What are you talking about? What mess?"

Davia's voice went up a notch in annoyance. "This mess! This . . . this . . . man coming out here . . ."

"Man? You mean Mr. Miles? That man?" Reba laughed devilishly.

Davia's agitation increased. "Yes, who else would I be talking about? He comes over here accusing my baby of gnawing on herself, and I'm defending her, thinking his niece is one step above a cannibal, and what happens?

Two four-year-olds make fools out of both of us. Anyway, what do two little girls know about vampires and Dracula and all of that . . ."

Reba sat watching the woman pacing in front of her rant about the events of the day. She'd known Davia for three years and she constantly marveled at this beautiful, poised, self-assured woman. The mountains that she had climbed would have stopped a weaker person, but she had scaled every one of them and survived. Davia Maxwell was the most determined person she had ever met. Nothing stood in her way and few things rattled her, but this man's presence today seemed to have shattered that calm. It was true that she was a fanatic when it came to Gabby, but to go on like this over a little misunderstanding? No, that wasn't Davia. There was definitely something else going on here.

"I felt like an idiot." Davia finished her tirade and flopped onto the love seat opposite Reba. "I really ought to punish her for not telling the truth. Don't you think?"

She looked at Reba expectantly, waiting for her reply. She valued Reba's opinion. Since this woman had answered her ad for a housekeeper, she had become much more than just someone to help keep the house clean and take care of Gabby. She had become a friend. Of course, she wasn't your average household employee. Not many housekeepers were pursuing a doctoral degree at Emory University. Reba was, but she was in need of a job when she showed up for an interview and Davia had been in need of assistance. The two women had clicked. Hiring her had been one of the best decisions that Davia had ever made. Now sitting across from her, waiting for her sage advice about Gabby, she was taken aback by the sudden light that appeared in the woman's eyes. It didn't quite match the seriousness of the moment.

"Uh-uh! So that's it!" Reba grinned like a cat that had trapped a canary.

"That's what?"

"Justin Miles is tugging at your drawers!"

"What?" Davia looked at her, dumbfounded. "How in the world did you get that out of me talking about Gabby fibbing?"

"I think that he liked what he saw, too."

Scooting to the edge of the love seat, Davia waved her hand in front of Reba's face. "Hello! Reba! Is anybody home? I was talking about Gabby telling a fib."

"I wonder if he's married. He wasn't wearing a ring, because you know I checked that out."

Married? Ring? Now she was going too far. "Earth to Reba. Earth to Reba. Can we get back on the subject at hand?"

Reba added a wink to her grin. "Honey, I was talking about the subject—Mr. Justin Miles and his marital status."

"Have you lost your mind?" Davia threw her hands up in frustration. "What has Justin Miles got to do with what I'm trying to talk to you about? I'm concerned about Gabby's fibbing, and how she found out about vampires and . . ."

Reba waved her hand dismissively. "Oh, forget that. You're making a mountain out of a molehill. Let's get to the important stuff, you and that man."

"There is no me and that man. He came over here to talk about . . ."

"Yeah, yeah. Girl, we've got to see how we can get you two together."

Davia decided that the realm of reality had vanished altogether in this conversation. Further discussion was impossible. The woman had lost her mind.

Reba Fray was a man magnet, attracting not only men her own age, but men years younger than she, and she took all applicants. During her years working in Davia's home, Reba had commented to her more than once that she was determined to find her employer a man. Just as she did with CeCe, Davia usually ignored Reba's attempts to play matchmaker, and today would be no different. It had been a long day, and she was too tired for this foolishness.

Without fanfare, Davia got up and headed to her second-floor office. "I'm going upstairs. Call me when you're back in your right mind."

Reba watched as she walked away in retreat. She called after her, "You can't hide behind that wall forever, Davia."

The words had their effect. Davia spun around to face her. "What wall?"

The smile on Reba's face faded to be replaced by a serious look and tone. "The one that you keep your emotions hidden behind. Oh, I'm not talking about your feelings as far as Gabby is concerned. You love that child to death, and you can't be any more devoted to your friends, but when it comes to members of the opposite sex, the wall is erected and the defenses go up. As long as I've known you, you've had absolutely nothing to do with men unless it's associated with business."

Davia wasn't going to deny it. "So?"

"So you're straight, and men are crazy about you. Taking that into consideration, I've always known that there's something else going on, and one day you're going to have to face whatever it is. You can't hide forever."

Enough was enough. Friend or no friend, Reba was stepping out of bounds, *again.* "Listen, I don't have time for this . . ."

"Of course, you never have time. You're too busy running."

"That's enough." Davia's tone had caused grown men to cringe, but the woman standing before her didn't. It was moments like this that made Davia regret having allowed the employer-employee relationship between them to get so far off course. Reba was getting her doctorate in psychology and Davia had no doubt that she was her major case study.

Reba continued. "There's no denying that Gabby and Small Sensations are the biggest miracles in your life, and if they're enough for you, then so be it. But if there are other miracles to be experienced, let them happen." This time it was Reba who got up to leave the room. "I'm going to start dinner."

Davia stormed up the stairway toward her office, mad enough to spit nails. How dare Reba Fray think that she knew her so well? What she didn't know about her could fill an ocean. Davia plopped into the soft leather swivel chair behind her desk, a replica of the one in her company office. Two of the walls in her home office were redwood, as well as the bookcases that lined a third wall. She had fallen in love with the large redwood trees on a business trip to California, and now her home office and the one at Small Sensations were both decorated with the beautiful wood. She felt at peace in both places, just as she had among those trees, but Reba's meddling had upset her sense of well-being. Switching on the computer, Davia tried to dismiss Reba's latest attempt to psychoanalyze her, but she found it difficult.

With angry strokes, Davia's fingers flew across the computer keyboard. *Put Pride in Your Child's Stride.* The words jumped out at her in a tableau of red, black and green letters as she checked the company's website. Putting pride in her own stride, that was what her sacrifices had been about. By sheer will she had turned Small Sensations into the largest manufacturer of Afrocentric clothes for children in the nation. At age thirty-four, she was the founder and the owner of a multi-million-dollar company. A sense of pride at that accomplishment coursed through her body every time she saw her company's name blazoned across the website, or on billboards, in magazine ads, or on the company's five-story building on Peachtree Street—a building that she owned. Small Sensations was a miracle. Yet, no one would ever know the price that she had paid for its existence.

Davia blinked back the tears that she was determined not to shed. Everything that she had sacrificed to build her company had been done with her child in mind. The company was to be her child's legacy, but—

It was better not to dwell on the past. It was the present and the future that mattered and it was time to attend to them both. Hitting a few more keystrokes, she watched as the company's latest sales figures appeared on screen. They were sensational. Davia smiled. The legacy was alive and well. The future looked bright.

Reba had been right about one thing. Gabby and Small Sensations were all that existed in her life. They were her life, and she was happy. She didn't need anything or anyone else, especially a gray-green-eyed man with an attitude.

The telephone rang. Absently, she picked up the receiver.

"Hello."

"Hello, Ms. Maxwell."

The voice on the other end was deep, masculine and familiar. Davia recognized it immediately. "Yes, Mr. Miles? Did you forget something?"

There was a slight hesitation at the crisp, business-like tone in Davia's voice. "Well, no, I didn't. I was just thinking that it's too bad that we've had this little misunderstanding and I'm glad that things have been settled amicably."

There was a pause as he waited for a response. When there was none, he proceeded. "I just want to say how much I enjoyed meeting you and your daughter, and I was hoping that . . ."

"It was a pleasure meeting you also, Mr. Miles, and your niece. But I'm afraid that you're mistaken about Gabby."

"Mistaken? Uh, I don't understand."

"Gabby isn't my daughter," Davia informed him. "She's my granddaughter. "

Hanging up the receiver, she let the dial tone sever the connection.

CHAPTER 4

Justin was stunned. The delectable *Ms.* Maxwell was a grandmother! She had to be kidding! At least that's what he tried telling himself after hearing her startling revelation. He had been glad to hear the dial tone after she told him because he had been at a total loss for words.

He had called her from his car phone after pulling up to an ice cream parlor where he stopped to treat Bianca to a cone. Not one to waste time, he had made the decision to ask the lady out shortly after leaving her house. He didn't know whether she was interested in him or not, but he was definitely interested in Ms. Maxwell. Her revelation didn't dim his interest; it only served to increase his curiosity about her.

How had she become a grandmother so young? She couldn't be a day over thirty-five and looked younger. What had happened to Ms. Maxwell? She wasn't wearing a wedding ring, so he assumed that she wasn't married. Where was the man involved in this? Where was Gabby's mother? The questions seemed endless, and the only one who could answer them was Ms. Maxwell herself. Perhaps the lady thought that by informing him of her grandmother status that his interest in her might lessen. Well, she was wrong. It might have thrown him off balance for a bit, but now he was back on track.

While Bianca sat beside him happily licking her treat, Justin thought about what his strategy might be in getting to know Ms. Maxwell. She had made it clear when he first spoke to her that she didn't know his sister, yet he couldn't rule Vanessa out as a source of information. Justin and Vanessa were the children of Katherine Miles. That alone meant that if one was African-American, lived in Atlanta and had any significant position of status, Katherine knew something about you. If their mother knew anything about Ms. Maxwell, she might have shared it with Vanessa. The only challenge was that if he mentioned the lady's name to Vanessa, she might alert their mother. Justin didn't want his mother knowing his business.

He knew that a grandmother of any age would not meet his mother's rigidly high standards for anyone dating her son, but what she thought about the women he dated had long ago ceased to be important to him. He was his own man, and he found Ms. Maxwell totally intriguing. She was a beauty, there was no doubt about that, and her story spurred his interest. His attraction to her had been instantaneous and he wanted to get to know her. *That* he was certain about.

As her son planted a kiss on her upturned cheek, Katherine Miles broke into a smile that softened her café au lait face. At age sixty, she was a beautiful woman, her face unlined by age. Her light auburn hair was streaked with gray, and the gray-green eyes she had passed on to her son were acutely alert. The stylish cut in which she wore her hair was youthful, and complemented her heart-shaped face. She wore little makeup. She had never needed it. She had always been a natural beauty. Katherine considered her features as being "all American." Her nose was small, sharp, and her lips were thin, attributes that she felt enhanced her attractiveness. She was fiercely proud of her white ancestry. The fact that it was the result of her great-great-grandmother, a slave, having been raped by her owner's son was ignored. Over the years her family had modified that incident to her having been *enticed*.

Before marrying the late Frederick Zachary Miles, the only son of one of Atlanta's most prosperous black physicians, Katherine Justin had been actively pursued by the most eligible bachelors in Atlanta. Katherine's parents had spared no expense on their only child. She got whatever she wanted and went about getting her way in any fashion that she deemed necessary. Over the years Katherine had become known as the "Queen of Black Atlanta Society." She even reigned over a small kingdom.

Shortly after Justin was born, Zachary Miles had purchased one hundred acres of land a few miles outside of Atlanta's downtown perimeter. After building a twenty-room showplace on the land for his family, he surrounded part of the lush acreage with a gate of stone and a higher wrought iron fence, then sold the remaining acreage in tracts to forty-nine of his wealthy friends. The result was Zachary Acres, an exclusive compound for many of the movers and shakers in Atlanta. This was Katherine's kingdom, and she ruled it with grace, finesse and a will of iron.

She now sat in her favorite wingback chair amid the luxury of her exquisite living room smiling up at her son. Justin returned her smile.

"Hello, Mother."

"Hello, yourself, mister. What took you so long getting this little one home from school?" She hugged her granddaughter to her as Bianca planted a kiss on her cheek.

The child's eyes met her uncle's silently. They had agreed not to divulge to Katherine the reason for their diversion to the Maxwell home. Vanessa should be the first person informed of today's events. If she wished to share the information with their mother, that would be her choice.

Justin was noncommittal. "Oh, we've been here and there."

"Buying ice cream, I see." Katherine gently wiped a dab of ice cream from the corner of Bianca's mouth. "And before dinner, too."

Justin grinned guiltily as he took a seat in the chair next to his mother. Katherine sent Bianca upstairs to get ready for the evening meal. They watched her lovingly as she scampered away.

"You spoil that child rotten," Katherine admonished, knowing that she was guilty of the same offense.

Justin didn't deny it. "That's what doting uncles are for."

Katherine sat back in her chair and gave a heavy sigh. This was the sign that criticism was coming. Justin braced himself for the forthcoming comment about either Vanessa or himself. Her children were the love of Katherine's life, but the direction he had taken, and that Vanessa seemed to be taking, did not meet with their mother's approval. So Katherine never missed an opportunity to let them know about it, and since Vanessa was absent, it was safe to assume that the censure would probably be aimed at her. He was correct.

"You're right, son, doting uncles are supposed to spoil their nieces and a doting grandmother's job is to spoil her grandchildren. That's why I can't for the life of me understand why Vanessa won't let me pay for Bianca to attend the Prescott school. It's the finest school in Atlanta, and Bianca would have the opportunity to associate with the children of the cream of Atlanta society."

Justin was blunt. "I don't want to hear it, Mom."

Katherine bristled. She hated being called anything other than Mother. "Your lack of respect is not appreciated, Justin, and it will *not* be tolerated." She paused for an apology. Katherine did not allow disrespect.

"Forgive me, oh mighty mother," he teased.

"Nor is your sarcasm amusing." She continued, "I was simply saying that Vanessa's decision to put Bianca in that . . . that . . ."

"Preschool."

She cut her eyes at Justin. Katherine did not allow interruptions either.

"I'm simply trying to say that Bianca would thrive in a better environment.

Vanessa's defiance of me is affecting Bianca, and if you were as doting an uncle as you claim to be, you would help me do something about it."

Justin wanted to laugh aloud. His mother knew better than to try and involve him in his sister's life. Unless it was life threatening, he believed in the adage "live and let live."

Actually, he was quite proud of Vanessa for having chosen Bianca's new preschool. Finally, at age twenty-eight, she was showing some backbone by making a decision in her life that hadn't been influenced by Katherine. It seemed that since losing her husband in an automobile accident two years ago, his sister had changed quite a bit. She had always been under her mother's powerful influence, but the hold appeared to be weakening. A few weeks ago she had ignored Katherine's wishes and placed Bianca in Playful Tots. This act of defiance had been the first independent decision he could ever remember Vanessa making, and he had been delighted.

Katherine had been livid when she discovered what her daughter had done, but Vanessa had held firm. She had explained to her mother that although the school was miles from Katherine's home, where she and Bianca resided, it was closer to where Vanessa worked as an interior decorator. Its convenience had been a factor in her decision. Yet, Justin knew that her action had been more than that. It had been a defining step in Vanessa's declaring her independence from their domineering mother.

He had always been the rebel in the family, the one his parents found impossible to control. His chosen career had been the bane of their existence. He was the only male member on both sides of the family who had not gone into medicine. Instead he had chosen a career in computer technology. It was a career decision that his mother still didn't understand.

Justin was also the only member of his family, on both sides, who had attended a graduate school outside the South. His master's degree in computer science was from the Massachusetts Institute of Technology, M.I.T. Until his recent move back to Atlanta, he was the only member of his family, on both sides, who had chosen to reside in the North, and Katherine was not shy about expressing to him the heartache that each decision he had made in his life had caused her. But he was back now and he knew that his mother's efforts to manipulate him would be greater than they had been when he lived in New York City. Katherine had been ecstatic over her son's return to Atlanta. She viewed his presence in her city as yet another opportunity to try to extend influence over him. Her only challenge, as it had always been, was his lack of cooperation.

Justin Miles carried the name of two of Atlanta's oldest and most influential black families. He was the only male heir to both the Justin and the Miles family fortunes, and he was the cause of constant frustration for Katherine Miles. To make matters worse, he had earned his own fortune as an entrepreneur and couldn't be controlled with her money. She was at a loss when it came to understanding her adored and beloved son.

She watched as his eyes twinkled at her expense, obviously amused by her heartfelt concern about his sister. She had tried every way she knew to elicit his assistance in getting Bianca removed from that school, but to no avail. She had run out of tactics other than outright begging, which she refused to do. She knew that her son would make some sort of inane remark to placate her, and he did.

"Mother, Bianca is doing very well in her preschool. I've been picking her up from there for two days now, and from what I've seen the teachers seem nice and so do the kids. The neighborhood surrounding the school consists of brand new homes, with upper-middle-class families doing the best they can to give their children a good start in life. So I don't see the problem. Vanessa made her choice, and it looks like a good one to me. You ought to go by the school and check it out instead of condemning it, sight unseen."

"Humph, you sound like Henry." Katherine sniffed, referring to Henry Gaston, the family chauffeur, and the father of Justin's best friend, Clark. Henry had worked for the Miles family for over forty years. He was like a second father to Justin. Henry's opinion mattered in the Miles family. "He said that I should go to this open house thing that this preschool is having this evening."

Justin's interest in the conversation took a sudden turn. "Open house?"

"Yes. Last week Bianca brought this gaudy, iridescent notice home informing anyone—anyone who wasn't blinded by the color—that the school is having an open house tonight. I'm surprised that she didn't say something to you about it. Hopefully she's forgotten it, because I certainly don't want to go."

Open house, at the preschool. That meant parents and significant others would be in attendance. Yes! Perhaps this would offer another opportunity to see the delectable Ms. Maxwell again. This was too good to be true.

Justin made a conscious effort to control his excitement. Any indication of interest would alert Katherine that something was afoot. "Perhaps you should go, Mother. After all, Bianca needs to have someone there to represent her family."

Just as he knew she would, Katherine resisted. "I have no intention of going to that place unless I absolutely have to. If you're so concerned, you go. After all, you're the one who's supposed to be baby-sitting."

Bingo! However, a little resistance was necessary to offset suspicion. "I've never been to a school open house before!" He hoped he sounded reluctant enough.

Katherine was encouraging. After all, Justin was right; somebody had to represent the family. It was important that the people at that school know the stock from which Bianca came. "Of course you've been to an open house, sweetheart, when you were a child. You loved them."

The statement was so ridiculous that they both laughed. Then, timing it just right, Justin relented. "All right, since I'm an expert in the area, I'll go. Just let me know the details."

Katherine gave a sigh of relief. Justin gave a sigh of satisfaction.

❧

As Davia and CeCe walked around the school that evening, enjoying the brightly colored decorations, warm punch and home-baked cookies, Davia thought about Stephanie, her beautiful daughter, the round-faced little girl with the incredible brown eyes. She remembered the school open houses that she had attended for her and wondered what her daughter would have thought of her own little girl at age four. Certainly she would have been as proud of her child as Davia would always be of them both.

Stopping at an abstract finger painting with Gabby's name scrawled neatly in the lower right-hand corner, she and CeCe examined it.

"Interesting," Davia observed.

"Genius!" CeCe declared. Her eyes took in the pictures surrounding it, then declared them to be the work of "amateurs."

Davia shook her head in amusement at the intensity of CeCe's assessment. "Girl, you ought to quit. I'm going to the bathroom before the kids put on their program. Grab a couple of seats so we won't end up standing against the wall."

Davia exited the classroom while CeCe moved to the folded chairs placed against the walls in preparation for the program the children would be presenting. She took a seat and claimed the one next to her with her purse.

As she looked around the room at the miniature desks and chairs that decorated the room, her thoughts drifted to Stephanie, just as Davia's had. She would be nineteen years old if she had lived. She would probably be as beautiful as her mother and certainly just as smart. What would Stephanie think about the woman with whom she'd had so much strife during those turbulent teenage years? The girl had accused Davia of being a bad mother, incapable of providing warmth and love. The words had nearly destroyed Davia, but only CeCe had been allowed to see her tears. She wondered if Stephanie was looking down from heaven bearing witness to her mother's determination to sacrifice her entire life as penance for what she perceived as the ultimate sin, being an inattentive mother. That's what it was, penance, a punishment that Davia had imposed on herself for feeling responsible for the death of her child. CeCe might not be a psychiatrist, but she'd bet her law degree that her friend's ban on men was Davia's ultimate form of atonement. Well, it was time for it to end.

CeCe gave a weary sigh and absently surveyed the room. If Davia would give her a chance, she knew that she could fix her up with the right man—a man who would love and cherish her and make her live for something else other than Gabby and work. She deserved at least that! If Davia wasn't interested in Kevin, then there were plenty of other hunks with good bods to chose from. Men like—CeCe's eyes stopped roaming as Justin walked into the room.

With his hand firmly gripping Bianca's, he tried to appear relaxed, but his appearance was deceiving. He was anxious, a bundle of nerves. What if Ms. Maxwell wasn't here? What if she was here? What would she do when he approached her? Would she reject him publicly? He'd see, because if she was here he definitely was going to approach her. His eyes took in the entire room with one swift glance.

There were only four other African-American adults in the room; a couple examining the room decorations, Bianca's preschool teacher, and an attractive woman sitting in one of the folding chairs lining the walls. She seemed to find him interesting, but his glance swept over her briskly. There was no sign of Ms. Maxwell. Justin quelled his disappointment. Perhaps she hadn't arrived.

He was momentarily distracted when Bianca's teacher greeted them both, then hustled his niece into another room to join the other children who were getting ready for a short program they were to present to the adults. Nodding politely at the woman in the chair, who continued to stare boldly at him, he turned to look at the pictures on display, searching for Bianca's drawings. He could still feel the woman's eyes on his back. She was quite pretty, with creamy, rich brown skin and dark hair worn in a sleek bob that stopped at her shoulders. The slight smile she had given him revealed a deep dimple in one cheek. Normally, he would have approached her and started a conversation. According to his sister, there wasn't a pretty woman alive for whom he wasn't on the prowl, but today he was interested in only one woman, and she wasn't the one.

As Justin gazed at the colorful array of pictures without really seeing them, he marveled at his dilemma.

He couldn't understand why he felt such an overwhelming attraction to Ms. Maxwell. No woman had ever fascinated him so completely in such a short time. He wanted to know her. He wanted to know her story. How had she come to be a grandmother so young? What were the circumstances that had brought her to this?

He had read and heard about the plight of teenage pregnancy. Too often it destroyed young, promising lives. His mother and her friends viewed pregnancy out of wedlock as deplorable behavior, unacceptable no matter the circumstances. Katherine relegated such behavior to the exclusive domain of the "lower classes." It was her contention that teen pregnancy did not happen among the "upper class." But Justin begged to differ. He had assured her that her observations about "upper class" morality had some definite flaws, and if he were a gossip he would have provided her with the names of "upper class" couples that he knew had aborted unwanted pregnancies outside of marriage. Of course, Katherine didn't believe him, so he had allowed her to retreat into denial.

He wondered if Davia had wanted her pregnancy. Whatever the case, she seemed to have survived young motherhood and she appeared to have prospered. Both accomplishments earned his admiration.

Refocusing his attention, he found Bianca's picture and smiled at the childish scrawling of her name at the bottom of the colorful drawing.

"Your daughter's?"

Justin looked around at the sound of the voice drifting over his right shoulder. It was the woman in the folding chair. He was surprised not only by her sudden appearance but by her height as well. She was tiny, a little over five feet. She hadn't looked so petite when she was seated. He returned the warm smile she bestowed on him.

"No, it's my niece's."

CeCe's smile widened. His niece! Good! That was three points in his favor. Fine as hell! No wedding ring! And no kids! At least she hoped that was the case.

"Oh, you don't have kids that go here?" She tried to sound casual.

Justin heard both unasked questions. "No, I don't have any kids. I'm not married."

It took everything that she had in her to keep from dancing a jig. Now, if he wasn't gay, on parole, a pervert, an intellectual midget or just a plain, everyday kook, he might be perfect for Davia. She stuck out her hand. "I'm CeCe Green."

"Justin Miles. Nice to meet you." His hand closed over hers briefly, careful not to linger too long. He didn't want to give her a false impression. She seemed nice enough, but she wasn't his reason for being here.

"You said this is your niece's work?" CeCe eyed the collage of swirls and squiggles, her eyes dropping to the name, Bianca. The drawing was okay, but she was no Gabby. "It's nice."

Justin nodded in agreement. The woman had taste. Bianca's picture was undoubtedly the best in the room. "Where is your daughter's picture?"

CeCe moved toward the blackboard to the left and pointed to a finger painting hanging above the board.

"Right here." Her voice was filled with pride. She noted the smile that started working its way across his handsome features. The smile froze as his eyes lowered to read Gabby's name.

Gabrielle! He didn't know there was another Gabrielle in Bianca's classroom. "Your daughter's name is Gabrielle? I bet that gets confusing for the teacher, having two Gabrielles in the room?"

CeCe frowned in confusion. "Oh, I didn't know there were two in here. I didn't see the other one's painting on display." She had looked at every hanging art piece, judging the competition. It had been sadly lacking.

Justin frowned this time. "Well, I think there are, your Gabrielle and Gabrielle Maxwell."

"What?" CeCe frowned, confused at the direction the conversation was taking. "Gabrielle Maxwell *is* my Gabrielle."

The man looked at her dumbstruck. What was his problem? Was Gabrielle's name that odd? She'd known when she first saw him that he was too good to be true. He was beginning to fall into the kook category.

Justin found his voice. He was certain he hadn't heard her correctly. "Did you say that Gabrielle Maxwell is *your* daughter?"

Not only was he a kook, but he had a hearing problem, too. It was best to dump this loser and move on. "I said Gabrielle Maxwell is my Gabrielle." She spotted a woman moving toward the chairs she had reserved for herself and Davia, and found her excuse to abandon this loser.

45

"Excuse me, I've got some seat saving to do. Nice meeting you, Mr. Miles."

Justin watched as she hurried over to the seat, which she previously occupied, shooed the intruder away and reclaimed her seat. It was obvious that he had been dismissed, but he didn't mind. He needed time to gather his thoughts and recover from the shock of her statement. How in the world could she be Gabrielle's mother and Ms. Maxwell be Gabrielle's grandmother? What had happened in that family? The child must be that of Mrs. Maxwell's son, but had he had that child by CeCe Green? The woman looked to be in her late twenties or early thirties. Had Ms. Maxwell approved of a relationship between her teenage son and this woman? What kind of woman would condone such a thing? Perhaps the mystery of the Maxwell woman was more complex than he realized. This might be more than he was willing to handle.

It was at that moment that the lady in question made her appearance and any doubts that Justin had harbored instantly vanished. She paused in the doorway for a moment to look around and Justin knew the exact moment that she saw him. Her eyes widened and her breath caught in her throat, just as his did. As he watched her, he wondered if her heart was beating as wildly as his own.

CHAPTER 5

Davia groaned at the sight of Justin Miles, but it was hard to tell if it was a groan of regret or of appreciation. Despite her lack of interest she couldn't deny that Justin was a very good-looking man. Rationalizing her reaction to his presence in the room as one that any woman would have toward him, she ignored the butterflies in her stomach, gave him a stiff nod and joined CeCe on the other side of the room.

CeCe hadn't missed the sign of recognition between the two of them as she slid her eyes from Davia to Justin. "Do you know him?"

Davia adjusted her oversized purse on her lap and got comfortable before answering, trying to sound nonchalant. "Yes, that's the uncle of one of Gabby's friends, Bianca Thomas. His name is Justin Miles. We met recently." She deliberately left out the reason why.

CeCe looked stunned. "You mean to tell me you met a gorgeous hunk of a man like *that* and never said a word to me?"

Davia shook her head at her lecherous friend. "I meet gorgeous men all the time and I never mention them to you. Why should this one be different?"

"Well, thanks a lot. It's nice to know that you think so much of me."

Ignoring CeCe, Davia readied herself for the start of the program. What she wasn't ready for was the company of Justin Miles as he took the empty seat next to her.

Davia couldn't contain her look of astonishment at his acknowledgment of CeCe. Her friend had already met the man and she hadn't been in the room more than five minutes. The woman was faster than the speed of light!

"You've met Mr. Miles?"

CeCe had the grace to avoid Davia's accusing eyes. "Yes, we met when he first came in. We were admiring the children's artwork."

Davia's eyes narrowed suspiciously. "Uh-huh, I just bet you were."

CeCe cut her eyes at Davia, annoyed by the look and the sound of suspicion. This was the last time she would do Davia a favor. She could find her own man after this! Looking past her and toward Justin, CeCe smiled, but Justin's eyes were riveted on Davia. It was clear that Davia didn't need her assistance to hook this one.

CeCe's gaze shifted to her friend, who sat stiffly clutching her purse, staring straight ahead. The woman didn't have a clue. It looked as if she'd have to help this along. CeCe opened her mouth to speak but Justin intervened.

"Are you two related?"

Davia turned cold eyes on him. What was this? Twenty questions? She didn't like strangers in her business. However, CeCe didn't seem to mind.

"We might as well be," CeCe answered coyly. "We're such close friends, we might as well be sisters."

That earlier look of confusion on Justin's face surfaced again. "Oh, so you're not in-laws?" He noticed that Davia actually looked him in the face this time. Progress was being made. Unfortunately, she was looking at him as if he were insane.

"What would make you think that we're in-laws, Mr. Miles?" She shot a glance at CeCe. What had the woman said to this man?

CeCe looked confused until the reason for his question dawned on her. She gave a guilty chuckle. "No, no, no! You think that I'm Gabby's mother, don't you?"

"Well, over there, you said . . ." Justin gestured to the spot where they had been standing when they had spoken earlier.

"No, when I said *my* Gabby, I meant that Gabby was my girl. I mean, my *girl*."

CeCe became flustered. "Oh, you know what I mean. Gabby's not my child. She belongs to her." She thrust a thumb toward Davia. "That's Grommy over there."

Confusion crossed Justin's face once again as he turned to Davia. "Grommy?"

Davia thrust her chin up proudly. "That's what my granddaughter calls me."

She tightened her hold on her purse and further stiffened her body, transmitting that he was dismissed. His time was up. The only problem was that Justin Miles didn't seem to get the message.

"So what's the word Grommy about? A combination of Grandma and Mommy?"

The man was astute as well as nosey. She didn't answer. It was none of his business.

"How did you know that?" CeCe's head swiveled between Justin and Davia. "Have you two met before on a personal basis?" CeCe grinned at Davia like a Cheshire cat, her eyes asking where the two had met and when. Davia's body language made it clear that she might never know.

"Ms. Maxwell and I certainly have met." The twinkle in Justin's eyes and the smile on his face transmitted a message that he made even clearer. "And I enjoyed the experience."

CeCe almost leaped out of her seat with joy. This man pulled no punches. He was interested in Davia. Maybe her friend had hit the jackpot! If only Davia was receptive. But it was obvious that she wasn't. Her posture had gone from stiff to absolutely rigid. When Davia opened her mouth to speak, CeCe interrupted her effort.

"There is no Mr. Maxwell, so I guess you could continue to enjoy it if you really want, Mr. Miles."

Davia wanted to sink into the floor. Her eyes radiated daggers of death at CeCe, who wisely chose to ignore her.

Justin took advantage of the situation as he turned up the charm a notch. He addressed CeCe, recognizing that he had found an ally in his pursuit of the lovely Ms. Maxwell. "Please, call me Justin."

"Well, Justin, I'm CeCe." They shook hands. "And my friend here is Davia."

Justin's attention returned to the object of his pursuit. "Davia, what a beautiful name . . ." he paused, ". . . for a beautiful woman."

Davia was trembling, she was so angry. How dare these two! What was she, a piece of meat to be auctioned to the highest bidder? She would kill CeCe later, but right now she was going to get rid of this two-bit playboy. She had opened her mouth to do just that when the teacher announced the beginning of the children's program.

Reining in her temper, she resolved to nip his little game of flirtation in the bud as soon as the performance was over. She'd put an end to *Mr. Justin Miles* in—she checked her dainty gold watch—approximately thirty minutes. There was not a man alive that would ever get close to her again. That was an absolute certainty!

Settling back in her chair she stole a glance at Justin. He sat beside her with a smug smile on his face. As he relaxed in his chair, his shoulder accidentally brushed Davia's shoulder. Electric currents charged through both their bodies. Each of them snatched away as if they had been burnt, both surprised by the small sensation.

Davia shuffled into the kitchen of her home half asleep. Business at Small Sensations had increased 15 percent in the past few weeks due to a new ad campaign, and it meant late hours both in the corporate office and in her office at home. The long hours were taking their toll. She was exhausted.

Sitting at the marble-topped table in the kitchen nook, Reba watched as Davia moved across the room toward the stove and the teakettle. Pouring the hot water into the cup, she dipped the tea bag, added a dash of honey, then came over to the table to join Reba. Settling on the cushioned chair, she offered a terse good morning.

"Good morning!" Reba's greeting was bright and cheerful.

Davia scowled. She was in no mood for cheerful this morning. "Is Gabby still in bed?"

"Uh-huh. After all, it is Saturday. I thought I'd let her sleep in." She paused dramatically. "Like you should be doing."

Davia took a sip of tea, avoiding the accusing eyes that bore into her. She didn't want to hear one of Reba's lectures today. However, observing her body language and the set of her mouth, she knew that she was going to hear one anyway.

Reba sat back in her chair, her arms planted firmly across her chest. "This does not make sense, Davia! You hired me to take care of that child, and here you are doing triple duty—super mom, super grandma and super nanny all at one time. You are needed at your place of business. You're not neglecting Gabby if I pick her up from school, help her with her school assignments, take her to the park, tuck her in. I mean, my goodness! What are you paying me for, anyway? You go to the Buckhead office, do your thing there, dash to pick her up from school, spend every waking hour with her, put her to bed, go to the upstairs office, take care of business there most of the night, grab two . . . three hours of sleep and start all over again! And this isn't the first time that this has happened. What's this about? What are you trying to prove? You're young and healthy, but even young and healthy wears out. "

Davia leveled her with one of her "I'm the boss, you're the employee" looks. As usual, Reba wasn't intimidated. She returned her look with a "so fire me" look of her own. It was a war of wills that each was determined to win. The thought drifted through Davia's mind that even if she won, she'd still be the loser. Her health and her sanity were at stake at the pace she'd been going lately, and she knew that Reba's admonishment was out of genuine concern. How could she be upset with her for that? However, what did upset her was what Reba said next.

"You ought to give that Justin Miles a chance. You need a social life, and I think he'd be good for you."

Davia slammed her coffee cup down and pushed away from the table. She definitely didn't want to hear this! Getting up, she stomped toward the stairs.

"He sent another dozen roses today. They arrived this morning."

The amusement in Reba's voice increased Davia's anger as she left the room without looking back.

"I put the newest ones on the dining room table in a vase!" Reba shouted after her. "I'm running out of vases!" Her words followed Davia up the stairs.

She could hear the echo of Reba's laughter as she slammed her bedroom door. It was a conspiracy! Everybody was conspiring against her in favor of that man. He had started his relentless campaign to get her to go out with him the day after the open house over a month ago. He had been annoying enough at that event.

Every time she looked up he was watching her. With that toothpaste ad smile of his, the arrogance he exuded was sickening. Just because he put all of the other women in the room in catatonic states didn't mean she was affected. At one point she had turned to him and whispered that she didn't like being "ogled." She had asked him politely to stop. He replied that he wasn't ogling, he was simply "mesmerized."

Mesmerized! How corny! Even if she was attracted to him a tiny bit, after that pathetic line, forget it! The next day he'd had the audacity to call.

"Hello, Ms. Maxwell. This is Justin Miles. How are you this morning?"

She had been too flabbergasted to speak at first. Why was he calling? The matter between the girls was settled. She had set him straight the night before about staring at her. Surely he had gotten the message that she wasn't interested in him.

"I won't beat around the bush, Ms. Maxwell . . . Davia. I hope you don't mind my calling you that?"

Silence.

"Anyway, I'd like to invite you to dinner tonight, if you're not busy. I'd really like to see you again."

Her answer had been short. *"I'm busy."* She had hung up.

He hadn't called again, but since then he had sent her roses every day. They filled the house with their delicious fragrance. Of course they filled the house, because Reba kept retrieving them from the trash, where Davia deposited them each time they arrived. He sent yellow roses. Yellow was Davia's favorite color. It wasn't difficult to track down the culprit who had provided Mr. Miles with *that* information—CeCe, although she adamantly denied it.

Gabby was excited each time a new delivery of roses appeared, anxious to know why Grommy was getting so many flowers. Davia told her that they were from a friend and left it at that.

She wanted the flowers to stop. When she threatened to stop the deliveries by calling the authorities, CeCe informed her that she had no case. Justin had never threatened her with harm. He'd only sent her roses. There was no law against that. Davia could have slapped that silly grin right off her friend's face when she offered her that piece of legal advice. She still wasn't sure it was true.

She didn't have time for this nonsense. Her life was too full, and she was exhausted. Davia lay in her unmade bed and pulled a pillow over her head. Closing her eyes, she quickly gave into sleep—a sleep that brought dreams interrupted by a pair of stunning gray-green eyes.

Davia Maxwell was on the run, and he planned on her running straight to him. Justin chuckled as he pulled his new Lexus sports car up to the front door of his mother's home. Getting the elusive Ms. Maxwell to go out with him had become a challenge, and it was one that he was enjoying. The bombardment of flowers was a calculated ploy to keep him on her mind.

She was adamant about not wanting to date him, and he wasn't used to rejection. That made her all the more fascinating. But he knew that his attraction to her was more than that. He just couldn't put his finger on what it was. No matter, they were going to get together one way or another. *That* he was sure about.

Jauntily, he jumped out of his car just as a sleek black BMW came roaring down the driveway from the back of the house. The beep of the horn drew his attention as the car came to a stop within inches of his tuxedo-clad frame. Justin smiled as his best friend, Clark Gaston, rolled down a tinted window. Clark's father, Henry, sat on the other side of him in the passenger seat.

Not only did Henry work as the family chauffeur, but his wife, Pauline, had worked as the family's housekeeper for almost as long as her husband. Clark was their only child, and at thirty-six, he was the same age as Justin. He and Clark had grown up together and had been inseparable since childhood. Social boundaries had never been an issue between them. Just as Henry was thought of as a second father to Justin, Clark was like his brother, and Justin's father had seen to it that Clark had shared many of the advantages that his son had enjoyed. The two men had attended different graduate schools, but they had graduated from Morehouse together. Now both were successful entrepreneurs in fields that they loved. Clark was an architect and his firm was one of the fastest growing enterprises in Atlanta.

Justin broke into a wide grin as he greeted Henry and then transferred his attention to the handsome brown face of his best friend. "Hey, my man, where are you off to?"

Clark smiled up at him. "I should be asking you the same thing. Look at you, all dressed up like a penguin and sporting a new ride, too! Nice! Real nice! What's the occasion? Another one of Katherine's charity events?"

Justin tugged at the onyx studs at the cuffs of his dress shirt. "Not this time. I'm escorting the prettiest little sister in town to some fancy awards dinner. What about you two?" His gaze took in both father and son dressed in matching Atlanta Hawks sweatshirts. "Aw, man, don't tell me I'm missing the game tonight!"

Henry's square-chinned face, an older duplicate of his son's, leaned across Clark and winked at Justin. "A true Hawks fan wouldn't have to ask."

Justin and Clark chuckled, both recalling the many games they had attended with Henry. He was a basketball fanatic. The three of them had spent countless hours playing basketball on the small court Zachary Miles had built for his son on the Miles estate.

Revving the engine, Clark gave Justin a "see ya" and left him standing on his mother's doorstep staring after them as they drove out the iron gate and disappeared. Inside the house he found not only his sister, but also his mother; both were dressed to the nines in formal wear. Although standing a few inches shorter, Vanessa closely resembled their mother. She had the same cafe au lait complexion and heart-shaped face, which was usually framed in a mass of light brown ringlets that she wore tumbling past her shoulders. Tonight her hair had been styled into an elegant French roll that complemented her sharp features. Unlike her brother, she had not inherited their mother's unusual eye color. Her eyes were a dark brown like their late father's. Justin remembered that when she was a child they used to sparkle, but over time the sparkle had gone out of her eyes and that saddened him. He'd do anything to bring that sparkle back. Despite that, she looked lovely this evening in a blue sequinned gown.

Justin greeted each woman with a kiss on the cheek, and then turned his attention to Katherine, who was dressed in a black, floor-length evening gown that fitted her shapely frame to perfection.

"What's the occasion? Are you going with us?"

"No, darling. Your old mother has plans of her own."

Justin raised an eyebrow. "Oh? Dr. Collier?" Hastings Collier was a friend of his parents and a resident of Zachary Acres. He had been smitten with Katherine for years, and after the death of Justin's father, he had often escorted the lovely widow to various affairs.

Katherine gave a mysterious smile. "No, it's not."

Justin glanced at Vanessa, who shrugged her ignorance. He grinned mischievously. "So there's a new love slave in the mix?"

Katherine took her son's teasing in stride. "No, simply a new friend I met at the recent Boule Ball."

"I see. And does this 'friend' have a name?"

Katherine smiled. "He certainly does, just like all of your dates that you never introduce me to."

Vanessa laughed. "She got you this time, Casanova. Come on, let's go."

Hooking her arm through her brother's, she guided him out of the room. The doorbell rang just as they reached the door. Justin opened it.

Standing in the doorway, elegantly attired in a tailored tuxedo, was a man who appeared to be in his fifties. About six feet tall, his pecan-colored face was long and angular, framed by black wavy hair, salted with gray. His eyes were dark, almost black, and Justin could see no warmth in their depths. For a moment the crooked smile he bestowed on them seemed uncertain, but he quickly recovered.

"I'm here for Katherine Miles." He paused. The cool eyes grew warm and the crooked smile straightened. "You don't have to introduce yourselves. I can look at both of you and tell that you're Katherine's children, Justin and Vanessa. Right?" He stuck out his hand. "I'm your mother's escort for tonight, Charles Cash."

Vanessa smiled and greeted him with a polite hello. Justin shook his hand.

The man's handshake was strong, self-assured. Yet, for a brief moment Justin felt uneasy about this stranger standing in his mother's doorway. Dismissing the feeling, he and Vanessa said their good-byes and left the house.

CHAPTER 6

The accolades had been bestowed, the awards presented and the acceptance speeches delivered. Rubber chicken, wild rice and asparagus tips were the evening fare, and after dinner a band took over to provide the evening's entertainment. The lights were dim and the dance floor was crowded as quiet conversation drifted throughout the ballroom.

The band was good, dispensing an eclectic mix of soul music and jazz. The entire evening was designed for fun and relaxation but Davia wasn't enjoying herself. She didn't like formal business affairs and this evening's event was made even more unbearable because of the presence of one man—Justin Miles.

If she hadn't known better, she would have sworn that CeCe had arranged his appearance here, but this was an annual event and invitations weren't easily obtained. CeCe's law firm and three other black businesses in Atlanta had received Business of the Year awards from the Atlanta Black Chamber of Commerce. It was an honor that Small Sensations had earned five years ago. But tonight was CeCe's night, and she had been beside herself with excitement since learning that her law firm was to be honored. Davia knew that Justin Miles had been the last thing on her friend's mind. Actually, CeCe seemed as surprised at seeing him here as Davia had been, but in less than an hour from the time Justin entered, CeCe had gathered information about him from her friends and acquaintances in attendance. Dutifully, she reported those findings to a seemingly disinterested Davia.

It seemed that Justin's date was his sister, Vanessa, whom Davia had still to hear from regarding the vampire incident. She wondered if Justin had told her about it. CeCe also reported that Vanessa was one of the interior decorators for Regal Designs, another of the evening's award recipients. So, there seemed to be no ulterior motive for Justin's presence at this affair.

Davia had expected him to make a pest of himself, using this very public event to continue his pursuit of her, but she had been wrong. When he first noticed her, he smiled and nodded politely. A few minutes ago, as he passed her table leading his sister to the dance floor, he had introduced Vanessa to her, noting that Bianca and Gabby attended the same preschool. He had excused himself and continued to the dance floor, where he was now dancing with his sister.

Davia tried to ignore him, but his looming presence even on the dance floor was hard to ignore. He towered over most of the men, and his dancing was smooth and flawless. To make matters worse, he looked good enough to eat in his tuxedo. Justin Miles was not the kind of man easily dismissed.

She had met Leroy Platten at the evening's affair. He was serving as her escort. His wife was out of town visiting her sister. Most of the night, he had been table-hopping, as he networked with the movers and shakers in the room. Returning to the table, he asked Davia to dance and she accepted.

The crowd on the dance floor was dense, and much to her chagrin she found herself dancing right next to Justin. The sleeve of his tuxedo brushed against her bare arm and for the second time a bolt of electricity passed between them. They each missed a dance step.

"Are you okay?" Leroy's bushy eyebrows rose in question. Davia nodded.

"Sorry," Justin apologized to his sister.

Davia retreated first. "Leroy, I'm sorry, I really don't feel up to dancing tonight."

Leroy studied her for a minute. He loved Davia like a daughter and was always concerned about her welfare "You're all right, aren't you? I know how you hate these kinds of affairs."

Davia gave him a reassuring smile. "Yes, I'm okay, just tired."

Leroy led her back to their table. A few minutes later the music stopped and the dance floor slowly emptied. Justin passed her table again as he escorted his sister to their table. This time he didn't acknowledge Davia's presence. She told herself that was the way that she wanted it.

Leroy excused himself to do more networking. CeCe and her date stayed glued to the dance floor, as did the rest of the table's occupants. Davia found herself alone at the table.

Turning down at least a half dozen men who asked her to dance, she noted, reluctantly, that with each new song Justin seemed to be whirling a different woman around the dance floor. She continued to try and ignore him.

To add salt to the wounds, CeCe bounced over to the table between dances to remind Davia how good Justin looked, and CeCe wasn't easily ignored, either. She was in her element tonight. She fairly glowed.

CeCe was dressed in a slinky sequined number, with a peek-a-boo neckline, and Emanuel, her date for the night, stuck like glue to the petite beauty. Davia knew that it was best that he did. All evening Davia had watched her girlfriend move from table to table greeting those whom she knew and drawing admiring male glances wherever she went. Girlfriend was working it! Watching her do her thing was amusing, but Davia hadn't been amused earlier when CeCe approached the table where Justin was sitting and he rose to greet her. That had been Davia's first inkling that he was in the room. He had been the last person she expected to see. His presence had rattled her composure. She had spent the rest of the evening trying to regain it. Now CeCe was back at their table with the latest installment of the Justin Miles Report.

With the skill of a private investigator, her friend had gathered even more information about Justin, and CeCe's breathless delivery made it obvious that she was impressed. "Girl! Do you know who Justin Miles is? He's Frederick Justin Miles, the son of the late Dr. Frederick Miles and Katherine Justin Miles, the *queen* of black

Atlanta society. Honey, the Justin and the Miles families are two of the oldest and richest black families in this city! I should have made the connection when we first met him. But, girl, let me tell you. He owns a computer company and you'll never guess which one, Complete Computers! It was featured in *Black Enterprise* magazine. I remember reading the article. Girlfriend, the man came from money and made even more on his own. Sweet Jesus! And he's after your butt hot and heavy. He's been watching you all night, although he's trying to be slick about it. I'm telling you, if you don't go after this one I will."

Davia heaved a disgusted sigh. At least she could give CeCe credit for trying to be discreet. She had whispered the unsolicited information in her ear rather than yelling it out to the entire room. But it didn't matter, Davia had heard enough. That cinched it. It was bad enough that Justin Miles was harassing her, but it was worse now that she knew that he was a member of one of the wealthiest and most socially prominent families in Atlanta. Attention from a rich, self-centered playboy was attention she didn't need or want. She could only guess what his game was, and he was crazy if he thought that she would be playing it with him.

Grabbing her wrap and matching evening bag, Davia started to get up from her chair.

"Where are you going?" CeCe asked, evidently surprised.

Davia started for the entrance. "I'm outta here. When you see Leroy, please tell him that I went home."

CeCe chuckled. "Okay, you coward, you can run but you can't hide. I'm telling you that man wants you badly, and my money is on him."

Davia continued walking without looking back.

Justin saw Davia leave as he led the latest woman with whom he had been dancing back to their table. He had tried all evening to ignore Davia, but he had found that literally impossible. His eyes seemed to stray toward her of their own volition, and the more he saw, the more he liked. The dress she wore was simple black chiffon, held up by two thin sequined straps and cascading down her shapely frame to end just above her knees. Her legs, encased in shimmering sheer stockings, were as firm and shapely as the rest of her. Black satin heels with a rhine-stone strap encased her feet. She was understated ele-gance from head to toe. The electric current that had passed between them during their brief encounter on the dance floor had rattled him. This was the second time such a connection had occurred. That had never hap-pened to him before. The woman was like a magnet grad-ually attaching herself to him.

He had learned more about her without having to ask. Women talked, and mostly about each other. When he returned Vanessa to the Regal Designs table, she men-tioned the lovely young woman to whom her brother had introduced her. That started the women at the table talking and they had plenty to say about Davia Maxwell.

None of them knew her personally but they did know that she was the vice president of Small Sensations Children's Clothing, an established business entity in the city. Davia worked very closely with the company's president, Leroy Platten. The women also discussed Leroy's marital status and implied that there was more to the relationship between him and his vice president than met the eye, but no one said so openly.

After hearing this Justin had turned his attention to Leroy Platten. The man appeared to be in his sixties. He was a rich mocha brown, with a high forehead distinguished by a rapidly receding hairline. His gray hair framed a round face dominated by a wide nose and bushy eyebrows. His eyes always seemed to be moving, missing nothing. His smile was broad and he appeared warm and friendly. Of average height, he didn't appear to be fit. The paunch where his waist should have been attested to that. He was an average-looking man and old enough to be Davia's father. Justin didn't size him up as being much competition.

Justin's discreet observation of Davia most of the evening led to that conclusion. The interaction between Davia and Leroy appeared close, but Justin failed to sense that special something that would identify them as lovers. From his observation, they appeared to be close friends, nothing more. Of course the man *was* married, and they *were* in a public place, and appearances were known to deceive. He would get to the bottom of their relationship eventually, but for now he wasn't concerned.

At the table, Vanessa informed him that she would be going out on the town tonight with two of the other women at the table. She asked if Justin wanted to accompany them, but he declined. Using her announcement as an excuse to end the evening, he said his farewells and headed toward the front entrance.

To his surprise Davia was standing outside the building. He assumed she was waiting for a cab. Maybe she hadn't come with Platten as he had suspected.

He glanced at her out of the corner of his eye. She didn't acknowledge Justin's presence as he handed his car key to a young valet. They continued to ignore each other as they stood side by side, both looking straight ahead, awaiting their separate transportation. Justin broke the silence.

"And how did you enjoy tonight's festivities, Ms. Maxwell?" He continued to look straight ahead as he spoke.

"Fine." Davia didn't look at him.

"And I assume that you have enjoyed the flowers I've sent you."

She turned to face him this time, her eyes narrowed. "They were lovely and I thank you, but I'd like you to stop sending them to my home. I don't like being harassed."

From her stance she expected an argument. He surprised her.

"Okay." Why argue? "But I would like to offer you one more thing, if you don't mind."

Her eyebrows shot up. Her calf-brown eyes were wary. "What?"

The brand-new, candy apple red Lexus he had picked up last week pulled up to the entrance right on time. He nodded toward it, unable to contain the pride he felt in his latest toy. "A ride home."

Behind his car a second valet pulled up in a shiny new silver Lexus, the same make, model and year as his own. Davia nodded toward it. "Thank you, but I have one."

Taking her key from the valet, she tipped him and slipped easily into the car's soft leather interior. She drove away, leaving Justin standing at the entrance. Shaking his head, Justin smiled. The lady certainly had good taste.

CHAPTER 7

Davia wasn't crazy about Chuck E. Cheese, the child-friendly theme restaurant Gabby had chosen for their regular Saturday morning outing, but her granddaughter loved the place. After the week Davia had had at work she had looked forward to spending this time with Gabby. They had started the morning with shopping, and "the Cheese," as Gabby called it, was their lunch stop before heading home.

It was a familiar routine for them. What wasn't familiar was the sight of Justin Miles sitting in "the Cheese" with his niece Bianca. He was casually sipping a soda. Gabby spotted Bianca before Davia spotted Justin and the child darted toward them before she could stop her. By the time Davia reached the table the two girls had made their plans to dine and play together. Within five minutes of having entered the restaurant, she found herself seated across the table from Justin Miles.

It had been two weeks since they each had attended the awards banquet. As she had requested, the flowers had stopped and she had almost managed to forget him—almost. Davia rationalized that the electricity between them was an aberration. She dismissed the fluttering in her stomach whenever he was near as nervous energy. The breathlessness she felt at the sound of his voice, that was simply exhaustion. Yes, there was an explanation for everything—almost.

Davia made an attempt to look relaxed as she sat across from him at the table. It irked her that he could sit back and look so cool and calm. He was dressed in a pair of jeans and a v-neck sweater that exposed wisps of hair on his chest. A well-worn leather jacket hung on the back of his chair. Davia didn't recognize the scent of the cologne he was wearing, but it was wreaking havoc on her senses. He looked and smelled just a little too good.

"I don't bite, Ms. Maxwell," he said with a cocky smile on his face. "So you don't have to look so distressed. I know that you would rather cut your arm off than come anywhere near me, but since the kids are having fun, perhaps you can grin and bear me for a while."

He had said it jokingly, but she recognized the truth behind his words. She hadn't known that her discomfort was so apparent. The fact of the matter was that she did not want to like this man. To like him might mean that she could be attracted to him, and she didn't want to be attracted to *any* man.

She tried to save face. "I'm sorry that you feel that way, Mr. Miles."

"Justin. Please call me Justin. My father's name was Mr. Miles." He flashed an engaging grin.

The flutters in her stomach flared. She swallowed. "Okay, Justin. I'm sorry that you feel that way. I really don't have anything against you."

"It's just that you don't like me." The smile remained on his face, but the gleam in his eyes dimmed.

"No . . . no, it's not that."

Justin leaned forward, resting his goateed chin in the palm of his hand as he looked at her intently. "Then what is it?"

From his expression she could tell that the answer was important to him. That surprised her. She didn't expect her feelings to make any difference to some rich playboy. Why should they? Davia's eyes shifted past him. How could she explain her reluctance to get to know him or any man? He would never understand. She just knew that she was better off having as few men in her life as possible. That's the way it was. That was the way it had to be.

"Well?" he prompted.

"Well, what?"

"Well, what is it about me that you don't like?" Sitting back, he spread his arms wide in an open gesture. "I think I'm a nice guy. I'm hard working, love my family. I'm a wonderful uncle. At least my niece says I am. Other people like me. Why don't you?"

Davia caught a hint of pain in his voice. Could her rejection really be bothering him? She doubted it. A man like Justin simply wasn't used to rejection and it was bruising his ego, not hurting his feelings. She knew from experience that men couldn't be trusted. They'd say any-thing . . . *do* anything.

"I never said that I didn't like you, Mr . . . Justin. It's just that I don't like being harassed, and at the open house that night your approach turned me off. I didn't like it. Then sending all the flowers was a bit overboard. I don't like a hard sell."

Justin's smile vanished. His expression grew serious. "I'm truly sorry, Ms. Maxwell. I really didn't mean to offend you."

His apology seemed sincere. "Your apology is accepted, Justin."

He flashed that smile again. She returned his smile with one of her own. Maybe he wasn't so bad after all.

The rest of the afternoon went well. Caught up in the excitement of the two little girls, she and Justin joined them in play and indulged their seemingly insatiable appetite for pizza. During much-needed rest periods they laughed and talked about everything and nothing. Davia had to admit that she had enjoyed herself. When they left the restaurant and said their good-byes, Davia told herself that she wasn't disappointed that he hadn't asked to see her again.

☙

Davia knew that if she wanted to keep her encounter with Justin Miles a secret from CeCe and Reba, she would have to keep her four-year-old quiet, which was easier said than done. On the way home from the restaurant, she tried to solicit a promise from Gabby to keep their accidental meeting with Justin and Bianca a secret. Of course her inquisitive little munchkin asked the inevitable question: "Why?"

She had to struggle for an answer that would make sense, and she found herself lacking. Finally she came up with, "Because some things that we do are just between you and me."

The explanation was weak, but Gabby pondered it for a second and seemed to accept it. With a sigh of relief, Davia put all thoughts of Justin aside. It was true that the afternoon with him had been fun and that he seemed to be a nice man, but she doubted that she would hear his name again. It turned out that she was wrong.

At the dinner table that evening Gabby made an announcement out of the blue. "Bianca's Uncle Justin said that he would love to take me and her to a fun park."

Davia froze as she wondered when that statement had been made and why it had to be brought up at this moment. Since Gabby offered no details as to where or when this had occurred, she resumed eating with the hope that her granddaughter would stop chattering if she ignored what she had said. She didn't.

"Bianca said that her uncle took her to Disney World." She turned to Davia. "Why can't we go to Disney World?" Not waiting for an answer, Gabby's eyes grew large with excitement. "Hey, maybe Bianca's Uncle Justin can take us all to Disney World, huh, Grommy?"

Enthralled by the possibility, she looked at Davia expectantly. She wasn't going to be ignored this time.

With a cursory glance at Reba, who was busy tackling a baked potato, Davia answered quickly, hoping to avoid the possibility that today's encounter might be mentioned.

"Who knows, Gabby, I might take you to Disney World myself. That would be fun." Davia really liked the idea. What she didn't like was Reba's question to Gabby.

"Just when did Bianca's uncle tell you this?" she asked nonchalantly as she cut into her meat loaf with relish.

"This meat loaf sure is good, Reba," Davia tried an intercept. "Did you put something different in it?"

"No, I . . ."

"At the Cheese."

Woman and child spoke simultaneously.

Reba frowned. "At the Cheese? Did you go there today?"

"Uh-huh, with Grommy." Gabby resumed eating.

Davia knew the second that the little girl remembered her blunder. She looked up at her grandmother with wide-eyed guilt, but Davia gave her a reassuring smile. It was bound to come out sometime. She then prepared herself for the inquisition that she knew was coming. Reba began with Gabby.

"So you saw Bianca and her Uncle Justin at Chuck E. Cheese today?" She was addressing Gabby, but looking at Davia, who answered.

"Yes, we did, Reba," Davia said defensively, "and Gabby played with Bianca while Justin and I talked. The four of us ate pizza and drank soda pop, and then we all went home. Okay?"

Davia speared her last piece of meat loaf, hoping that the information that she provided would keep her nosey, overly analytical nanny's mouth shut. It was too much to wish for, but instead of asking more questions Reba began to laugh, catching Davia and Gabby both off guard.

"What's wrong, Miss Reba?" Gabby began to giggle as her nanny's laugh became infectious.

Reba shook her head, indicating that there was nothing wrong, as she continued to chortle at Davia's expense. Davia rolled her eyes at her, giving her the silent message that as far as she was concerned the subject of Justin Miles was closed. She didn't want to hear any more about him. But it came as no surprise when after dinner Reba pointedly announced that she had a telephone call to make. A full half hour hadn't passed before Davia received the expected call from CeCe, who drilled Davia like an army sergeant, requiring that she omit "absolutely nothing about the day." She was vehement in her efforts to determine whether Davia had "scared the man away."

Sitting at her desk in her Peachtree Street office two weeks later, Davia gave a wistful sigh as she thought about Justin Miles. CeCe was probably right. She had scared the man away, but that was for the best. She had no social skills in male/female relationships. Every man who showed any interest in her over the years had been soundly rejected. Why should this one be any different? So what if he was charming and appeared to be warm and sincere? Appearances deceived. Trusting a man only meant heartache, and she had experienced more than enough heartache in her life.

Justin sat in his office at Complete Computers, concentrating more on Davia Maxwell than on the papers before him. It seemed that she was all he could think about. Their unexpected meeting couldn't have gone better if it had been planned. She was everything he'd thought she would be and more. He couldn't remember when he had enjoyed being with a woman more. She seemed to like him. Maybe he had a chance.

Crossing his large office, he walked to the bar located in front of one of the three floor-to-ceiling glass windows. Grabbing an apple juice from the small refrigerator behind the bar, he twisted the top off and in one motion drained half the bottle. Dropping onto the sofa opposite his desk, he stretched his long legs out in front of him, leaned his head back against the sofa and stared across the room at the Atlanta skyline outside the window.

Davia. He liked her name. It was as beautiful as she was. To say he was smitten was putting it mildly, and he had only seen the woman four times in his life. He knew so little about her, and there was so much he wanted to know. She had told him that she held a business degree from Clark Atlanta and an MBA from Emory. He also knew that she was very well read and extremely intelligent. Oh yes, he wanted to know her better. He had made no secret of that. Good Lord, when she stepped into that restaurant with those jeans riding those shapely hips . . .

Justin sat up suddenly, jolted by the tug in the front of his pants. He blew out a long-agonized breath and finished his juice. Discarding the bottle he walked back to his desk.

He had convinced himself that it was best to give Davia Maxwell some breathing room, since she had indicated that he had come on too strong. But two weeks had passed and he still hadn't called her. The truth was that he didn't want to face another rejection. She was the first woman who had ever rejected his attention, and it had been hard on his ego. There was no denying that, but something told him that this woman was well worth taking the chance on another ego bruising. He wanted her, and if she rejected him again he would survive.

Picking up the receiver, Justin began pushing buttons on the telephone. As he dialed, it didn't dawn on him that he was dialing her home number from memory.

When the call came she didn't know what to do or say. Davia had resigned herself to retreating into her self-contained world. It was comfortable and safe. If she allowed Justin Miles to penetrate her defenses, then he could turn her world upside down. She wasn't sure if she was ready for that, but she was willing to try. So, gathering all of the courage that she could muster, she accepted his invitation to dinner and prayed that she hadn't made a mistake.

They agreed to meet at a restaurant. She had chosen not to have him pick her up at her house. She didn't want Reba or Gabby to know that she had a date with him. Gabby had never seen her go out with a man before, and she wasn't sure of her reaction. It could be confusing for her. As for Reba, she knew what was on her mind; when it came to Justin, Reba would tell CeCe, who would start making wedding plans. So tonight's excursion had been explained as a business affair, and neither woman nor child questioned the explanation.

For the date, Davia slipped on a silk turquoise slip dress that stopped just above her knees and accentuated her womanly curves. She marveled at the rich color and how it complemented her dark complexion. CeCe had picked the dress out for her months ago and had oohed and aahed when Davia modeled it.

Fixing small diamond studs in her pierced ears and the matching thin necklace around her neck, she completed the trio of diamonds with a shimmering ankle bracelet. She stepped into turquoise file pumps that matched her dress, checked her hair and makeup, then nodded in approval. She was ready.

It wasn't until she was heading for the bedroom door that her legs nearly buckled from under her. Catching herself just before she hit the floor, she struggled to a chaise lounge in a corner of the room and fell onto it heavily. Her chest heaved violently as she found it difficult to breathe. Taking gulps of air into her lungs, she leaned forward, resting her head on her knees and whispered a silent prayer. "Please God, let this fear go away. Let it become a thing of the past."

CHAPTER 8

As soon as she walked into the restaurant, Justin knew that his player days were over. He was hooked. This woman had him under her spell and there was nothing he could do about it. There was no doubt about it. Davia Maxwell could be *the one*.

As he stood in the shadows of the lounge adjacent to the restaurant watching her, his heart was pounding loudly in his chest. The dress she was wearing, the glittering diamonds, her hair, her makeup, all perfect. Everything about her was right. If there were any doubts, the amount of male attention she was getting by simply standing in the entranceway confirmed it. Finishing the soda he had ordered, he placed the glass on the bar and with determination headed for Davia. Walking up behind her, he bent and whispered in her ear. "Hello."

Davia jumped, startled by the unexpected greeting. Turning, she opened her mouth to reply but clamped it shut as her eyes traveled down the length of his body. He was dressed in an expensive gray suit, just a shade darker than the gray in his spectacular eyes. A white shirt with thin gray stripes and a gray, silk tie complemented the suit. A white handkerchief peeked at her from his jacket pocket. He looked so good. She felt her stomach flutter at his nearness. Self-consciously, she took a step backward, too nervous to speak.

Although she smiled at him, Justin could tell that she was anxious. He was touched that someone who appeared to be so confident would be unnerved by a date with him. The two of them stood looking at each other until the maitre'd salvaged the awkward moment by showing them to their table.

As they followed him, Davia noted the quiet elegance of the exclusive restaurant that Justin had chosen for their evening together. Candles adorned each linen-covered table, lighting the darkened room like fireflies. A pianist, discreetly sequestered in one corner of the room, played softly, adding just the right touch of ambiance to their surroundings. Once they were seated, the wine steward came to their table inquiring about their selection. Both declined.

"I'm not much of a drinker," Davia confessed, feeling less than sophisticated as a result of the admission.

Justin nodded. "I understand. I don't drink at all. I don't like the taste. That makes it difficult at times, especially since I attend so many social engagements due to my business." He noticed that she sat a little straighter at the mention of his business.

"If you don't mind my asking, what services does your company provide?"

That was all it took for him to start talking. Complete Computers was his baby, and he relished any opportunity to talk about his company.

Davia watched the animated expression on Justin's handsome face as he talked about his pride and joy. He had mentioned his company only briefly during their conversation at Chuck E. Cheese, and she had avoided discussing Small Sensations. She listened with great interest while he told her how, after coming from three generations of physicians on both sides of his family, he broke tradition to become a computer entrepreneur. Now, a decade later, Complete Computers employed hundreds, boasted an international clientele and offered a range of computer services.

"And the best part of all is that I did it on my own," he concluded, "with no help from my family. After Morehouse I never took another penny from my folks, although few people outside of my family believe it."

Davia pondered his words for a moment, looking at him thoughtfully. "You know something, Justin, I'm going to be honest with you. When we first met I thought you were just a rich, idle playboy, but I'm reconsidering that assessment."

Justin smiled, pleased at her candor. "Oh, really?"

"Yes, really. After being with you and talking with you a little more, I sense a substance in your character that's hard to overlook." She paused, looked at him and smiled. "I know what it takes to pursue a dream, and for you to go after yours and reject your family's help while doing it took a lot."

Justin savored Davia's words. He sensed that the admission of having prejudged him hadn't come easily for her.

They dined on a meal of succulent roast duck, snow peas and au gratin potatoes while engaging in conversation. Justin avoided getting too personal as they talked, hoping that by respecting her privacy the nervousness that she had displayed earlier would wane. He wondered if she was aware of how nervous he was being here with her. If she thought that he was in control of this present situation she was wrong. He could only hope that things would go well and that she would want to see him again, because he was certain that he wanted to see more of Davia Maxwell.

Justin blinked rapidly, startled out of his contemplation by the sound of Davia calling his name. He looked into her questioning eyes. "I'm sorry, I'm afraid that my mind was somewhere else. What did you say?"

"I asked why you don't go by your first name, Frederick."

Her question took him by surprise. Had she been interested enough in him to ask others about him? Again, he hoped. "How do you know my name is Frederick?"

"That night at the Black Chamber of Commerce dinner, CeCe did some detective work and found out that you go by your middle name."

She took a spoonful of the strawberry shortcake they had ordered for dessert, licking at a dab of stray whip cream at the corner of her mouth with a swipe of her tongue. Justin's eyes followed the gesture as, instantly, his body reacted. Shifting in his seat, he took a sip of water and then cleared his throat.

"Actually, my name is Frederick Justin—two names that came from my mother's side of the family. My second middle name is Zachary, after my dad. Now, I know that Frederick Justin Zachary is a mouthful, but if you want to call me that, I don't mind." He winked. "As long as you call me."

Davia chuckled. "There you go coming on strong again."

Justin looked chastised. "Oops, sorry."

Having finished her dessert Davia sat back in her chair and eyed him speculatively. She liked Justin Miles. It wasn't just the fact that he stirred her senses and upset her entire equilibrium. She liked his easygoing manner. The fears she had harbored about this date now seemed silly. This was the second time she had spent a long period of time with him and nothing drastic had happened. She relaxed a bit more.

Justin noticed the change in her body language. "So am I forgiven for that momentary slip of decorum? Do you still like me?"

"I didn't say I liked you in the first place," Davia retorted, pleased with her ability to be playful with him. "If you want me to say it, I will. I like you."

She was shocked by her own admission and quickly drank from her water glass to cover her embarrassment. Justin was pleased by her comment but recognized some reservation in her response.

"Well, I like it that you like me, *Ms.* Maxwell, yet I hear a *but* in that forced confession."

Davia looked at him solemnly. "You're very perceptive. The *but* is that we come from two different worlds."

"Oh, do we? So you're the human being and I'm the alien? Is that it?" He grinned, but she remained somber. He got the message.

Folding his hands on the table, he leaned forward and looked her in the eyes. "You haven't told me much about your world, Davia, but I think that any difference we might have makes us more interesting. Yet, you're right. I do come from another world. I've been taught since childhood that I'm a member of what my mother calls the black elite."

"The Talent Tenth was what W.E.B. DuBois called it."

"Ah, the lady knows her history."

"Quite well."

Her sharp tone caused Justin to pause. Their eyes held each other steadily. It was obvious that she was hostile to the concept and he prayed that his background wouldn't put a wedge between the possibilities he saw for them. He continued. "Then as you probably suspect, as a member of this so-called black elite, my parents tried to structure my life so that I came in contact only with people like myself—those who were wealthy and privileged. I was expected to engage in activities with the children of others just like me. I had to belong to the right clubs, the right fraternity. My sister and I weren't allowed to mingle with anyone else."

"That must have been boring."

Justin laughed. She was astute.

"You're right, it was. That's why I rebelled."

Davia raised an eyebrow. "For some reason I'm not surprised. What did you do?" Justin had her full attention.

"I didn't like the kids in those clubs and organizations, so I refused to put up with them. Instead, I ran with my best friend, Clark."

"I remember your mentioning him when we were talking at Chuck E. Cheese. Wasn't he a rich kid, too?"

"No, not with money, but rich with love and family. His parents work for my folks. His father's the chauffeur and his mother is the housekeeper. We're only a few months apart in age and we were inseparable. We got in a couple of scrapes we shouldn't have, but nothing criminal. Finally my parents got tired of it all and decided to quell my rebellion. My mother talked my father into sending me to a boarding school. They said that it would expand my horizons."

"Did it?"

"Oh, I got a few friends from the experience, but mostly it sucked."

It was Davia's opportunity to laugh. Justin seemed to take life's experiences with a grain of salt. Of course he could afford to do that. Life had not afforded her the same privilege. She would not be telling him her story with the same casual abandon. Not that she was going to tell him her story at all. That was in the past. Of course it would be nice if he was the type of man that she *could* trust with her past. Was it possible? She doubted it. Life had taught her not to trust any man.

Justin noted the myriad of emotions crossing Davia's face, the last one being a shadow. Concerned, he reached across the table to take the hands she had folded carefully on the table. At his touch she snatched her hands away quickly and jumped back in her chair. Her eyes were wide with fear. Justin was baffled by her reaction.

Davia's face heated in embarrassment as she looked into Justin's questioning eyes. "I . . . I . . . I'm sorry. I . . . I don't know why I did that. I . . ." Noting that her actions had attracted the attention of fellow patrons, her humiliation became more acute. Horrified, she whispered, "I've got to go home." Grabbing her purse off the table, she rose from her seat and rushed out of the restaurant, leaving Justin behind.

At a loss as to what had just happened and why, Justin paid the bill and hurried after her. What had spooked her? What had he done? He made it to the parking lot just as Davia was entering her car.

Slowing his pace, afraid that he might spook her again, he spoke quietly as he drew near. "So I'm such a bad date that you're running away without saying good night?"

With her hand on the open car door, Davia froze at the sound of his voice. Emitting a shuddering sigh, she shut her eyes and wished that this whole night would go away. She had made a fool of herself in front of him and ruined what was turning out to be a pleasant evening. How could she face him again? She was a novice when it came to dating, and she should have foreseen the potential for disaster. She wanted to disappear.

Justin watched the look of distress on her face. It was so acute that he wanted to take her into his arms and comfort her. Instead, he jammed his hands into his trouser pockets. If only he could get her to tell him what was wrong, because something was *definitely* wrong.

"I hope you'll accept my apology before we part for the evening." The weight in his heart lightened as her long lashes lifted and her dark eyes settled on his face. He could see the silent review of the evening in her head as she considered his statement.

She frowned. "Why are you apologizing? You didn't do anything."

He stepped a bit closer and reached for straws. "I touched you, without your permission. You didn't like it."

Davia gave a sardonic chuckle. "Yes, I would say that was quite obvious to you and everyone else, but you didn't do anything out of place. It's just . . ."

"It's *just* what, Davia?" he whispered, daring to step closer. They stood only inches apart, only the open car door standing between them.

The sound of her name on his lips was like liquid fire—soft, sensuous. Justin placed his hands on the top of the car door next to her hand. She could feel his heat.

"Tell me, Davia. Tell me what's wrong." He looked into her pain-filled eyes, wanting to eliminate that pain. He wanted to increase the joy in her life. He wanted her to see the desire for her in his eyes.

Davia did see the desire and it was disconcerting. She had been duped before by silver-tongued words from someone she thought would be kind to her. She had been tricked. She would never let that happen again.

She had been young then and starved for affection. She was a grown woman now and her senses were much more acute. Yet the ability to trust still eluded her. Could it be possible that Justin Miles could be trusted? Could he stand up to scrutiny? She searched those gray-green eyes carefully. Could she trust Justin Miles with her present? Could she trust him with her past? The burden of not trusting anyone was getting heavy, but she wasn't yet ready to give it up.

She took a deep breath. "I'd rather not say what's wrong, Justin. But, who knows, maybe someday I will be ready to talk about it."

"I'll settle for what I can get."

Davia offered him a handshake and thanked him for the evening. "I'm afraid that's all that I can give you for now."

Justin nodded, suppressing his disappointment, as he watched her get into her car and start the engine. Before pulling away she rolled the window down and leaned out. His hopes soared.

Davia smiled at his expectant expression and for reasons she couldn't fathom, she decided to take an invisible step forward. "Next Saturday, the date is on me."

As he watched her drive away, Justin couldn't wipe the grin off his face.

"Who is Davia Maxwell?"

Justin lifted his eyes from his dinner plate to look at his mother. It was ironic that she should ask the same question that he had been asking himself. The only difference was that the motive behind each of their questions was different.

Taking a sip of his soup, he answered nonchalantly, "She's a friend of mine."

Nothing in his voice or his actions betrayed the fact that he wanted her to be anything more than that.

Katherine nodded; her senses were attuned to the slightest indication that this Davia Maxwell might be something more than a friend. Men could be so naive sometimes, and a rich, handsome man like Justin was a prime target for some tramp. Justin had always been independent to a fault, defying her and his father at every turn, but when it came to the important matter of choosing a mate, she meant to have some say-so in who would be the mother of her grandchildren. They would be the ones to carry the history and heritage of two of Atlanta's most prominent black families. His choice for a wife must be impeccable.

"Vanessa tells me that her daughter goes to Bianca's school."

Justin's eyes slid to Vanessa, who appeared to be very interested in the pattern on the china. He had wondered when Davia's name might come up. He'd never mentioned the biting incident to his sister or mother and neither had Bianca, but the two little girls had developed a growing friendship over the past few weeks and Gabby's name was already a household word. After meeting Davia, Vanessa had asked him about her, noting how attractive she was, but he had been noncommittal, just as he was being at this moment with his mother.

Katherine continued her probing. "Vanessa mentioned that she met this Davia at the Black Chamber event, but hasn't seen or spoken to her at the school."

"She drops her daughter off and picks her up at a different time, Mother." Vanessa sounded defensive.

"It doesn't matter, Vanessa. I've always told you about the importance of knowing the parents of one's children." The censure in her voice was evident. "Bianca tells me that your brother and this Davia person met at Chuck E. Cheese with the children. Although we really know nothing about this woman, it seems that Justin has no objection to having your child spend time with her." She looked at her son disapprovingly.

Justin refused to take the bait. Vanessa already knew about the Chuck E. Cheese meeting. He had nothing to explain. He kept eating as the inquisition continued.

Katherine took another tactic. "Gabby, what a peculiar name, but at least I'm able to pronounce it." Katherine threw an amused glance across the table at Charles Cash, who had joined them for dinner this evening.

Charles took the cue. "It's better than Shanequa, or Charmain, or Quetta, some of the names I've heard." He joined Katherine in condescending laughter.

Justin's jaw tightened. He didn't like their laughter at the expense of others, and he wasn't too fond of Charles. It seemed that every time he visited his mother the man was there. He was always polite and seemed very respectful toward Katherine, Vanessa and Bianca, and his mother seemed to enjoy his company. If she was happy Justin was happy for her. Just as he didn't want her prying into his love life, he wouldn't pry into his mother's. She had been a widow for six years and deserved to be happy again. Yet, there was something about Charles Cash—

Their laughter drifted into his thoughts and disturbed him. His eyes narrowed as he looked at his mother. "We as black people have always been creative. Why wouldn't it continue in naming our children? After all, oftentimes a name is all a person might have to give his or her child. Why not make it as unique and as special as possible? And Gabby is a nickname for Gabrielle, which, as you know, Mother, is French. I think it's a beautiful name."

Katherine's laughter turned into a coy smile. "Is that all that you find beautiful in the Maxwell household?"

Justin wasn't falling for that one. "I find beauty everywhere I go, Mother, especially in this room." He winked at her.

Vanessa laughed at his clever retort. Katherine pouted. "Justin, I'm not trying to get into your 'business,' as you so crudely put it. I simply asked a question!"

He knew that he was tiptoeing through a potential minefield. Katherine wanted information, and if she couldn't get it from him, she would get *mis*information from somewhere else.

"Actually, Davia Maxwell is quite attractive." *That was an understatement.* "And if you're trying to ask me about her family background, I don't know anything about it. All I know is that she seems like a nice lady." *And that she turns me on totally!* Justin resumed eating his dinner.

Katherine nodded thoughtfully. "I see."

She returned to her own meal, but she had watched her son closely as he talked about the Maxwell woman.

He had displayed little or no interest, and that was his big mistake. Justin Miles displaying no interest in a beautiful woman was like a child leaving a candy store without asking for a treat. It didn't happen. Something was going on.

Meanwhile, this little friendship Bianca had developed with this Gabby child had to be closely watched. She doubted if her grandchild could learn very much from people outside of their social circle. Justin was a grown man, and if he wanted to hobnob with the masses, that was different, but Bianca was a baby, and it was her duty as the child's grandmother to see to it that she was not unduly influenced by those unlike herself. She regretted the day that Vanessa had enrolled the child in that *school*.

Why she had to fight to maintain family traditions and mores was beyond her comprehension. Young people today didn't seem to understand tradition and the importance of knowing one's place in life. With her marriage to Zachary, the Justin and Miles families had become *the* social and economic forces in black Atlanta. She would go to her grave before she would let all that both families had worked for be easily compromised.

CHAPTER 9

The cat was out of the bag at the Maxwell house about her date with Justin Miles. Both Reba and CeCe were ganging up on her today, and she was about at the end of her rope. It had been an early morning phone call from Justin that had done the deed. She had been asleep when he called and Reba had taken the message: *Tell Davia that I enjoyed our date Saturday and I'm looking forward to this Saturday.* Reba had given her the evil eye when she delivered the message and Davia had confessed to CeCe without any prompting.

Now it was Friday, the evening before their second date, and the three women sat on the deck of Davia's house overlooking her fragrant garden while CeCe and Reba pressured her to tell all.

"I cannot believe that you would go on a date with Justin Miles and not tell your friends anything about it." CeCe was hurt and wanted Davia to know it.

"And she lied to me," Reba added, sounding just as wounded. "She told me that she was going to a *business* affair last Saturday. I should have known she wasn't wearing that turquoise dress to impress any *business* acquaintance."

CeCe squealed. "You wore the turquoise dress? Humph, humph, humph." She shook her head slowly from side to side. "You could have killed the man because, honey, he wants you."

Reba added. "Yes, he does, and when a man wants a woman like that, nothing is going to stop him." Reba addressed CeCe. "You should have heard him on the telephone." She put an imaginary telephone receiver to her ear to dramatize. "Uh, is Davia Maxwell home? Uh, this is Justin Miles." She grinned at the thought of the flustered caller. "He was hesitant, uncertain. Not sure that his call would be accepted. I could hear it in his voice. And I assure you, a man like Justin Miles is not the kind who lacks confidence. It's not in his character. The only thing that would make a man like him hesitant is a woman who has gone against the grain of everything he's known."

CeCe shook her head in agreement. "Uh-huh, the girl done put a whippin' on that tail and he doesn't know which way to turn." She turned to Davia, looking at her with a new sense of admiration. "Girl, what did you do to that man?"

"She's got what it takes, that's all." Reba grinned at Davia approvingly, and picked up an empty pitcher that had contained lemonade. "Let me go fix us another round."

As soon as Reba disappeared into the house, CeCe scooted her deck chair closer to Davia's and whispered teasingly, "You and Justin didn't get it on, did you?"

"What!" Davia jumped from her deck chair so quickly that it overturned. Birds nesting nearby scattered. Butterflies fluttered away. "How could you think that I would do something like that? I don't even know him! We've seen each other two or three times! I won't be thought of as a whore!"

Shocked by Davia's reaction, CeCe sat frozen.

"I was only teasing," she said weakly, realizing instantly that she had gone too far.

Davia stood trembling with anger at the accusation that she felt had been hurled at her. CeCe had never seen her like this. She was at a loss to how her words had caused such a reaction. However, she knew that there were secrets in Davia's life to which she was not privy. Not once in their friendship had she pressed her to confide those secrets. She had always hoped that eventually she would do it on her own. Their friendship was based on the unspoken agreement that there were areas of their lives that would not be discussed. CeCe wasn't certain what her own areas were. She seemed to have confided her entire life to Davia, from her disastrous three-month marriage at nineteen to the death of her baby shortly after its birth. It was Davia who had the untouchable topics. Now sex must be added to the list. With her reference to the last of those taboos, CeCe could tell from her stance that Davia was willing to challenge their friendship. CeCe wasn't.

Rising from her chair, she approached Davia cautiously, measuring each step. There was pain and defiance in her friend's eyes. CeCe spoke softly. "I'm sorry, Davia. I didn't mean anything by what I said."

"Then why did you say it?" Davia's nose flared, and her breathing was heavy. She declared emphatically, "I will *not* be thought of as a whore!"

CeCe stopped in front of her. "It was a bad joke, my friend, a sad attempt to be flippant. I apologize. I would never think of you in those terms."

Feeling foolish about her reaction, Davia took a deep breath. She and CeCe had gone through too much together for her to react like this, especially when her friend had no idea what was behind her response. Perhaps this was the time to change that and take a step out of the past.

She sat back down at the table. CeCe joined her. Reaching across the table, Davia placed her hand on top of CeCe's. "No, I'm the one who's sorry. You're my best friend and I wouldn't hurt you for the world."

CeCe flashed an understanding smile. "I know that."

"It's just that there have been so many things that I don't want to remember." Davia paused. Like a kaleidoscope, brief moments of her tumultuous life flashed before her. "But maybe it's time that I did."

CeCe stilled, unable to believe what she was hearing after all of these years. Davia spoke quietly.

"Before last Saturday, I haven't dated anyone since I was fourteen years old, if you want to call what I did dating." She paused, traveling back in time. "His name was Mark Cattrell, and he was sixteen years old. We met at a fast food restaurant in downtown Chicago. He was smart, well spoken and well dressed, and he told me that I was pretty and made me feel like I was. We used to meet at the restaurant every weekend and he would take me to the beach, to museums. He opened up a whole new world. It wasn't until he took me to his parents' home on Lake Shore Drive that I discovered that his family were wealthy. He told me that the difference in our backgrounds didn't matter, that he loved me. That's all I needed to hear. No one had ever loved me before. His folks weren't at home the day he took me over there, so we took advantage of that and we ended up in his bed. That's where his parents found us."

Davia stopped, not certain that she could continue without breaking down. She took a shaky breath. "I don't have to describe the scene that took place when they discovered us, but I never expected to hear the things that they said to me." She closed her eyes, the events of that day still painful. "His parents called me a whore. They said that I was ghetto trash who had seduced their son. They assured me that I was beneath them and their son in every way. To make matters worse, Mark never said a word in my defense. Not one word." Davia opened her eyes, brought back to the present. "A week later Mark and his parents died in a small plane crash. It was two months after that I discovered I was pregnant."

Davia watched CeCe closely, searching for the slightest sign of condemnation. She saw none; instead, her friend's eyes glistened with tears.

"It must have been difficult, being all alone—a child carrying a child."

"I survived."

"Yes, you did," CeCe concurred. As a matter of fact, Davia had done more than that. Now pieces of the puzzle that formed her friend's life made sense, especially her reluctance to get involved in emotional entanglements with men. Davia had something to prove. *"I won't be thought of as a whore!"*

CeCe ached for her friend and what she had endured in the past. Life had dealt her some harsh blows, but she had fought back and she had won. CeCe squeezed her hand in reassurance. "Thank you for sharing with me."

"Like I say, it was time." Davia gave a sigh of relief. The burden of silence had been lifted. She had finally told her best friend almost everything.

Justin couldn't get enough of Davia Maxwell. She was on his mind constantly.

At his weekly Wednesday night dinner at his mother's house, she mentioned that he seemed distracted. Vanessa also noticed, as did Bianca. His niece complained that he wasn't playing with her at the dinner table the way he usually did. The ever-present Charles Cash tickled her and said that maybe he could take her uncle's place. Justin scowled at the comment. *Not likely.* Still, his family was right. His growing fascination with the lovely Ms. Maxwell had his mind in a constant fog.

Saturday evening finally arrived, and it hadn't come soon enough for him. They met at a movie complex in a suburban shopping mall. This second date turned out to be less strained than the first. The film that they saw was a comedy, and they left the theatre thoroughly entertained. They were still laughing at the antics in the movie as they walked to their respective cars.

"I like that comedian," Davia declared, feeling much more relaxed than she had when the night began. "Of course there are guys coming up that are just as funny, but he still has what it takes to make me laugh."

She glanced out of the corner of her eye at Justin. He was simply overwhelming. It wasn't just his height; he was just so attractive. He was dressed casually in all gray, and he had to know how good he looked in that color, especially with those gray-green eyes. More than one woman at the theatre had given him surreptitious looks, yet Justin's attention had been focused completely on her. He had made her feel very special.

"You know, I was thinking," he said, breaking the brief silence between them as they strolled. "A lot of these comedians got their big breaks on television, but I can't see it replacing the comedy clubs. These guys need a place to hone their craft."

"Well, I guess you're right, but I can't say. I've never seen a stand-up comedian live."

Justin came to a stop and his eyebrows shot up in surprise. "You haven't!"

Davia shook her head, unsure if that was good or bad from his reaction.

He grinned, obviously delighted. "Hmmm, I was just wondering where I could take you next." In his excitement he forgot the no touch rule which he had practiced religiously throughout the evening. Taking her hand he pulled her toward the parking lot. "Come on, let's take my car and come back and get yours later. We'll grab a couple of burgers and be at the club in time for the last show." Wordlessly, Davia trotted alongside him. Caught up in his excitement, she forgot the no touch rule as well.

Hours later as he pulled up in front of Davia's house, Justin felt a sense of loss at having to part with her for the evening. The night had been perfect. Davia seemed to have had the time of her life. She had been fascinated by the comedy club and the comics and he had enjoyed sharing the experience with her. The truth was that he enjoyed everything about Davia. The lady was too good to be true. She listened well and had a positive view of life—all of that and an exquisite face and body, too.

Davia had objected to his following her home. She didn't want Gabby to see them together. But he had insisted, noting that at this late hour Gabby should be in bed. Suspecting that her fear of his following her home wasn't based on Gabby's curiosity, his departure at her front door consisted of the simple words "Good night." But, not kissing those luscious lips had been an exercise in self-restraint. As he strolled down the walkway to his car, he vowed that he would be back, and the next time that they parted at her front door, a kiss would be in order.

CHAPTER 10

"These dogs are killing me!" CeCe fell back in her chair and slid her feet out of the heels she had been wearing.

Davia took a sip of her soda, letting it wash down the remainder of her sandwich. She looked at CeCe unsympathetically. "It serves you right for wearing heels to the shopping center. You're the only person I know who gets dressed in heels to go shopping. You're going to be short, no matter what you wear."

"I ain't thinking about you, girl. I do not go out of the house looking bad, even to go shopping. That's a no-no." CeCe bit into her own sandwich with relish, chewing as she spoke. "I am starved to death. Spending your money is hard work."

Davia rolled her eyes at her friend. Justin had called and asked her for a third date this Saturday and she had accepted. Unfortunately, CeCe had been in Davia's office when the call came. Overhearing the conversation, she had insisted that Davia shop for something new to wear on her date. CeCe had picked her up this morning and whisked them to so many of her shopping haunts, Davia had lost count.

Shopping was an activity in which Davia rarely indulged. CeCe, on the other hand, thought of it as her patriotic duty. This was the day that Davia was to go out with Justin, and she and CeCe had spent half of it in shopping malls. Although she had grumbled at first, Davia had to admit that she was having fun. She liked taking time to do simple things. For too long, she had been busy working, following her dream, acquiring the material things that she thought would make her life perfect. It had taken quite a while for her to realize that absolute perfection was a futile pursuit. The lesson had cost her dearly. But she was changing and she was beginning to appreciate the results.

"Hello."

The deep timbre of his voice startled her out of her pensiveness. She had come to recognize Justin's voice as readily as she had come to recognize those gorgeous gray-green eyes that now stared down at her. Unable to conceal her surprise, or her pleasure, she smiled up at him.

"Hello."

Her heartbeat accelerated and silently she berated herself for her reaction. Her mind was still trying to resist her attraction to Justin, but her heart knew it was useless. He stirred something inside of her buried long ago. It was frightening because she didn't know what to do with the feeling.

Glancing across the table to see CeCe's reaction to Justin's sudden appearance, she discovered her usually animated friend sitting frozen in place. Her sandwich was suspended in midair. Her eyes weren't riveted on Justin but on the man standing next to him. Davia glanced at him briefly. He was almost as tall as Justin and just as well built. He was a rich chocolate brown, with penetrating black eyes, a broad nose and well-defined lips. His head was shaved and a diamond stud pierced his left earlobe. He was a handsome man, and CeCe was making it obvious that she thought so, too. Acknowledging his presence with a nod, Davia returned her attention to Justin.

Justin's grin could have lit up Mt. Everest as he stood basking in Davia's smile. Clark's eyes moved from Justin to the dark-skinned beauty smiling up at him, then back to his friend. Slowly it dawned on him what was up with Justin, what was *really* up.

He had wondered about his friend's sudden urge to shop this afternoon after their one-on-one basketball game. Unlike himself, Justin was not a shopaholic. Although just as fastidious about his dress as Clark, Justin used the same tailor that his father had used. Rarely did he buy off the rack. So when Justin had claimed that he was turning to Clark for his assistance, Clark knew something was afoot. Now here she was in the flesh, and she wasn't alone.

"Won't you gentlemen join us?" CeCe asked, giving Justin a dimple-cheeked smile while eyeing Clark speculatively.

"Sure." Justin's answer was casual but he was barely containing the excitement he was feeling at seeing Davia. He took a seat in the empty chair next to her, while Clark sat down next to CeCe. Justin made the introductions. "Davia Maxwell, Charlotte Green, this is my friend, Clark Gaston. Clark, Davia and Charlotte."

"Call me CeCe." Her eyes twinkled as she held out her hand to shake Clark's. Neither Justin nor Davia noticed the sparkle in Clark's eyes. They were each too entranced with the other.

"We'll have to stop meeting like this, Ms. Maxwell," Justin teased.

"Like what, Mr. Miles?" she retorted with an impish grin.

"By accident, Ms. Maxwell. If I didn't know better, I'd think that you were stalking me. I know I've been stalking you." He winked and settled back in his chair as she blushed.

"That's some way to break the ice, man." Clark chuckled, taking note of the smitten expression on Justin's face. "Declaring yourself a stalker." He turned to the petite CeCe and shook his head slowly. "I can't take the man anywhere."

CeCe gave him another dimpled smile and Clark felt like a snowflake melting in the heat of summer. He'd thought Justin was in trouble! He'd been at the table two seconds and was going down for the count. Trying to appear calmer than he felt, he returned his attention to Justin. "Hey, man, if the ladies don't mind us joining them, let's go grab something to eat." He looked at CeCe, praying that she didn't show that dimple again until he regained his senses. "You ladies don't mind if we share your table, do you?"

His prayers weren't answered. CeCe flashed that smile. "Of course not."

Clark made a fast retreat. An amused Justin caught up with him as they surveyed the choices of eateries. "Is something wrong, my man?" He couldn't keep the teasing out of his voice.

Clark ignored the implication. "I was going to ask you the same thing. Why haven't I heard the name Davia before? It's obvious there's something going on between you two."

They stopped in front of a gourmet hamburger stand. "Yes, there is. We met a couple of weeks ago and we've been out twice. As a matter of fact, we're going out again tonight."

Clark smiled. "I see, so that's the sudden interest in upgrading the wardrobe."

Justin didn't deny it. "Man, this woman has put the whammy on me, hard and fast. I can't even explain it." He glanced over at CeCe, then returned his attention to Clark. "I think you know what I mean."

Clark couldn't deny it. "Yeah, maybe I do."

At the table an excited CeCe addressed Davia. "Girl, we've got to get those two hunks out of here quick before these sophisticated heifers stomp us into the ground making their plays." She glanced around the eating area of the upscale mall at the women whose eyes were firmly fixed on Justin and Clark. "We've got to come up with a plan."

Davia was amused at CeCe's demeanor. Her normally unflappable friend was flappable after all, and it was obvious that Clark Gaston was doing the flapping. She could relate. "I don't know what your plans are, but mine are already made. I'm going out with Justin in about . . ." she checked her gold wristwatch, ". . . seven hours."

CeCe glared at her. "I know you're gonna hook a sister up."

Davia laughed. "From the way that man was looking at you, I don't think I have to do any *hookup*."

CeCe leaned across the table and whispered accusingly, "Why didn't you tell me about Clark? He's gorgeous!"

Davia agreed. Clark Gaston was cute, but Justin—he defied all of her preconceived notions about men. His mere presence turned her on, and that was proving to be a problem. She didn't know what to do about it, or how to react. In her thirty-four years of living, self-preservation was the sharpest instinct she had honed. It was the only thing she knew. She had protected herself with it all of her life, but with Justin, she felt the armor she wore was in serious danger of being penetrated.

She answered CeCe's inquiry. "He mentioned Clark as being his best friend, but I hadn't met him, and I don't know that much about him."

CeCe wiggled her eyebrows. "Then I'll just have the pleasure of doing some hooking up by myself. Ssshhh. Here they come. Just sit back and watch the master at work."

"You don't have to pour it on too thick. He's obviously interested."

"Interest and pursuit are two different things, sweetheart." CeCe giggled wickedly. "I mean to encourage pursuit."

Justin and Clark reached the table and were sitting down when Davia's cell phone rang. She answered it. Leroy was on the other end.

Her table companions watched her intently as her demeanor changed. It was clear that the news from the other end wasn't good.

She answered tightly, "I'll be there shortly." Terminating the call, she noticed the expectant looks on the faces of her companions. "I'm sorry, I've got to get down to my office. It's an emergency."

"Nothing serious, I hope?" asked Justin.

Davia gave him a grateful smile. "Nothing that can't be handled."

"Who was that, your assistant?" CeCe sounded concerned.

"It was Leroy."

Justin felt a lurch in the pit of his stomach. Why would Leroy Platten call Davia on a Saturday? Didn't she get time to enjoy herself? How much *did* he rely on her? He heard himself saying. "If you didn't drive, I'll take you to your office."

She looked surprised at the offer. "That's nice of you, but I rode with CeCe and she'll . . ."

"Make sure that Clark gets home," CeCe completed her sentence. "I assume that he was riding with you?" Although her comment was directed at Justin, her eyes and her smile were on Clark.

"Yeah, you're right," Clark quickly answered for Justin. "I'd appreciate the ride." He turned to Justin, his eyes daring him to say a word. He didn't.

Wrapping his burger to go, Justin stood and held his hand out to Davia. "That's settled. Shall we?"

Justin sat in Davia's spacious office, pretending to leaf through a magazine while discreetly watching her as she took care of business. What he saw was impressive.

A large shipment of clothes had been lost in a trucking accident. The Small Sensations truck driver had been seriously injured. The client to whom the clothes were being shipped had a large backlog of orders for Small Sensations apparel and was unsympathetic to the unforeseen accident that was holding up his order. A small fortune in merchandise had already been lost and an even larger fortune would be sacrificed if the matter wasn't settled to the customer's satisfaction. With astute efficiency, Davia settled the matter.

As he watched her, Justin's admiration and respect for the woman's prowess grew by leaps and bounds. Was there nothing she couldn't do? She was raising her grand-daughter with love and complete devotion. She handled business with the skill and finesse of a person twice her age, and she had captured his heart with little effort, a feat he couldn't have imagined for any female a few short weeks ago.

Right now she sat at her desk talking on the telephone to the wife of the injured truck driver, assuring the woman that she shouldn't worry about a thing. She reiterated that he would receive full pay during the time needed for his recovery. Her voice was soft, soothing, sympathetic, and, for Justin, arousing.

How many company vice presidents would take the time to make such a personal call? Her kindness and consideration opened a place for her in his heart that he doubted could be easily removed. He liked everything about this woman and wanted her to know it. He wanted her to become part of his life and wasn't going to wait any longer to tell her so.

Tossing the magazine aside he focused his entire attention on her. She sat in the oversized swivel chair with her blue jean-clad legs crossed as she rubbed her brow, which was furrowed in worry. Her beautiful face was etched with weariness. He wanted to hold her, caress her, and take the weariness away. They'd been in the office over six hours and he had resisted every attempt she had made to get him to leave her. The time that their date was to officially begin was in less than an hour, but she was exhausted. It would have to wait until another day. The best recourse was to see that she ate something and then get her home where she could get some rest.

Davia took the telephone headset off and disconnected the call. She felt as if she had done battle with a two-ton elephant. She was tired down to her bones. Placing the headset on her desk, she looked up to see Justin staring at her. She could feel the sexual tension emanating from him clear across the room. She wanted to dismiss his heated stare, but she didn't. Instead, she returned his gaze with one that held just as much fire.

Justin rose from his seat and stole across the room. Davia didn't move as their eyes locked. As he drew closer, his eyes darkened with growing passion while hers widened with uncertainty.

Rounding the desk, he turned her chair to face him and braced his palms on each arm of it. Their faces were mere inches apart.

"I'll never hurt you, Davia," he whispered in answer to her unspoken doubts.

His words brushed across her heart like a summer breeze. She closed her eyes to enjoy their essence and then opened them to dispel their myth. "Men always hurt me."

Her words were filled with such torment that Justin drew back against their assault. Just then the door to Davia's office opened, and Leroy burst into the room.

"Davia, thank goodness you got here. I was . . ."

He stopped short as Davia and Justin jumped apart at the unexpected intrusion. The older man's expression was one of confusion at the sight of Justin. Then it gradually turned to one of recognition.

"Hey, I know you." He snapped his fingers, trying to make a connection. "You're . . . you're . . ."

"Justin Miles," Davia said. "Justin, this is Leroy Platten."

Leroy pumped Justin's hand eagerly. "Yes, yes, Katherine Miles's son. A friend of mine pointed you out to me a couple of weeks ago at the Black Chamber of Commerce Awards Banquet. I wanted to come and introduce myself then, but didn't get the opportunity. It's very nice to meet you."

"It's nice meeting you, too, Mr. Platten."

"Call me Leroy."

"And I'm Justin."

Leroy nodded agreeably. There was an awkward silence as he glanced at Davia, expecting an explanation for Justin's presence. Receiving none, he returned his attention to the visitor. "Well, to what do we owe this honor?"

"Uh, he . . ." Davia was tongue-tied. Justin came to the rescue.

"I ran into Davia at a shopping mall earlier today with her friend, Ms. Green. The three of us were talking when you called her. Since Davia hadn't driven, I offered to bring her here to the office so that Ms. Green wouldn't have to interrupt her day."

The explanation was short and to the point and Davia was grateful. She didn't know why she was at such a loss to explain his presence. She owed Leroy no explanations, but for some reason she felt like a kid being caught with her hand in the cookie jar.

Leroy nodded. "Oh, I see. I didn't know you two knew each other."

Another awkward silence filled the room. Leroy's years of life experience told him not to pursue the course of this conversation. He retreated to safer ground.

"That was certainly nice of you, Justin, to give her a ride." He turned to Davia. "I cut the meeting in Savannah short to come back and see what I could do to help, but I should have known that you wouldn't need me. I called the client from the limo coming here from the airport, and he couldn't say enough good things about you." He turned back to Justin. "I'm telling you, this woman is a miracle worker. She's the best thing to happen to me since water and sunlight!"

Going to Davia, Leroy pulled her up from her chair and hugged her. He then planted a kiss on her cheek. "You're one great lady."

Justin stiffened as he noted Davia's acceptance of Leroy's affection. She didn't recoil from his touch. Instead, she patted the man affectionately on his back. *Leroy could hold her. He could even kiss her, but she won't let me do either!*

Happily rubbing his hands together, Leroy turned from Davia just in time to see the jealousy that Justin was trying to conceal. Leroy fought the smile trying to force its way to the surface. So that's how it was? Davia had finally found someone special, and from the look of it Justin was about two seconds away from kicking his tail. It was time to make a hasty retreat and let nature take its course.

Leroy headed toward the door. However, he decided to provide a little reassurance before he left. He didn't want those silly rumors about him and Davia to get in the way of progress.

"I've got to get home to the little woman. I can't wait to see her. Two days away from her is more than I can stand."

He offered Justin his hand. "Nice meeting you."

Justin shook his hand. "Same here."

Leroy squeezed the younger man's hand and looked him in the eye. "Good luck." His words were sincere, but the look transmitted to Justin made it clear that if he hurt Davia, he was going to need more than luck.

Both approval and warning had been communicated in their polite exchange. Justin had nothing to worry about here. The older man cared about Davia and he wanted her to be happy with the right person. The two men exchanged knowing smiles.

Justin returned the man's steady gaze. "Thank you."

Leroy closed the door behind him, leaving a satisfied Justin and an upset Davia behind.

"You two must think I'm stupid!" she fumed as she came from behind the desk. "I saw what was going on between the two of you. You were standing here in *my* office going through some little testosterone thing. I saw him giving his approval of your being here, as if I want or need his approval."

Justin chuckled. "So you peeked at that little exchange, did you? Like you, I neither need nor want his approval, but I can tell that you respect him. So, I'd rather have him on my side than vice versa." Slowly, he began to advance toward her.

She pointed a finger at him. "You hold on. Stop right there, mister!"

With his hands clasped behind his back, Justin stopped right in front of her and gently kissed her fingertip. Startled, Davia snatched her hand away.

"Don't . . . don't do that." Blinking furiously, her eyes flew to his.

"Don't do what?" Justin replied quietly.

"That! Kissing. Don't!" It was hard to think.

"Are you asking me not to do this?" He planted the sweetest of kisses on her temple. She stiffened. "Or this?" His lips moved to her eyelids. Pushing against his chest, Davia forced him away from her.

"No!" On shaky legs, she backed away.

"No, what?" Justin didn't retreat.

"I can't . . . I can't . . ." Davia stuttered.

"Care for me?" Justin finished her sentence. "I disagree." He reached out to her.

Davia's heart was beating out of her chest. Could it be possible? His words were so reassuring.

"Trust me, Davia," he crooned. "I won't hurt you."

The words pricked her soul. *Was it possible? Could she really trust him?* Davia's stiffness began to recede.

Justin's body was now flush with Davia's as her eyes closed involuntarily. Gently, he wrapped an arm around her waist.

"Believe in me." He kissed both eyelids.

She wanted to believe.

His kiss moved to the tip of her nose. "Trust me."

She swayed and a sob caught in her throat. *Lord, she needed to believe in the possibility!*

Cautiously, Justin's lips touched her lips. She didn't resist. He increased the pressure and her lips slowly parted.

CHAPTER 11

The kiss was brief. Davia was the first to pull away. Justin could see that she was frightened and he wanted to reassure her that she had no reason to be. He wanted to hold her close to him, to let her know that he had anxieties too. He reached out to caress her cheek, but she backed away. His hand halted in midair.

"I know that you've been hurt, Davia."

"No, you really don't know anything about me," she corrected him. Her voice was shaking. *How could he know? How could he have a clue?*

"I can't argue that, but I want to get to know you." He dared a step toward her. "I want to know everything about you because I care." The sincerity in his eyes confirmed his statement as he dared another step toward her.

Despite her continued uncertainty, Davia didn't retreat. She had already opened up to this man more than she had to any other man in her life. Justin's kindness and concern overwhelmed her. The qualities that he seemed to possess indicated that he might be different from other men she had known. He threatened to penetrate defenses that she had perfected. She could feel them crumbling. Still, she challenged his resolve.

"So you want to know about my life. You, the son of privilege who couldn't possibly understand." She shook her head. "No, Justin, you only *think* you want to know. You see, my life has been very different, and the picture isn't pretty."

Wanting to put distance between them, Davia moved across the room to the refrigerator built into the wall. Opening it, she withdrew a can of soda. Popping the top, she took a swig, more in an effort to squelch her rising heat than to quench her thirst.

On the other side of the room, Justin witnessed Davia's attempt to withdraw, but he was determined not to let her. He was falling hard for this woman, and there were matters that needed to be discussed before he succumbed completely.

Walking across the room, he took a detour to the office door and turned the lock. He could hear Davia's intake of breath.

"Don't lock that!" Her voice was strangled.

Turning, Justin was stunned by the look of panic on her face. Her eyes were riveted to the lock on the door.

Disturbed by her reaction, he quickly unlocked the door. "I just wanted us to talk. I thought about how Leroy came in . . ." He faltered in his explanation.

Davia gripped the back of a chair to steady herself. She took a ragged breath in an effort to regain her composure. She didn't like locked doors.

Not wanting to upset her further, Justin moved toward her cautiously. "Are you all right?"

She nodded, but the look on her face made a lie of her claim. Justin didn't believe her for a second. He fought to control his emotions. Who or what could have caused such a reaction? He chose his words carefully.

"You said that men always hurt you," he said quietly, his voice unable to contain his anger. "Some man abused you."

Davia's body jerked. The soda can slipped from her hand and tumbled to the floor. Soda spewed like a fountain from the can onto the Berber carpet. Davia didn't notice.

She had said too much to him.

"That's why you don't trust men."

She shouldn't have said anything.

"Or is it just me that you don't trust?"

Noting that she didn't answer him, he drew closer as she stood staring at him. He spoke in a soothing voice.

"If you don't want to tell me what happened, that's fine, but I want to help you. I want to offer my support and my friendship. I've never known anyone like you and I want you in my life. But the barriers between us have to come down."

Justin now stood face to face with Davia, whose eyes were glazed with unshed tears. Yet, the hard set of her mouth revealed that she was still resistant.

Bending, Justin picked up the fallen soda can, and then, finding a roll of paper towels, he wiped up the spill. Tossing the towels into the trash, he washed his hands at the sink, wiped them dry, and then, under Davia's watchful eye, he sat in a chair and got comfortable. He was prepared to be as stubborn as she was.

"So, you're not going to talk to me. Am I being punished because you think that I'm from a different world and that I would be shocked by what you have to tell me? Perhaps I'm more aware of the world than you think I am. After all, I am a full-grown man. I know that our lives have been different . . ."

"Very different," Davia corrected him, "and I'm not punishing you."

Justin's mouth lifted into a small smile. "It certainly feels like it. You've taken pains to tell me practically nothing about yourself. It's evident that you were a teenage mother and that you've been deeply hurt by a man." Justin rose and walked over to stand before her. "But, Davia, I'm not the man who harmed you. I'm the man who wants to ease your pain. That is, if you'll let me." He reached out to caress her cheek and she didn't move away.

Justin's whispered promises summoned Davia's every need and desire. She was tired of holding onto a past where love was nonexistent. She wanted desperately to throw aside the shackles of distrust which had bound her for so long. Here was a man who was offering her a different reality, one that she had never dreamed could exist for her.

Davia's silence led Justin to wonder if he had blown it. Would she continue to reject his plea, or should he remain hopeful? He was persistent.

"I don't know where a relationship between us will lead, Davia, but I'm asking you to give it a chance. I'm crazy about you, and all I ask is that you allow us to get to know each other better."

The room vibrated with the silence between them as trust struggled to make its presence known. Then, without a word, Davia started walking toward the door. Hope dimmed for Justin. He had gambled and lost. Steeling himself for her departure, Justin closed his eyes and sighed deeply as he listened for her exit. Instead, he heard a click. His eyes flew open. Having locked the door, Davia walked back across the room and stopped in front of him. Taking an uncertain breath, she forced herself to take the boldest step of her life—a step into the future.

"I was raised on the south side of Chicago by a cousin named Phyllis. She was a drug addict and a prostitute . . ."

Katherine Miles was perturbed with her son. He was supposed to come by her house and pick up two tickets he had purchased to one of her charity events. He had yet to arrive. Actually, she hadn't seen much of him in the past few weeks. His telephone calls to her had become less frequent, and she didn't like it at all.

Upset by what she perceived as her son's neglect, she had summoned Henry and had asked him to drive her to Justin's office building when she couldn't find him at home. If he was there, she would deliver the tickets personally and then give that boy a piece of her mind.

They were on their way there when Katherine noticed a red Lexus sports car waiting for a red light on the opposite side of the street. The distinctive license

plate that announced Justin's name to the world identi-
fied the car as belonging to her son.

"There's Justin!" she alerted Henry.

"It certainly is," he concurred.

"I wonder where he's headed," she said absently.

"Do you want me to blow and get his attention?"
Henry asked, poised to obey her command.

She was about to ask him to do just that when she
noticed movement on the passenger side next to her son.
From this distance, she couldn't identify the facial features, but it looked like it could be a man or a woman—
a woman with very short hair. Justin confirmed that the
person was the latter when he leaned over and gave his
passenger a kiss.

"Uh-oh, it's obvious that he's not headed to his
office." There was a note of male pride in Henry's voice.
"Should I blow?"

"No, don't bother. He probably wouldn't stop
anyway." Katherine's eyes stayed glued to her son's car.
She watched as it accelerated on the green light, turned
the corner and disappeared from sight. She should have
known. Justin was on the prowl again. She could understand why women loved her son. After all, he was rich
and very good looking. Nevertheless, she did not appreciate being ignored by him for one of his little flings. The
only name that she had heard connected with him lately
was that of Davia Maxwell. Was that the woman in the
car? If so, from what she had just witnessed, this woman
might be more than a casual acquaintance.

Between this Davia person and her child, Gabby, half of the Miles family seemed involved with these Maxwell people. She made a mental note to find out more about Davia Maxwell, but she was certain that there was no need to worry. Justin was never serious about any woman for very long. For years, Katherine had let him have his harmless dalliances. However, it was past time for him to start thinking seriously about finding a wife. It looked as though she would have to get busy and help the situation along.

As Henry turned the car back toward home, Katherine mentally began to compose a list of acceptable women—ones with the *right* bloodlines. The name Davia Maxwell was definitely not one that would be on the list.

❧

Justin sat in the restaurant across the table from Davia, watching as she brought her salad fork to her lips and chewed languidly. He was continuously amazed at the effect that she had on him. Everything she did seemed to turn him on. The kiss she had allowed him in her office had been like kerosene poured on a burning flame. He had contained the flame before it burned out of control, but it was still smoldering. Unable to resist, he had stolen a kiss from her in the car and she had offered no resistance. Davia was beginning to trust him, and he was floating on Cloud Nine until she asked a question that he had never expected.

"What would your mother think of me if you were to introduce us? Do you think that she would like me?"

Justin fell from his cloud with a thump. Chuckling, he shook his head. "You do have a way of starting in the middle of a nonexistent conversation, don't you?"

Davia grinned. "I usually say what's on my mind."

"And my mother was on your mind?"

"Yes, and the fact that you called her on your cell phone before we were seated. Were you checking in?" From what she knew of Justin, he didn't appear to be a mama's boy, but for her own sense of security she needed to hear it from him.

Justin guffawed at the very idea. "Checking in is something I haven't done since I was a teenager." He laughed again, still tickled. "No, I was supposed to pick something up from her and I just remembered it. I just wanted to make arrangements to follow through. Anyway, I didn't reach her. Mommy Dearest must be out doing her own thing."

Davia didn't respond to his teasing tone as she watched him with serious eyes. It was clear that she wanted an answer to her question. Pushing his unfinished salad aside, Justin leaned back in his chair and studied Davia for a moment. He could tell that the answer was important to her and it deserved to be addressed honestly.

"Would Katherine Miles like you?" He echoed reflectively. With a deep sigh, he leaned forward and looked her straight in the eyes. "No, she wouldn't want to like you. But it doesn't matter, because I like you very much."

A smile crept across Davia's face. "What do you know, an honest man. You and I might be able to make a go of this."

Justin returned her smile. Reaching across the table, he took her hands into his and massaged them gently. "*Ms.* Maxwell, I *know* we will."

A few hours later Justin parked the car in front of Davia's house and turned off the ignition. It was the end to a long and eventful day, but he sensed that it wasn't over. He was right. Davia had been silent during the ride from the restaurant. He knew that she was exhausted, but it was obvious that there was something else on her mind. So he waited. It was a short one.

"I think that my daughter would have liked you, Justin. Her name was Stephanie Renee, and she was fifteen years old when she died."

Justin was taken aback. There it was again, information delivered out of the blue, unrelated to any conversation. She was a master at it, and if catching him off guard had been the intent, her words were successful.

He had wondered about Gabby's mother. Davia had never mentioned her and he had never asked. He had trusted her to tell him what she wanted him to know, when she wanted him to know it. He had been right.

"I was only fifteen when I had my daughter—a child having a child. I didn't know how to be a mother. I had only seen what mothering was on television or in the movies. My cousin told me that my own mother died when I was four years old. I don't even remember her."

Pausing, Davia shifted her attention from the distant past back to the present. She looked over at Justin. "I never knew my father. Phyllis said that no one knew who he was." She waited for his reaction to her words. There was none. Justin sat stoically, holding her eyes. His silence urged her to continue.

"Like I told you before, I was raised by my cousin, Phyllis. I think she was my mother's first cousin. She really never made that clear. All I know is that somehow she got custody of me—for the welfare check, I'm sure—and she never mentioned any other relatives. She never showed me any love or affection. I don't think that she knew how. Surviving was all she knew and that's what she taught me to do—survive. For the first half of my life, that was my code. Having a relationship was something foreign to me. It was difficult for me to express emotion even with my own child, who loved me without conditions."

Davia's eyes misted. "Stephanie was a beautiful child, inside and out. She had this cute little round face, with incredible brown eyes." She paused, remembering the child that she had adored. "She loved to tell me her little made-up stories. I couldn't get enough of her, but there never seemed to be enough time for us to spend together. When I moved to Atlanta, I never asked help from anybody. I got through school with loans and by working two, sometimes three, part-time jobs. I worked even harder when it came to financing my business and making a go of it. There was just never enough time in the day."

Closing her eyes, she fought the tears that threatened to flow. She had shed so many tears in her lifetime that she was surprised that she had any left. Justin moved to hold her in his arms and she accepted his offer of comfort as she continued.

She told him how her teenage daughter had hidden her pregnancy from her. Racked with guilt and with her body shaking with sorrow, she confessed how she had been so busy trying to build a life for the two of them that she had not noticed the change in her own child's body. She recalled the nightmare of Gabby's birth, relived the terrifying ride in the ambulance to the hospital and how her daughter—who'd had no medical care during her pregnancy—hemorrhaged. By the time they reached the hospital, Gabby had been born and Stephanie was dead.

She didn't know what to expect from him when she finished her story. She didn't think that there was anything he could say to her that could ease the unbearable pain, guilt and sorrow. She was a woman who had sacrificed her child's life for her own success. What could be worse than that?

When she quieted, Justin tenderly wiped her tears away. He kissed her brow. His words of comfort were simple.

"Forgive yourself."

It was exactly what Davia needed to hear.

CHAPTER 12

Davia sat at her desk at the Small Sensations office staring at sketches of the latest designs for Teen Sensations, her company's expansion into the country's adolescent market. The effort was less than a year old, and the clothes were flying off the shelves of every retail outlet carrying her product. Orders were pouring in. Over the past three months her ability to meet obligations at home and at the office had been stretched to the limit. Yet, somehow, she found the time for Gabby and for Justin.

He had become a very important presence in her life. Each time they were together, the two of them continued to learn more about one another. With each passing day they grew closer.

Justin seemed to accept her in every way, and once she let down her guard she found that trusting him became easier. He wasn't perfect, but neither was she. Justin was kind, warm, sensitive and quite demonstrative. The latter took some getting used to. He had no reservations about giving her a kiss or a nibble in public, and while she resisted his efforts initially, she had to admit that once she had grown accustomed to his overt displays of affection, she had begun to enjoy them. What a change! She had transformed from a woman who couldn't stand to be touched by a man, to a woman who craved the touch of only one man—Justin. It was wonderful. *He* was wonderful.

The ring of the telephone and a knock on the door tore Davia from her musings. Picking up the receiver, she pushed the blinking button on her private line, simultaneously granting permission to enter. Justin's voice greeted her on the other end of the phone line, just as Leroy entered her office.

"Hey, beautiful." She could hear the smile in Justin's voice.

"Davia, I've got a question for you," Leroy said at the same time.

"Are you busy?" Justin could hear the sound of a voice in the background.

"Hi, Justin, give me a minute, please, Leroy just came in." Putting Justin on hold, she turned her attention to Leroy.

On the other end Justin felt that tinge of jealousy that always seemed to plague him at the mention of Leroy's name. He was certain that he was no threat to his budding relationship with Davia, but he had to admit that he couldn't help feeling resentful toward any man who spent more time with her then he did. As a businessman he knew the value of a smart, talented employee, but the man worked her to death. He didn't like it. Didn't he ever give her a break? Yet she never seemed to complain. She was truly one of a kind.

Davia wasn't the kind of woman that a man could take for granted, that was for sure. Nor was she one of those little fluff balls his mother loved to fix him up with. Davia kept him on his toes. She challenged him and he loved every minute of it. Yes, Davia Maxwell was all woman, *his* woman. He was in love with her. There was no doubt about it. Frederick Zackary Justin Miles had found *the one* and he hadn't even been looking.

Her return to the telephone brought a smile to his face. "Hey, pretty lady, you were out of town on business last Saturday, so you owe me a date."

Davia could feel his gentle spirit through the telephone line. She grinned. "Oh, yeah? And what do you have in mind?"

"How about having dinner with me at my home this weekend?"

Davia's grin faded. "Dinner? At your house?"

"That's what I said." Justin could hear her anxiety. "Would you do me the honor?"

Davia tensed. She hadn't been in a house alone with a man since—No! She was learning to put the past behind her. This was another opportunity to take a step forward.

She sighed. "All right."

"Are you sure?" Justin prompted. She sounded hesitant.

Clearing her throat, Davia spoke with increased confidence. "Thank you, I'd love to have dinner with you at your home."

Her grin lit up the office. Stepping forward sure felt good.

After Justin introduced Davia to his housekeeper, Mrs. Holland, he gave Davia a tour of his house. It was a contemporary structure nestled in an affluent suburb; the four-bedroom house was a splendid stone structure with plenty of windows and skylights. The floor plan was spacious. Walls and doors separated the bedrooms, and his home office, but the kitchen, living, and dining areas were open spaces separated by furniture arrangements. Justin guided her through each of the rooms, ending the tour in the family room, where a beautifully crafted, wrought-iron staircase led up to a loft.

"Your home is gorgeous." Davia said, running her hand over one of the two soft leather sofas placed opposite each other before an adobe-style fireplace.

"Thank you." He was pleased at the compliment but even more pleased that she was here with him. He had delighted in the light dancing in her dark eyes as they toured each room. He wanted her to love his place as much as he did. Who knew? Maybe one day this might be her home, too.

"I'm glad you like it." He planted a kiss on her forehead.

Immediately, Davia's body warmed. Her body always seemed to respond whenever Justin was near. The touch of his hand, the sound of his voice, the kisses that he so readily shared with her were all exhilarating, but her apprehension still remained. Self-consciously, she moved toward the unique staircase.

"What's up there?"

Noting her retreat, Justin grabbed her hand and led her toward the stairway. "Come on, I'll show you."

The iron steps leading upward were covered in the same gold carpeting that ran throughout the rest of the house. The carpet was so thick that Davia's feet sank into it as they climbed upward. To her surprise, Justin's bedroom was at the top of the stairs. Like the rest of the rooms in the house, it was open and spacious. Decorated in various shades of gold, the space was dominated by a huge iron bed with a headboard that sported the same design as that on the winding stairway. Knowing it was best not to linger in this room, Davia moved quickly to a pair of etched glass double doors.

"What's in there?" She nodded toward the doors.

"Open them."

She did, and revealed a master bathroom that looked as if it came out of *Architectural Digest*. It was a world of black marble accented with gold. Even the fluffy black towels were trimmed in gold braid and embroidered with Justin's initials in gold. A stained glass skylight was above a black marble garden tub with brass fixtures. Standing beside her in the doorway between the bedroom and bathroom, Justin swiped his hand and, like magic, a mirrored wall in the bathroom opened automatically to reveal a huge walk-in closet.

"I'm impressed." Davia was fascinated by the entire effect. "The towels are a bit narcissistic, though. Were they your idea?"

Justin chuckled at her observation. "No, actually I really can't take credit for anything in this house. Clark designed it and Vanessa decorated the rooms. All I did was move in."

Davia smiled at the mention of Clark's name. From what CeCe had told her, Clark Gaston was an architectural genius. Of course, to CeCe everything he did was extraordinary. As far as her friend was concerned, the new man in her life practically walked on water.

Justin guessed where Davia's thoughts had taken her. "Vanessa decorated Clark's house, too." He winked. "I'm sure that CeCe has told you all about his place."

He knew that Davia's best friend had become a frequent visitor to his best friend's home. Clark had confided in Justin that he might be going down for the count. He had succumbed completely to the charms of CeCe Green. Meanwhile, Justin had no doubts that he had surrendered his heart to Davia. It seemed that the ladies were threatening to put two of Atlanta's most eligible bachelors out of circulation, and neither of the gentlemen had any complaints.

"Your sister has very good taste," Davia replied as she took one last look around. Turning, she prepared to leave, but as she moved past Justin, he snaked an arm around her waist and drew her against his body.

"Her brother has good taste as well," he whispered. He placed a tender kiss on her lips. Then, to her surprise, he released her.

"I don't want you to think that I've invited you here to take our relationship to the bedroom," he explained in answer to the quizzical look on her face.

She swallowed and admitted the truth. "I was sort of nervous about that."

Justin stroked her cheek. "Don't be. I'd be a liar if I said that I didn't want to make love to you, because I do. But if or when we do make love, it will happen when it's supposed to. As for now, all I want is to be with you and spend time with you, and I hope that's what you want too."

Davia nodded, feeling somewhat disappointed that she didn't feel more relieved about his gallantry, but recalling the reasons why this man was special. "Yes, that's what I want, too."

Justin took her hand. "All right then. Let's go eat."

He led her down the spiral staircase, through the house and into the dining room. There they feasted on a melt-in-your-mouth meal left for them by his housekeeper.

After dinner, they retreated to the family room to listen to music. Their listening eventually turned into a songfest. Off key and loudly, they sang an eclectic mix of songs highlighted with a duo of Whitney Houston's version of "I Will Always Love You." At the song's end they collapsed into fits of laughter.

"You know I will, don't you?" Justin asked, wiping tears of mirth from his eyes.

"You will what?" Davia questioned, recovering from her own laughter.

"I will always love you." Justin looked at Davia thoughtfully as his manner and tone turned serious. "I am in love with you, you know."

Davia breath caught in her throat, but she managed to give him the coldest gaze that she could muster. "Don't be."

She made a move to get up from the sofa, but Justin stayed her with a touch. His gaze didn't waver. He hadn't meant to confess his feelings for her so soon, but it was done and he was glad. He *was* in love with her. He had no doubts about it. Her response wasn't what he wanted to hear, but he was realistic. There was a reason for her reaction, and he was determined to know what it was.

"Why don't you want me to love you, Davia? Why do you want to deny yourself the joy of being loved?"

Her answer was simple. "Because love hurts."

The look in her eyes was gut-wrenching. They were filled with a lifetime of sorrow. She shut them in an attempt to hide the pain, but he wouldn't let her. Justin cupped her chin in his hands and held it until she was forced to open her eyes and look into his. It was then that he spoke.

"Not *my* love. My love will never hurt you."

"Your words are the right ones, but . . ."

His lips descended on hers before she could finish. The kiss was gentle, and they parted breathlessly. His mouth hovered above hers. "There are no buts. I place a high value on two things in life—keeping my word and pledging absolute loyalty to those I love. You have both from me. You have my word that I love you and the loyalty and devotion that come with that love. So, I'm asking you to trust me. I'm asking you to give love a chance."

Davia swayed. She could feel herself wavering. "If only I could."

Justin captured her lips again, this time with more intensity. His heart threatened to explode in his chest as he put everything that he felt for her into the kiss. Her heart beat with the same rhythm as his. Once again, he broke their connection to look at her.

"I love you, Davia. Love me."

Love him? Davia closed her eyes, as she pondered what love could mean. *Could she? Did she know how?*

Justin saw the conflict and the confusion on her face. "Open your eyes for me. Let me see what you feel."

She did, so that Justin could see the truth that she was unable to verbalize but was no longer able to hide. She loved him too, and it was Davia who took the lead this time. Drawing Justin's lips to her own, she gave him a kiss that would seal their fate.

When they parted, Justin mustered all of the self control that he possessed. "For the sake of self-preservation, I think we'd better go. It wouldn't take much more for me to break my word about the intent of my invitation. So, as soon as I can walk, we're out of here."

Davia smiled at his attempt at levity. He was right. This was all too tempting. She moved from his embrace, presenting them both with the opportunity to clear their heads.

Rising, Justin reached his hand out to her. "We'd better get you home." His hand remained suspended in midair as Davia ignored it.

The night's events had helped her to come to a decision and she made a quiet request. "Have a seat, please. I've got something that I want to tell you."

Justin complied. Davia took a breath to gain her composure and continued.

"You asked me once if I had been abused. I never really answered you." She paused, trying to gather the courage to say the words she had only articulated to one other human being in her life. She swallowed hard. "When I was a teenager, someone did hurt me . . ."

"Who was it?" Justin's jaws tightened. He looked as though he was ready to wreak revenge on the offender then and there.

Davia's heart was beating double time. How could she tell him? Would he ever understand? "You see, there was this . . . this . . ." She wanted to say the word. She wanted to tell him what had happened. She wanted to tell him everything, but the words wouldn't come. It had been decades, and the memory was still too painful. Tears pushed past her valiant effort to stifle them, and a sob caught in her throat.

Justin pulled her into his arms, unable to bear her distress. "It's all right. If you can't talk about it yet, you don't have to."

"I know it's just that . . ."

"Baby, really. It's okay." He massaged her back soothingly.

"I have to make you understand. I used to hide in the basement in the dark . . ."

"Why?"

"It was safer there." She choked as she swiped at her tears.

The sound nearly ripped Justin's heart from his chest. "Davia, please, I can see how hard it is for you to talk about."

She nodded against his broad chest. "Yes, it is. It's just that it's important for you to know that this is not your fault."

Justin's brows furrowed. "What's not my fault?"

"My reluctance . . ." Her voice trailed off as she looked away in embarrassment.

"My inability to love . . . to make love."

Justin gave her a sad smile as he turned her face to him. "Davia you don't have an inability to love or to be loved. Your family and friends prove that, and the look on your face a few minutes ago when you looked at me tells me that you have an enormous capacity to love. As for making love, your reluctance is understandable. Sweetheart, you've never been made love to by someone who truly adores you."

Davia pondered his words as she looked into his eyes and saw the passion that lay there. He believed in her, and, miracle of miracles, he loved her.

She shook her head slowly. "I guess you're right."

"I *know* I'm right."

She sighed heavily. "Justin, I bring so much baggage with me."

He tweaked her nose. "Just call me your baggage handler."

It was so tempting. "So you're Mr. Fix-It, huh?"

He smiled. "I could be if you'd let me."

If she would let him. Davia held Justin's eyes, and in them lay the love that he had confessed for her—love that she needed so badly. The load was so heavy, and she had been carrying it alone for so long. How would it feel to have it lifted?

"Prove it."

Justin drew back in surprise. Was she saying what he thought she was saying?

"Prove what?"

Davia swallowed all of the doubt that she felt. "Prove that you can fix it. Make love to me."

Justin looked at her, dumbfounded. Was she serious? "I'm not a child to be toyed with, Davia. I told you, I didn't bring you here to make love."

Her eyes widened in bewilderment. "You don't want me? But you said earlier—"

Justin would have laughed aloud if he hadn't seen that she was serious. If he thought she was ready for it, he would let her feel just how much he did want her. "Then if you remember what I said earlier, you know the answer to your question. But I have one for you. Are you ready for this? How can you be sure that the time is right here and now?"

"I know that you value honesty, and I'd be lying to you if I said that I am sure." She moved closer to him and laid her head on his solid shoulder. "But I do know that the only man I want to be with is you. I have no doubt about that." This man had turned her whole world around.

Justin swallowed his emotions as they threatened to turn into tears. Her words meant everything to him. She was letting him know that she trusted her heart to him. What more could he have asked? The kiss that he gave her held all of the love and gratitude that he felt for her and the gift that she was about to bestow on him. He wanted her to know that that her gift would be cherished.

Scooping her up in his arms, Justin carried her up the stairs to his bedroom and placed her in the center of his large bed. He rained kisses on her bared flesh as he slowly undressed her, caressing away her fear and anxieties, determined that she would soon be trembling with want and desire.

Inflamed, Davia lay pulsating as Justin stripped her of her undergarments. Then, removing his clothing to his briefs, he rejoined her on the bed. The sight of his chiseled body was a pleasant surprise. She'd had no idea that he was so beautifully built. He had mentioned working out at the gym, but she had never expected this. Tentatively, she reached out and let her hot fingertips touch his bulging biceps. Justin stilled as she trailed a finger across his chest and encircled a nipple. Justin quivered. Uncertain, she tried to withdraw. He caught her hand and with his eyes alone, he urged her to continue.

Emboldened, Davia traced a finger down the length of his muscled torso, pausing at his intake of breath. Her eyes traveled downward until they came to rest on the large bulge outlined in his black briefs. It was intimidating. It had been years since she had been with a man sexually, and the experience hadn't been a pleasant one. Would this one please her? Could she please him? Was she capable of satisfying Justin's needs?

In one brief move, she lay beneath him as he hovered above her. Looking down at her, his mouth lifted into a lazy smile, and instantly another far more sinister expression flashed through Davia's mind. *Money!* She clamped her arms tightly across her bare chest. Her eyes widened in alarm as tension raced through her body.

Justin saw the panic. He felt the tension. Neither came as a surprise. He drew back to his knees and, with exceptional tenderness, he uncrossed her arms. Taking her hands into his, he kissed each palm with a reverence that nearly brought tears to Davia's eyes.

"We don't have to do anything you don't want to do," he assured her. "Say the word and we both walk away right now."

Davia lay still for a moment digesting his words. It was now or never. It was Justin, or there would be no one.

She rose to her knees and faced him. "I want to touch you."

He nodded. "Be my guest."

Guiding her hand, Justin helped her explore his body. It glided across his broad chest, stopping to tease each nipple to turgid rigidity. She flickered her tongue across each hardened nub, eliciting a moan of pleasure from him. Her hand plowed through the hairs on his chest, descending to his flat stomach, past the elastic band of his black briefs to rest on his burgeoning desire. It was there that her hand took on a life of its own, stroking and kneading, clumsily at first, then gradually acquiring an intensity that brought Justin close to release. Grasping her errant hand, he stopped the wayward exploration he had helped initiate. His tremulous body was a testament to how successful their trip had been. Now it was his turn to do some exploring of his own.

It started with kisses that were meant to challenge her inhibitions and vanquish her fears. He took her dark, distended nipple between his teeth and proceeded to tease, cajole and mold her into submission. Agile fingers stroked a fire within her, while his potent tongue turned a bonfire into an inferno. Justin worshipped her body as though it were an ancient temple before which he was paying homage. Spirals of ecstasy consumed her. Justin took her to places that she had never known existed, and in gratitude it was his name that she screamed.

Engulfed in a haze of rapture, she lay shimmering with pleasure as Justin removed his briefs, donned protection and returned to her.

"We're going to take it easy, sweetheart. Like I promised, I'd never hurt you in any way." With that he entered her, moving slowly as he felt how tight she was. As if in prayer, he whispered her name. "Are you all right?" He inched in further. "Let me know if . . ." Justin's thoughts drifted into oblivion as his pleasure increased. He moaned. She felt so good.

As the tip of his hardened shaft teased and pleased her, Davia was doing some moaning of her own, and when he entered her completely, she felt possessed. Justin's loving was slow, gentle and deliberate. He whispered words of love and adoration into her ear, against the cotton softness of her hair, the sculptured curve of her neck. They were words captured in impassioned kisses against parted lips.

"I'm going to take you on a journey," rasped Justin breathlessly. "Come . . . come fly with me."

And she did. Davia barely clung to consciousness as they soared higher and higher and higher until they reached their destination together.

In the early morning hours, as a satiated Davia slept in the curve of Justin's arm, he lay awake filled with the wonder of having made love to her. She was a part of him now. She had blossomed into a flower as fully as those growing outside her home. He was grateful that she had chosen him to share this most intimate part of herself.

Davia had been through a lot in her life, and she deserved everything that was good. He had promised that he would never cause her pain, and he wouldn't. He further vowed that he would also make certain that no one else would harm her again.

CHAPTER 13

"What do you mean, there's no such person as Davia Maxwell?" Katherine gripped the telephone receiver so hard the veins in her hands strained against her skin. "Is she using an alias?" She listened to the voice on the other end as Charles Cash moved across the sitting room to the mahogany bar on the other side of the room. He took two long-stemmed crystal wineglasses from the selection hanging over the bar and poured white wine in each. Then, meandering in that slow, lazy manner to which she had become accustomed, he returned to where he had been sitting next to her and placed her glass of wine on the highly polished coffee table in front of them. Crossing an ankle over one leg, he began sipping his wine as he massaged the tense muscles in her neck with his free hand.

Katherine responded to his touch, rotating her stiffened neck as she listened to the private investigator she had hired to gather information on Davia Maxwell. She remembered when Zack used to give her massages and where they eventually led. Well, Charles was no Zachary Miles. Oh, he was handsome enough, with his devilish good looks and that crooked smile of his, and he was sophisticated in a roguish way. Charles was also well versed in lot of areas, but he was a social climber, a wannabe among people who already had theirs. No, he was no Zachary Miles.

She wasn't sure what Charles wanted from her, but she knew that he would use her, or anyone else, to get it. He was correct in his belief that she could pave the way for him in acquiring whatever he might want, but she really had no intention of assisting him, although he didn't seem aware of that fact. Oh, he was good for a few laughs. They had a good time together. He was a present-able escort, and he kept her bed warm. Other than that, Charles Cash was of no value to her. She found it amusing that he actually thought that she was mesmer-ized by his charm. Well, she wasn't. She would keep him around for a while longer. After that she was sure that Charles would find another wealthy widow he would try to use.

Smiling, she patted his hand indulgently. Then, brushing it aside, she returned her attention to the caller.

Charles watched Katherine as she hung the receiver on its cradle in disgust and proceeded to prowl the room like an angry lioness. It seemed that lately her precious Justin had found himself some honey that didn't meet with his mother's approval, and that was all Katherine talked about. Hell, he was tired of hearing about it! If Justin had found himself a good lay from the other side of the tracks, hooray for him. He wished that Katherine would go about the real business at hand, helping him out. He'd invested a lot of time and effort into wining and dining her. He expected some return. What he really needed were introductions to more of her friends—rich friends—who could be talked into putting money into his investment firm. He was a man with expensive tastes, and lately his expenses had been exceeding his income. He'd been forced to borrow against some of his firm's investment funds and needed additional capital to offset those debts.

Katherine Miles had been a gold mine. He hadn't garnered any money or trinkets from her, but her circle of friends were among the most influential in Atlanta, and his association with her gave him the credibility he needed. His past was dead and buried. He had spent years building his future, and presently it looked pretty good. Things had been sailing along smoothly until her son's sex life got in the way. Since then, she'd turned her attention away from assisting him to concentrate on Justin—but enough was enough!

He had smiled and tried to sound interested and concerned when Katherine would rant about her precious son as she was now doing, but there were real issues—important issues—that needed attention. Specifically, *him* and his need for more investors. This frivolous situation with her son was getting in the way.

Sipping the last of his wine Charles set the glass on the coffee table and turned his attention to Katherine. What the hell was she saying?

"And according to the PI, this Davia Maxwell doesn't seem to have had a past prior to coming to Atlanta. If so, she's very tight-lipped about it. How in the world could anyone . . ."

Charles tuned out again as Katherine droned on. Occasionally he caught snatches of her tirade about how she was going to "nip this little romance in the bud." He was getting a headache, and his nerves were on edge as she went on and on.

There was a knock on the sitting room door. It opened and the energy in the room changed as Bianca entered. Katherine stopped her angry pacing as the child ran to her grandmother, anxious to give her a picture she had drawn for her. Charles's dark eyes followed the child, taking in everything about her—the golden skin, the long, wavy braids, the big bright eyes. His eyes slid slowly down the length of her lithe little body. Unconsciously, he licked his lips. She was beautiful, and showed signs of developing quite a figure when she matured.

Hugging her granddaughter fondly, and thanking her for the picture, Katherine admonished the child lightly as she turned her to face Charles. "Now, precious, Grandmother is delighted with your present, but when you entered, you forgot your manners. What do you say to Mr. Cash?"

Bianca looked down at the floor, avoiding the man's eyes. She didn't like this man, even though her grandmother seemed to think that he was okay. So she didn't tell her how she felt. She hadn't even told her mommy. Instead, like the good little girl everybody described her as being, Bianca minded her manners and spoke. "Hello, Mr. Cash."

Charles's smile broadened. "Hello, Bianca. It's nice seeing you." *Yes! Bianca!*

Now that was a member of the Miles family worth talking about.

Davia sat in the middle of her king-size bed reading a financial report while Gabby played with her dolls at the other end. Her ability to concentrate was almost nonexistent. All she could think about was Justin.

She had never met anyone like him. He respected her intelligence and valued her opinions. He had made love to her last night as if she were the reason for his existence. He had told her repeatedly that he loved her and had proved it to her in every way. Justin had taught her what love was about. In her wildest dreams she never would have believed that any man could mean so much to her.

The telephone rang and Davia's heartbeat accelerated. *Justin!* She answered the call on the first ring with a smoky "Hello."

"Child! This ain't that man calling you. It's your mama, so you can cut the crap!"

Davia couldn't help but laugh. "Hi, Mama." It was her foster mother, Mama Willa, matriarch of her foster family, the Johnson clan.

Davia's greeting grabbed Gabby's attention immediately. Dropping her dolls, she scampered to the head of the bed to join Davia, crowding her in an attempt to speak on the telephone. She squealed into the receiver, "Mama Willa! Mama Willa!"

Willa responded to the child's loud request. "Is that my baby I hear calling for me? Let me speak to her!"

Davia yielded the telephone. There would be no peace on either end if she didn't.

"Wait a minute, Mama Willa," Gabby commanded with all of the authority of a four-year-old. With one small hand tightly clutching the cordless telephone, Gabby used her free hand to adjust the pillows behind her back, as she had seen Davia do. She then settled herself against them, ready to enjoy her conversation, taking pains to cross her legs at the ankles just as any other "adult" getting ready for a gabfest would do. Returning her attention to the matter at hand, she put the receiver to her ear and resumed her conversation. "Oooooh, Mama Willa, do I have something to tell *you!*"

Shaking her head at the child's antics, Davia moved to the center of the bed and lay stretched out on her stomach, prepared to resume her reading. She was ready to let Gabby's conversation with Mama Willa fade into the background until the little girl said . . .

"I'm going to get a daddy!"

Davia's "What?" was as loud as Mama Willa's "What?" on the other end of the line. A beaming Gabby continued her conversation.

"You know that Grommy's been seeing Mr. Justin, and he's my friend Bianca's uncle, and when they get married, me and Bianca will be sisters, and Mr. Justin will be my daddy. You did know that, didn't you, Mama Willa?" Gabby took a breath. Pride was written all over her face. She had delivered news that nobody else knew.

Trying to recover from her granddaughter's startling revelation, Davia untangled herself from the bed linen in an attempt to reach the telephone before further disclosures could be made. She was too late.

"And you know what? I saw them kissing one time." A pause interrupted the conversation just as Davia reached for the telephone. A beaming Gabby handed the telephone to her. "Mama Willa wants to speak to you."

A shaken Davia took the receiver and managed a weak "Hello."

"What in the world is going on out there?" Mama Willa demanded to know. "What is that baby talking about? What does she mean, she's gonna get a daddy? You better tell me something, girl, and say it quick!"

Davia recognized Mama's no-nonsense tone. Everybody in the family knew that when they heard that, the answers had better be good.

"I don't know where she got that from, Mama. I really don't. Hold on, please."

Gabby had settled on her knees beside Davia with one arm thrown around her grandmother's back and her head resting on her shoulder. She was literally breathing down her neck. The little girl had no intention of being left out of this conversation, but Davia had other ideas. She patted the child's pajama-clad knee. "Sweetie, will you go down and see if Miss Reba has lunch ready? I'm hungry, aren't you?"

Rearing back on her haunches, Gabby looked suspicious as she shook her head. "No, I want to talk to Mama Willa. I got more to tell her."

More? "You can talk to her later. Now go do what I asked you to do." Davia used her own tone this time, and Gabby recognized it immediately. Climbing down from the bed she reluctantly left the room. Davia resumed her conversation.

"I don't know where the child got her information from, but you know that I'm not about to get married. Justin and I are just getting to know each other. I didn't even know Gabby knew about us dating. He picks me up at the house and brings me home long after she's gone to bed. I haven't even mentioned it to her yet. I didn't want to confuse her. I didn't know she saw us when he kissed me. Anyway, I'll find out what this is all about. She just told me that she has *more* to tell you."

"I bet she does." Mama Willa chuckled on the other end. "You've got to remember that little people have big eyes and bigger ears. Don't ever take a child for granted."

"You're right, but I can tell you right now there is absolutely nothing else she has to tell you that I haven't already told you." *Except about last night.*

"Would you marry him if he asked you?"

The question caught Davia by surprise. She'd never thought about marriage to Justin or anyone else. A lifetime of being loved by one man had never been on her agenda. She wasn't sure that it was possible. Daydreaming of such things had always been for others, not for her. Yet she found herself saying, "In all honesty, I don't know."

There was a moment of silence in which she could hear Mama Willa thinking. "It's that serious, huh?"

Davia wasn't sure how to answer that. "I think I'm in love with him."

"You *think* you're in love! You don't *know*?"

"I've never been in love before, Mama. How would I know? Anyway, it hasn't been that long. I've only known him a couple of months."

"I knew I was in love twenty-four hours after I met Joshua Johnson."

"I'm not surprised. Who wouldn't fall in love with Papa Josh? In some ways, Justin reminds me a lot of him." She smiled as she pictured Mama's husband. He was a quiet man who spoke only when he had something to say; when he did speak, everyone in his household listened.

Joshua Johnson was the son of a Mississippi share-cropper, and unlike his wife, he had never graduated from high school, but he was one of the smartest men Davia knew. He read incessantly, everything from the Bible to Chaucer. He had worked for forty years as a construction worker to support his large family, and he saw to it that each one of his six children graduated from college. He was a kind, gentle, patient man. His family adored him, and so did Davia.

"Well, if Justin Miles is anything like my Josh, then he must be quite a man. Now tell me, how much have you told him about yourself?"

Davia knew what was being asked. Mama Willa was the only other person who knew all of her secrets. She knew about the emotional scars that Davia bore—scars that still needed healing. "I've told him what I wanted him to know."

"I see. Maybe that's best for now. It's not always good for folks to know all of your business, but when truth begins to stand in the way between you and your happiness, then that's the time to do what you've gotta do."

Davia sighed. "Yes, I know." She hesitated before continuing timidly. "He says that he loves me."

The silence on the other end was a long one. Mama Willa was thinking. Then she spoke. "This man sounds like he's got good instincts, and it's obvious he has good taste. I like that. I think this Justin Miles might be the one for you. I need to meet him. Bring him home."

That was it. Willa Mae Johnson had spoken. No member of the Johnson family in their right mind ignored her request. Davia would be taking Justin to Chicago.

Katherine was near hysterics. It was inconceivable that her son would run off to some godforsaken cow pasture with some woman and practically ignore his family. This was the last straw.

"I don't know who this *Davia* is, but your brother has completely lost his mind!"

Sitting across the table from her mother, Vanessa recognized the extent of her mother's distress and was grateful that they were having lunch in public. Katherine Miles did not like public displays.

Looking at the older woman with what she hoped was empathy she nevertheless defended her brother.

"Mother, Justin left a message on your voice mail that he was going to Chicago on business."

"That's precisely what I mean. I know that's a lie and he didn't have the decency to tell me face to face. He left the lie on my voice mail! You know good and well what kind of *business* he's conducting in Chicago with that slut." Katherine took a sip from the gold-rimmed teacup in front of her. The brew was cold. She frowned and continued, "It's been weeks since he and I have sat down and talked with each other. When's the last time you spoke to him in person?"

Vanessa opened her mouth to answer, but realized that she couldn't remember.

"You see! He's neglecting us. Worst of all, he's neglecting Bianca! My goodness, we saw and heard from him more when he lived in New York City."

Vanessa sighed. "Well, he's a busy man. He just got his business settled here in Atlanta and . . ."

"Oh, for heaven's sake, Vanessa! Stop making excuses for him. You're always doing that. Nothing has changed with you. Whenever he was in trouble with your father or me, you came up with some excuse for his behavior. So just stop it!"

Vanessa recoiled at the admonishment while inwardly chastising herself for doing so. She was a grown woman with a child of her own and no longer had to feel that she must please her mother to win her love. Yet she still felt that way, and she still tried.

Although she would go to her grave denying it, Katherine made it no secret that Justin was her favorite child. Vanessa had accepted that fact long ago. Yet, in spite of that, any words her mother uttered that did not express pleasure with her still had the ability to reduce Vanessa to tears. She was fighting the threatening flow even now as she pretended to be preoccupied with her meal. As usual, Katherine was oblivious.

"Well, I'm not going to put up with this. He could traipse all over New York with any tramp he wanted to. Who knew and who cared? But he's back in Atlanta, and I won't have him sully our family name by taking up with some gutter trash from the ghetto."

Vanessa twisted her pasta in circles. It was useless talking to her mother when she was like this, but she tried anyway. "From what I hear, she doesn't live in the ghetto. As a matter of fact, she's the vice president of Small Sensations. Bianca wears that label."

Katherine sniffed. "Those abominable clothes with all of the loud colors. You and your brother ought to be ashamed of yourselves for buying that baby those clothes. I am not impressed. The woman *came* from the ghetto. That's the point. What she does now doesn't answer the question about who her people are or what she's done in the past. My goodness, she was raised in the projects, with those gangbangers and such. And that little girl, Gabrielle, where is her father? There's no record of a marriage license in Chicago or here in Atlanta."

Vanessa frowned in confusion. "How do you know so much about her, Mother? You haven't met her yet."

Katherine sniffed. "Don't worry about it. I know what I need to know, and I'm going to know much more shortly. If that woman thinks that she's going to worm her way into *this* family, she is very much mistaken."

Vanessa tried again. "Mother, I think . . ."

"Good afternoon, ladies. Sorry I'm late."

Katherine and Vanessa looked up into the smiling face of Charles Cash. Katherine returned his smile. Vanessa was more reserved. She wasn't sure about her mother's friend. He seemed nice enough. He certainly was attentive to Katherine, and he was very good with Bianca. Katherine didn't have much to say about him except that he was an investment consultant whom she had met at a charity event. Vanessa had never had an entire conversation with the man, so she chose to withhold her opinion about him until she got to know him better. She watched as Charles settled in the chair next to Katherine.

As he and Katherine engaged in chitchat, Vanessa thought about the information her mother had revealed about Davia Maxwell. It was a little disturbing that she knew so many details about the woman. As a matter of fact, she knew too many details and Vanessa was certain that Justin hadn't told her. The only conclusion to be reached was that she had had Davia investigated, something that Katherine would not hesitate to do. Vanessa knew her mother well, much better than Justin did. Her big brother still held the mistaken belief that there were some areas in which their mother had boundaries. She knew better. There were very few boundaries that their mother wouldn't cross, and who was in a better position to know than her own daughter?

Katherine Miles had orchestrated almost everything in her life, including her marriage to Bianca's father. Vanessa had never loved her late husband, but that hadn't mattered to Katherine. It was a good social match. That was all that counted. And, like the dutiful daughter that she had always been, she had simply gone along and married the wrong man just to garner her mother's approval. It had been a dreadful mistake and an unhappy marriage.

She wished that she was more like her brother. She envied him. He didn't care about social boundaries and he cared even less about his mother's antiquated ideas. Of course he had one advantage that Vanessa didn't have. He didn't have to earn their mother's love. He already had it.

Vanessa sighed and took a sip of water as the conversation between Katherine and Charles continued, excluding her. If only she had Justin's nerve. If only she had the courage to challenge Katherine, just once.

When Davia told Justin about being summoned to Chicago by Willa Mae Johnson, he couldn't wait to meet the person who meant so much to the woman he loved. In their many talks over the past few months Davia had brought Willa Mae Johnson to life for him with stories of how this woman had touched her. She greatly respected this formidable woman. So, no request from her beloved foster mother was too big or too small as far as Justin was concerned. He went to the Windy City as ordered and was in for a pleasant surprise when they arrived.

The Johnson home was a two-story brick colonial, located in an integrated suburb of Chicago. Davia had told him that their children had purchased the home for their parents as an anniversary gift. What she hadn't told him was that instead of walking into a household that he had envisioned as warm and loving, but barely literate, he would be walking into a home that was not only over-flowing with love, but with a passion for learning.

Willa Mae and Joshua had married as young teenagers and had become parents early. Both of them held an appreciation for learning that had never faltered. Willa Mae had finished high school after her first three children had been born. Books were treasured and learning was coveted in their home. All six of their biological children were well educated and had excelled in their chosen professions. Justin met two of them during the weekend.

Rev. Darius Johnson was the esteemed pastor of God's Grace Baptist Church located in Chicago. Years ago, Justin had read about Darius in *Ebony* magazine in an article titled "Is This the Next Martin Luther King?" A renowned speaker, Darius held a master's degree in theology and a PhD in economics. Under his leadership, his church had become one of the largest and wealthiest African-American churches in the United States. In his early forties, he had earned the admiration and respect of millions and his influence extended nationwide.

Justin also met the second oldest of the Johnson children. Her name was Judge Donna Hawkins, and at the age of thirty-eight, she was one of the youngest judges in the country to serve on the state supreme court. The other four Johnson children did not live in Chicago. They were scattered all over the country and held positions that were equally as prestigious as those of their older siblings. Joshua and Willa Mae Johnson had done their job as parents well.

When Justin met Joshua Johnson, he looked much as he had pictured him, average in stature, with a quiet, unassuming personality. Willa Mae was nothing like Justin had pictured her. Shamefully, he had envisioned her as large in size, sound and personality, based on nothing more than a distorted stereotype regarding her humble beginnings. His introduction to Mrs. Johnson proved him wrong.

In her late fifties, Willa Mae's cocoa-brown skin was smooth and line free. Her five-foot, six-inch frame was shapely, despite having given birth to six children. She had hazel eyes set in an oval-shaped face framed by dark brown hair sprinkled with gray. She wore it in a cropped cut close to her head, much like Davia wore her hair, and the effect was striking. She was as attractive as Justin's own mother, yet she was as different from Katherine as night was from day.

There was no pretense to Willa Mae Johnson, and she didn't mince words. She spoke her mind with little prompting. She made no pretense and put on no airs, yet there did seem to be one thing that she and Katherine appeared to share—when family was threatened, she took no prisoners. From the moment Justin stepped over the threshold into the Johnson household, there was no doubt that he was there to prove that he was worthy of Davia.

A few hours before he and Davia were to depart for the flight back to Atlanta, Willa Mae had cornered him alone in her kitchen. She got straight to the point.

"Are you in love with Davia?"

Justin almost laughed because the question was so easy to answer. He looked the beloved matriarch in her eyes and answered truthfully, "I love her mind, body and soul."

Willa Mae's gaze never wavered as she finished her morning coffee and studied him. A hint of a smile teased her mouth as she placed the empty cup on the table and then said, "I'm going to tell you up front, Justin Miles, I like you. You seem to be honest. You say what you have to say, and like my Joshua, you don't waste words. I like that. I've been watching the way you look at Davia and the way you touch her." She paused, her eyes boring holes into him like lasers. "Either you *are* in love, or you're a very good actor." She rose from the kitchen table. "But, baby, let me tell you, when it comes to actors, I've seen the best. All I want you to remember is that when you mess with my children, you mess with me. And you don't want to do that."

With that she left the kitchen. The talk was over. Justin had gotten the stamp of approval.

CHAPTER 14

Davia snuggled up in the cushioned comfort of the soft leather sofa in Justin's family room. After landing in Atlanta, the two of them had stopped at his house for some time alone together before she went home. Shutting her eyes, she reviewed the weekend that they had spent in Chicago. Justin had been a hit with the family.

Papa Josh and he had gotten along right away and Mama Willa, much more suspicious of everyone, had been impressed. Darius had told her in private that he thought that Justin was a "fine man," while Donna called him a "hunk." Yes, things had gone well.

Giving a contented sigh, Davia opened her eyes and looked straight into Justin's eyes. He had taken a seat beside her. Smiling down at her, he wrapped an arm around her waist and pulled her to him.

"What are you thinking about?"

Davia snuggled up to him. "Oh, I was thinking about our weekend and how much everyone liked you. The Johnson family saved my life, and their opinion means a lot to me."

"I know. Darius told me how his younger sister, Tina, brought you to their home."

"If she hadn't, I don't know where I would have ended up. I know it's hard for you to understand just how hard my childhood really was. So I don't expect someone like you . . ."

"Someone like me?" Justin pulled back. He wasn't happy with her description.

Davia didn't retreat. "Justin, I know you *try* to understand, and I appreciate it, but you come from a world of economic security. It's so beyond where I came from that there's no way you can understand what my life was like. Most children have families who are there for them. As a child, I couldn't even conceive of such a possibility until the Johnson family came along."

Justin nodded. "I see." He hated to admit it, but she was right.

"I was a runaway, Justin." She hesitated, reluctant to relive the pain of the past.

"You ran away from your cousin?"

"No, it was something else." *Someone* else. Davia took a shaky breath. Like a serpent, thoughts of Money slithered to the forefront of her consciousness. She pushed them back. "I don't want to go into it, but I did live on the streets for a while. I slept and ate where I could. I was a child carrying a child and I didn't even know it. I was completely alone. That is, until one day, when an eleven-year-old girl came up to me while I was sitting in the park."

"Tina Johnson," Justin stated, referring to the youngest of the Johnson clan.

"Yes, and she took me home to Mama Willa." Davia recalled. "I used to hang out in this little neighborhood park nearly every day. Don't ask me why, but for some reason I felt safe there. Lord knows it was filled with as much danger as the rest of the places I called home, but it had trees and flowers—Anyway, I would see this little girl in a plaid hooded jacket cutting through the park nearly every time I was there. She would walk back and forth to the store, carrying bags filled with this and that. She would smile at me, and I'd smile back, even though at the time there wasn't much to smile about. Then, one day, Tina stopped and sat down on the bench next to me without being invited. I just looked at her, shocked by her boldness. You know, this little kid approaching me, a big, bad teenager of fourteen. She didn't say anything to me. She didn't look at me either, but she opened this grocery bag, and took a loaf of bread out, then opened this package of thick-sliced bologna. She made two sandwiches and handed one to me." Davia paused to savor the memory.

"We sat there eating those sandwiches. Then, when we were finished, she said, 'Come with me.' Just like that, and I did. I was so tired of being alone." Davia swallowed the lump in her throat and glanced at Justin.

"I bet Mama Willa and her husband welcomed you with open arms." Justin's voice was husky with emotion.

Davia tossed him a grin. "They lived on the tenth floor of this high-rise apartment in the most notorious housing project in Chicago. When Tina opened the door to that place, noise seemed to be everywhere. The TV was playing in one room, the radio in another room, and the record player was on. Mama was in the kitchen singing church songs at the top of her lungs, and the smell of her fried chicken nearly buckled my knees."

Justin's mouth started to water involuntarily. "Yes! That woman can *cook*!"

Davia nodded in agreement. "Papa Josh was in a lounge chair with a kid on each knee. When I walked in everybody looked up, said hello, then returned to what they were doing, like my being there was the most natural thing in the world. Mama asked me my name and told me I was staying for dinner. I lived with them until the day I moved to Atlanta."

They were silent for a moment. Then Justin asked, "Did they adopt you?"

Davia shook her head. "No, I wouldn't let them."

Justin waited for an explanation, but when none came, he didn't push. Instead, he placed a tender kiss on her lips.

"Thank you for introducing me to your family. I loved meeting them."

"Like I said, I know it might seem childish, but their approval was very important to me."

"And what's important to you is important to me." Justin caressed her cheek. "You see, I may not understand everything about your life, but I do understand you. And now that I've met your family, it's time for you to fasten your seat belt and batten down the hatches. I want you to meet my mother."

❧

The hotel ballroom was a glittering paradise of silver and gold, accented by a dazzling array of tiny gold lights as Justin and Davia entered the annual Charity Ball. The decorations were exquisite and Davia voiced her delight, but Justin hardly noticed them. He hadn't recovered from the daze he had been in since Davia met him at her front door. The dress she was wearing was killing him.

The floor-length gown was white crepe, and it clung to her form as if it had been made for her. The sleeveless gown's scooped neckline made it appear almost demur until she turned. The back plunged to the small of her back. A split bared one shapely leg whenever she walked. Diamond teardrop earrings and a delicate matching necklace glittered against her flawless skin. She was gorgeous.

All Justin could think about since seeing Davia in that dress were ways to peel it from her body so that he could make passionate love to her. He hadn't wanted to attend this affair anyway, preferring to spend the time alone with Davia. Unfortunately, his mother was the chairperson of the ball committee, and he knew that for Katherine his attendance tonight was mandatory. Besides, it offered the perfect opportunity for two of the most important women in his life to meet.

Earlier that week Davia and Vanessa had arrived at the preschool at the same time to pick up their girls. The chance meeting had given them the opportunity to chat. Later that evening his sister had called him on his cell phone, eager to express her approval of the woman who had stolen his heart. He was pleased that she liked Davia, and appreciative when his sister had issued him a warning. Their mother was aware of his dating Davia.

She suspected that Katherine was up to something and wanted him to be aware. He thanked her for the forewarning, and this evening he was ready to face whatever Katherine Miles might pull.

Surveying the ballroom for his mother, he was glad that this social gathering was the setting for their meeting. Katherine could be a handful at times, but in public she was always the consummate lady. She would never embarrass herself in front of Atlanta's elite. It was his hope that after meeting Davia, she might try to get to know her and—miracles of miracles—perhaps even like her, but he was a realist. Katherine was a snob. Davia's present social and economic status didn't matter. It was her background on which his mother's opinions would be based.

Justin tolerated his mother's idiosyncrasy but adamantly disagreed with her. He was a man in love, and he would not put up with any effort on her part to interfere in his relationship with Davia.

His eyes shifted to the woman in question. How could he not love her? His hands trembled as he removed the evening wrap from her shoulders. She had become everything to him. His lips brushed the nape of her neck as he whispered, "Did I tell you how beautiful you look tonight?"

Davia flashed him a heart-stopping smile over her shoulder. "You've told me about a dozen times, but of course I love hearing it."

Turning to the coat check-in counter, Justin swallowed hard. He had to regroup.

It had been two weeks since their weekend in Chicago and their busy lives had kept them apart. Telephone conversations could never replace seeing or being with Davia, and his libido was stretched to the limit.

Glancing at his watch, he decided that it would be a short evening. He had attended too many of these society events as it was. When he weighed being here against being alone with Davia, there was no contest. They would be leaving early.

Checking her wrap, he returned to Davia. With his hand on the small of her back, he guided her into the main ballroom where his mother would be waiting.

From across the room, Katherine spotted Justin's entrance. Her eyes shone with pride. He was so tall and so handsome. The pristine white dinner jacket he was wearing fit his broad shoulders to perfection. He looked so much like his father that her heart constricted as he moved across the room. He walked with the same fluid movements as Zack. He possessed the same self-assurance that she knew so well. Katherine had been madly in love with Zachary Miles when he was alive, and she loved him no less in death. Their son was the personification of the love she and her husband had shared. Whenever she saw Justin, she saw Zachary. With a note of satisfaction she noticed the wistful looks on the faces of some of the women in the room as he passed their tables. This was Zachary's son, all right. This was her heart.

Her eyes shifted to the dark brown woman walking beside him and the light shining in Katherine's eyes dimmed. Justin *was* her heart, and this little nobody would never have him. Rising from the table she had been sharing with the other committee members, she went to meet the couple. She certainly didn't want her friends to meet this tramp. It was bad enough that they were drawing attention simply walking across the room. She forced a welcoming smile as the couple drew near.

"Well, finally." She turned her cheek for a kiss from Justin. He obliged. "I was wondering when you were going to get here."

"Now, Mother, don't start." Justin shook his head in amusement. Katherine was a stickler for time. "We're fifteen minutes late. That's not even late enough to be fashionable."

He turned to Davia and with a gentle prod brought her to stand between him and Katherine. Placing his arm possessively around her waist, he made the introductions.

"Mother, this is Davia Maxwell. Davia, my mother, Katherine Miles."

Davia smiled warmly and held out her hand, somewhat awed by the beauty of the older woman. "It's very nice meeting you, Mrs. Miles."

Looking the younger woman in the eye, Katherine took her hand and shook it firmly. "The same here, *Ms. Maxwell*."

Davia noticed the emphasis Katherine put on her name, but chose to ignore it, making certain that neither her smile nor her gaze wavered.

"Thank you, but please call me Davia."

Katherine's eyes swept over the dark beauty, taking in the touch of makeup accenting her sculptured features.

The short, wiry haircut that framed her face was very becoming. There was no doubt that the woman was pretty in an *African* sort of way. Her eyes fell briefly to the form-fitting dress. Her other attributes were also obvious, although her taste in clothing was questionable. Katherine's eyes swept upward to note the glittering diamonds. They were real and quite expensive, if somewhat gaudy for her taste. Once more her eyes met the younger woman's gaze.

"Davia, that's such an interesting name, quite exotic. Is it a *family* name?"

Davia's expression didn't change. There was subtext in the words that the woman spoke and Katherine knew that Davia knew it. A quiet war was being declared. It was a sophisticated one, but war nonetheless. Davia was up to the challenge.

"I'm glad you like my name, Mrs. Miles. I'm quite fond of it."

"I'm sure you are, my dear." There was a smoldering fire in Katherine's eyes despite her smile, and the interplay between the two women did not go unnoticed by her son.

"Is there some problem here, Mother?" he asked, subtly warning her that it was best that there be none. Whatever his mother had up her sleeve, it wasn't going to work.

Katherine feigned ignorance. "No, son, everything is just fine." And it was. Katherine had taken her stand and the woman had seemed to get the message.

Justin knew that it was time to retreat. These were two women who would battle to the death. Drawing Davia back against his chest, his lips caressed her hair.

"We need to find CeCe and Clark, sweetheart. They'll be looking for us."

His voice and touch made it clear to anyone observing what he felt for this woman. Justin was taking a stand of his own.

Davia smiled up at him gratefully. "All right. It was very nice meeting you, Mrs. Miles, and congratulations on this event. I'm certain we're going to have a good time."

"I'm sure." Katherine dismissed Davia, disturbed by the energy passing between this woman and her son. She looked past Davia to address Justin. "And, darling, I want *you* to come by the committee table later this evening. Your old flame Jane and some of the others in your crowd are here and would love to see you." With a final air kiss to Justin she turned and walked away. Davia gave a sigh of relief.

The rest of the evening was perfect. Davia and Justin joined CeCe and Clark and the two couples talked, laughed and danced the night away. This was the first time that Davia had spent any time with CeCe and Clark as a couple, and despite CeCe's contention that she and Clark were just having fun, the interaction between them said that there was more.

There was no doubt about the seriousness of the relationship between Justin and Davia. Sparks were flying.

Before the affair was half over, they had decided to call it an evening. CeCe and Clark had left long ago. As they took one last spin around the dance floor, Justin and Davia were too wrapped up in each other to notice

Katherine's searing gaze following them. She started as Charles slipped up behind her and tapped her on the shoulder.

"A penny for your thoughts," he quipped.

Katherine turned toward him coolly. "I was just thinking that it would have been nice if you had come to this affair *on time.*" She turned her back on him.

A flash of anger passed across his handsome features. *Who did this uppity bit . . . ?* Charles caught himself before the anger took over. The mask reappeared. He smiled.

"Now, Katherine, I told you that I had business to attend to."

She didn't acknowledge him as she directed her attention toward the dance floor.

Charles followed her line of vision. Her precious Justin was wrapped so tightly in the embrace of some woman that a piece of paper couldn't have gotten between them. Charles's eyes slid back to Katherine's tight expression. It was clear from the look on her face that she didn't like what she was seeing. His eyes returned to the striking couple.

"The mysterious Davia Maxwell, I presume."

The look that Katherine gave him confirmed his observation. He watched as Justin's lips brushed against those of the delicious beauty and she smiled up at him.

"She's a looker." Charles hadn't realized that he had spoken aloud until Katherine bristled.

"He's dated better, and I'm going to put a stop to this little fling, if it's the last thing I do."

Charles chuckled to himself. It was obvious to a blind man that Katherine's efforts would be in vain. From the look of it, her precious Justin had a love jones, and it was coming down on him hard. Aloud, he tried to sound sympathetic. "It looks like you might be too late."

Oblivious to everyone around him except Davia, Justin decided that he couldn't wait one more minute to be alone with her. Pulling her closer, he whispered in her ear, "Let's ditch this dump."

Davia grinned. "I thought you would never ask."

Taking her by the hand, Justin practically ran off the dance floor. As they made their way through the crowd, Davia looked over her shoulder to where Katherine was standing.

"Aren't we going to say goodbye to your mother?"

Justin kept moving. "I'll apologize for being ungracious tomorrow."

Uncertain about their breach of etiquette, Davia glanced back at Katherine once again to gage her reaction to their obvious departure, but she had turned to speak to the handsome, middle-aged man standing next to her. Davia blinked. He looked familiar. Her mind raced. She stumbled.

Justin turned, tightening his grip on her hand and stopped her from tumbling to the floor. "Are you all right?'

She quickly recovered. "Yes . . . yes. I'm fine."

Looking her over from head to foot, he winked. "Yes, you are."

Davia blushed at the stark look of desire on Justin's face. They continued toward the entrance. As they entered the lobby, retrieved their coats and stepped out into the starry night, all else was forgotten except each other and the evening that lay ahead.

Most of her life Davia had feared her own sexuality. In her mind that was what had caused so much pain in her life. Never would she have imagined that it could also bring so much pleasure, and that was the promise that danced in the depths of Justin's eyes as they stood in the foyer of his home and he whispered, "I want you."

With one finger he traced the curve of the bodice of the dress that had kept him enraptured most of the evening. He could feel her body quiver as her eyelids slowly closed.

Davia's legs threatened to buckle beneath her as sensations rippled through her body. Only Justin could make her feel this way. Opening her eyes, she looked deep into his. "I want you, too."

He gave her a sensuous smile. Taking her by the hand, he moved with purpose through the house to the spiral staircase that would lead them to paradise. At the foot of the stairs, he turned her to face him. Those swaying hips and that round derriere that had teased him all evening had him so worked up that he could stand it no longer. He had to have a kiss, just one kiss, to nourish his escalating need. He eased her against him, and then crushed her lips to his, taking possession of her mouth.

Davia curled into Justin. The feel of him, the taste of him, invaded every pore. She moaned with pleasure. He responded. She groaned with desire. So did he.

Breathless, they broke the kiss. Davia turned her back to him and indicated the zipper of her dress. "Please."

Enticed by the smell of her perfume, he nuzzled her neck. "My pleasure." Slowly, he lowered the zipper as he pressed his lips against her heated skin and confessed, "I've been dreaming of nothing else all evening but stripping this dress from your body." He placed a kiss between her shoulder blades and Davia's breathing became labored.

"I want to make love to you like no one has done before me." Slowly he trailed the path of her spine with the tip of his tongue.

Davia threatened to incinerate. She couldn't breathe. She couldn't think. All she could do was feel.

As his mouth reached its final destination, Justin placed a reverent kiss on her flesh. His large hands slipped inside the loosened gown and languidly removed it. The dress slithered down her body to pool at her feet.

"You didn't have on a bra." His voice held his surprise and delight.

"It's sewed into the dress," Davia croaked. She leaned back against his hard chest for support.

"Step out of the dress." His hot breath singed her jeweled earlobe.

She did as asked, kicked the dress aside and then turned to face him. The reward for her compliance was a kiss.

Justin eased her down onto a step. His eyes were ablaze as Davia lay beneath him clad in nothing more than satin bikini panties, thigh-high stockings and sparkling diamonds glistening like raindrops against her dark skin. This was his fantasy come true.

"Beautiful," he rasped.

As Justin rained kisses of devotion along the contours of her body, with trembling fingers Davia disrobed him, until his nude body hovered above her. The proof of his want and need was plainly evident. Having taken a condom from his discarded pants, he dangled it in front of her, wiggling his eyebrows suggestively, soliciting a giggle.

Heat quickly replaced humor as Davia's eyes stroked him, followed by her hand. Her touch was hesitant and uncertain at first, but as she heard his sharp intake of breath, saw his eyes drift shut and felt his body tremble, she felt empowered. Withdrawing her hand, she took advantage of Justin's momentary distraction and backpedaled up the winding staircase. Justin quickly recovered.

"Oh, no, you don't," he growled, delighted at her unexpected playfulness. Grabbing at her to halt her progress, he caught the edge of her satin bikinis.

"Justin!" Davia squealed as he slid the flimsy fabric down her legs, along with her stockings. She helped his determined effort with a slight wiggle. His look scorched her.

"You don't know what you do to me, do you?"

Dazed by the darkening of his eyes, she shook her head. "No, I don't."

"Let me show you." Justin parted her thighs and knelt between them. Bringing his lips to her unbridled breasts, he licked and suckled each potent nub until they hardened in anticipation. With knowing fingers he parted her moistened folds and worked his relentless magic. All she could do was moan and mewl. Heat ricocheted throughout her system until she exploded into microscopic particles hurling into space. Justin held her tightly until she spiraled slowly back to earth. Crooning from pleasure, Davia lay spent in his arms.

"That's what you do to me," he rasped. "You make me lose all control."

Having recovered a bit, an embolden Davia pushed away from him gently and tossed him a challenge. "Let me show you what you do to me."

Gripping the handrail, she stood on shaky legs and began backing up the stairway, her eyes never leaving Justin's eyes. As if in a trance, he followed her, advancing one step for each step she abandoned until they both reached the top of the stairs. It was there that she allowed herself to be captured as she took control. Tentative at first, then with increasing confidence, she proceeded to turn Justin's body into her personal playground.

His body quivered as her mouth captured his nipples, and what she did to his navel with her tongue nearly sent him toppling down the stairs. When her hands caressed his engorged shaft and with his help slipped on the condom, it took all of the willpower Justin possessed to keep from exploding in her hands. His legs gave away, and they slid to the floor. As they writhed in pleasure on the carpet, the bed was all but forgotten.

Davia was molten lava as Justin slid his shaft into her welcoming warmth. She wrapped her legs around him, deepening his penetration until he pierced her inner core. He gave a guttural moan as her heat engulfed him. His strokes were slow, escalating gradually as their moans of pleasure became the music by which they danced.

Never had anyone given him such pleasure. "I love you, Davia." He buried his face against her silken skin.

Dazed, delirious, Davia dug her nails deeper into Justin's back. She was on fire, consumed by the fuel of each powerful stoke. Justin increased the pace. Davia screamed and he answered her call with a ravenous kiss. Again and again they came together in a frenzied, unquenchable need for each other that ended in a mind-altering completion.

Much later, when they finally abandoned the floor for Justin's large bed, they lay entwined in each other's arms. Justin's body was still tingling with the power of what they had discovered together. He drew Davia closer to him.

"I love you so much." His voice quivered with passion. "I never want to let you go." Silently he vowed that he wouldn't. Davia Maxwell would be Mrs. Frederick Justin Miles. Davia could hear the truth in his declaration. She could feel the depth of his emotion. Tears threatened to flow. She snuggled closer to him, joy infusing every fiber of her being as she whispered the words that she had never thought she would say to any man.

"I love you, too, Justin." And she did—completely.

CHAPTER 15

So this was how it felt to be in love—this insatiable, incredible, indescribable all-encompassing feeling of caring so deeply for someone that you never wanted that feeling to end. Davia turned her head slightly to look at the man in whose arms she lay. Justin Miles was that *someone*.

"A penny for your thoughts." His lips savored the curve of her neck. She smelled so sweet. She *was* so sweet.

Davia smiled. "I was thinking about love and what it means to be in love."

Justin adjusted his body so that his head rested in his hand. "What about being in love? Specifically, what about being in love with me?" He wanted to know. No, he needed to know, because never in his life would he have imagined that three little words from a woman could mean so much. *I love you.*

Davia saw the adoration in his eyes and felt overwhelmed by the feelings she was experiencing. She caressed his cheek, and thrilled at his response to her touch as his aroused manhood began to throb against her bare flesh. This love had power that she had yet to fully comprehend.

"I was thinking how love has freed me. I can feel and I can trust now. I'm not afraid like I used to be."

Justin looked confused. "Afraid of what, baby? You don't ever have to be afraid as long as I'm here. I'll protect you with my life."

His words brought tears to her eyes. What had she done to deserve such devotion? If this was love, it was wonderful. She kissed his Adam's apple. "Thank you for that. But, I'm not talking about being afraid for my safety. I've just been afraid of so many things. My life has been so . . . so . . . ." She took a tremulous breath. "I can't even explain it."

"But one day you will."

Davia looked into his eyes. His words were prophetic. "Yes. One day I will."

"So you're saying that there is more that you have to tell me about yourself?"

Davia lay back on the bed with a sardonic laugh. "If you only knew."

Justin gazed down at her thoughtfully. "You're right, if I *only* knew." He gave her a sad smile. "But something tells me that tonight is not the night."

"No, it's not." Davia could hear the pain that she had caused by continuing to shut him out. It was time to lighten the conversation. "Tonight I've got to come up with a plan to stop your mother from killing me."

Her words had their intended effect. Justin broke into a gale of laughter. "You've got her number, that's for sure."

"If she had stared any more daggers at me at the dance, I'd be dead now."

Justin squeezed her derriere. "No, you wouldn't. I wouldn't let you die."

Davia whispered seductively, "And what would you do to save me?"

"I would have given you mouth to mouth."

She growled, "Show me."

He did.

&

The call that came from Katherine Miles a week after the ball didn't surprise Davia. She had known that it would come. Unfortunately, it arrived at a bad time.

Business at Small Sensations was skyrocketing, and Davia's workload was heavier than ever. Sleep was at a minimum as she continued to spend long hours at the office. She was on overload, and it was compounded by her refusal to skimp on her time with Gabby. She had vowed that it would never happen again. Yet, that left little time for Justin. Since their night of passion, telephone calls had been their means of communication and they each anxiously anticipated the next time that they could be together. Absence did make the heart grow fonder.

Despite the lack of time, Davia made a special effort to comply with Katherine's request to see her. If there were any stumbling blocks between Justin and her, it would be his mother and time, in that order. Time she could handle. Katherine might prove more difficult.

Katherine had invited Davia to her home for lunch. That request concerned Davia. Justin's mother was not the type of woman to engage in public confrontations, but Davia had no doubts that she had no qualms about private ones. Well, the woman had better be careful, because Davia was overworked and stressed out. The combination could prove to be dangerous.

Things went well on her arrival. Katherine was a gracious hostess. They exchanged small talk about the ball and the weather. Davia let Katherine take the lead and started to relax a bit, but not too much. She knew that Justin's mother would show her hand at the appropriate opportunity. She was right.

Sitting back in the elegant French provincial dining chair, Katherine pushed her half-eaten salad aside and folded her well-manicured hands on the table before her. Giving Davia a wan smile, she got straight to the point.

"You appear to be a very astute young woman, *Ms. Maxwell*, so something tells me that you know why we're here."

Davia pushed her salad aside, folded her well-manicured hands on the table and returned Katherine's smile. "You're correct about my being astute, *Mrs. Miles*, but just in case there might be a misunderstanding as to why I am here, why don't you clarify the reason for me."

Katherine paused and made a visual assessment of Davia. "Who are you, *Ms. Maxwell*? It is obvious that you come from the streets. One can acquire polish, but one can't acquire breeding." She paused, waiting for a reply that did not come. She continued. "I happen to know that your name is *not* Davia Maxwell. So who are you? And what are you after?"

Davia willed her body not to respond to Katherine's revelation as she held her gaze. "My name is Davia Maxwell, Mrs. Miles. If you can prove otherwise, do so."

Katherine sneered. "Oh, I can prove otherwise, my dear. You can tell my son that lie, but I know differently."

Davia's demeanor remained calm. "And what is it that you *think* you know about me?"

Katherine's smile wavered at Davia's unruffled manner. Could it be the information that she had been given was wrong? "I know that your first name is *not* Davia. You changed it. It was Shanay or Nay Nay or some such nonsense, and your former address was in some project in Chicago. You have no parents. You appeared to just have shown up one day at the home of a Mr. and Mrs. Johnson, who took you in. There is no record of a formal adoption or guardianship. Yet you were bold enough to use their last name until you moved here to Atlanta. *But* when you moved here, you changed your name legally to Davia Maxwell. You even enrolled in college here under that name. Shall I go on?"

Davia didn't answer. Her body had gone cold. Fighting to maintain control, she refused to waver from the steady gaze of the woman sitting across from her.

Unable to get the response she was expecting, Katherine's tone turned deadly.

"As you can see, *Ms. Maxwell*, I've had you investigated, and I am appalled at what I've been told. A birth certificate at Cook County hospital in Chicago has a Shanay Johnson giving birth to a baby girl about nineteen years ago. This Shanay Johnson couldn't have been more than fifteen years old."

Davia's gaze didn't falter, but her breathing did. It escalated. Katherine noticed.

She smelled blood.

"The birth certificate had the child's name listed as Stephanie Johnson."

Davia leaned back in her chair at her child's name tumbling from the lips of this hateful woman. The fire in her eyes ignited.

Katherine leaned forward, ready for the kill. "Lo and behold, four years ago at Grady hospital a baby girl was born to a girl named Stephanie Maxwell. A girl who was the same age as Stephanie Johnson would have been. I say *would have been* because, unfortunately, the poor girl died giving . . ."

"Stop it!" Davia hissed. Her chest felt constricted as her lungs fought for air.

Katherine turned the knife. "Stephanie's child's name was Gabrielle, Gabrielle Maxwell. Father *unknown*."

"I told you to stop it!" Davia slammed her fist on the table. Silverware jumped. China rattled as she leaped from her chair. "Don't you dare say another word!" Her eyes seared Katherine, who sat back in her chair in triumph.

"What's going on here?"

Katherine looked startled as Justin walked into the room. Like a chameleon, her manner changed as she smiled up at him sweetly. "Justin, darling, what are you doing here?"

He ignored her as his eyes stayed on Davia, who didn't move or acknowledge his presence as she stared daggers at Katherine. Looking from one woman to the other, he approached them cautiously, his brows furrowed in uncertainty.

"Davia? What's wrong?" He noted her rapid breathing, the look of rage on her face. She remained immobile. Her silent fury permeated the room. Justin turned to Katherine.

"I had some free time so I thought that I would stop by and say hello." He turned back to Davia, who still hadn't acknowledged him. "I called your office and you were out. I had no idea you were here until I pulled up and saw your car outside." His gaze took in the table and the half-eaten meals before transferring back to Katherine. "So tell me, Mother, what is this all about? It's obviously not about sharing a friendly meal. I could hear Davia's voice as I walked down the hall. What did you do to her?"

Katherine looked taken aback. "I beg your pardon? You make me secondary on your 'to do' list, then come to my home and accuse me of doing something to *her*?" She glared at Davia's defensive stance. "She was the one raising her voice to me like some uncouth barbarian, not vice versa. Your concern should be for your mother and not this . . . this . . ."

"That's enough, Mother." Justin's warning was stern. Moving to Davia, he put his hands on her shoulders and gently eased her rigid form back into the chair.

Katherine's eyes widened in disbelief as she rose to face him. "How dare you speak to me in that tone of voice? What has gotten into you? Has this woman become more important to you than I am? You don't know anything about her. Believe me, you don't."

Justin shook his head in exasperation. "I know what I need to know, and I don't need your approval about who I date."

"You're flippant and rude, Justin, and I won't tolerate it, especially in light of the information I've uncovered about this person. My Lord, I don't even know what to call her." Her malicious gaze settled on her nemesis. "Davia Maxwell isn't her real name."

"*Whatever* my name is, Mrs. Miles, it's personal and it belongs to me."

Both Katherine and Justin seemed surprised at Davia's interjection. Having recovered from the shock of Katherine's verbal assault, she was grateful for Justin's intervention. It had given her time to regain control of her emotions.

Justin's hand squeezed her shoulder in renewed support. "Sweetheart, maybe you can tell me what's going on."

Her eyes never left Katherine's. "I'm certain that your mother would be more than happy to fill you in."

Katherine grunted. "As I said before, you *are* astute."

"Well, I would appreciate it if someone could fill me in." Justin threw his arms in the air in mounting frustration.

Katherine sat down in her seat with a look of satisfaction. "Well, son, I have come across some important information about this woman that I think you should know."

With a sigh, Justin took a seat next to Davia. Leaning back, he crossed his arms across his chest. "Okay. Mother, just what is it that I need to know about Davia? Because right now I know what she *wants* me to know, and I'm sure she'll tell me anything else when she's ready."

For the first time since his arrival, Davia looked at Justin, and the tension in her body lessened. God, did she love this man. He was solidifying his support for her and she was grateful. But would it continue? Katherine was determined to turn him against her, as her next words proved.

"Did you know that the little girl she passes off as her daughter is really her granddaughter?" Katherine delivered this bit of news smugly.

Justin didn't falter. "Yes. Gabby is Stephanie's child. Stephanie was Davia's daughter."

The look of surprise on Katherine's face was worth Davia's having sat through her vicious tirade, but she didn't have time to savor the moment as the woman continued.

"Did she tell you that Davia isn't her first name? And God only knows what her last name is."

Justin didn't miss a beat. "Justin isn't my real first name, either. So what's your point?"

"Oh really!" Katherine rose from her chair angrily. "How naive can you be? For goodness sake, this woman comes from nothing. She was an unwed teen mother who crawled from the gutter and bred another unwed mother . . ."

"That's it!" Davia braced herself on the dining room table, leaning toward Katherine. Despite her stance her voice was calm—*deadly* calm. "I have had enough. I love Justin, Mrs. Miles, and I wanted to respect you as his mother, but I can see that I'm not going to get the same courtesy. You had no right to invade my privacy . . ."

"That's where you're wrong, Ms. Maxwell. I have every right to protect the fortune and good names that two great families left behind. As for respecting you, why should I? You're a little gold digger who saw my son and lured him into your seductive trap. You're a little nobody who doesn't deserve my respect."

"She's not a nobody! And I'm not a child, Mother. I make my own choices." It was Justin who leaped from his chair this time. "Davia has overcome obstacles that you and I couldn't begin to imagine. She's a top executive in one of the largest black businesses in this country."

"Some little business that makes loud clothing," sniffed Katherine. "Please, spare me."

"Yes, but it's *my* business, Mrs. Miles." Davia's eyes scorched Katherine as she inched closer to her. "*I* own Small Sensations, lock, stock and barrel. I own the building that houses it, the land the building stands on, every truck that delivers its products and the plane that transports our executives. It's all *mine*, lady, built on my blood, sweat and tears. You can be damn sure of that!"

Davia ignored the gasp of surprise coming from Justin. She was on a roll. "I built what I have at a cost greater than you can ever imagine. Do you think that I'm going to sit back and let you malign me? Insult me? Investigate me? If so, you've got another think coming."

Snatching up her purse, Davia prepared to leave. "And for your information, I've never hidden the fact that Gabby is my granddaughter. I'm quite proud of that fact. But if you should repeat in public a word of what you've said to me today, I'll slap a lawsuit on you so fast your head will spin."

Davia stalked toward the door. Justin stood looking from one angry face to the other, not sure what to do at this point. Davia was in a state of controlled fury, while his normally unflappable mother was seething with rage.

"Who do you think you are?" Katherine's voice trembled. She wasn't used to being challenged. "You don't know who you're dealing with."

Davia stopped dead in her tracks and slowly turned. Her eyes were blazing daggers. "No, lady, you don't know who *you're* dealing with. So don't try me."

She left the room without looking back. The sound of the front door slamming echoed through the hallway. Katherine turned angry eyes on Justin.

"So *that's* what you claim to love? She threatened me, your own mother!"

"No, that's who I do love. I love her with everything in me, and from what I've seen and heard you did your part to encourage the threat." Justin started toward the exit. "But I'll talk with you later about this. I've got to go."

Katherine looked incredulous. "I don't believe that you're running after her. Didn't you hear the way she spoke to me?"

"I said I'll talk to you *later*," Justin tossed over his shoulder as he hurried out of the room, leaving Katherine alone to sulk.

Charles Cash pulled up in front of Katherine's house just as Justin rushed out the front door. He watched as the younger man leaped in front of a gleaming new sports car as it was about to pull off. The driver slammed on the brakes.

As Charles got out of his car, he watched with amused interest what looked like a lover's spat. Justin rounded the car and spoke to the driver, and then reached in the open window, unlocked the door, and opened it, awaiting the driver's exit. There seemed to be some hesitation on the driver's part, but after another exchange of words the driver complied.

It turned out to be that cute little girlfriend of Justin's behind the wheel, and she didn't seem happy about what was happening. As Charles walked toward the house, Justin slid into the driver's seat, while she rounded the car and got into the passenger seat. Charles chuckled. Attitude was evident in every move that she made.

By the time Charles reached the front door, the two lovers had driven off. *So the pampered prince had found a princess that he couldn't handle. It looked like the breakup Katherine wants so badly could be near; I'm not sure how I feel about that.*

As he rang the doorbell, Charles felt relieved that he had missed the favored son. He didn't feel like playing second fiddle to him today. Although their contact had been minimal over the past months, he had discerned that Justin wasn't the kind of man he could easily deal with, and he tried to avoid him as much as possible.

However, Vanessa, the disfavored daughter, was another story. He had managed to have several conversations with her, as well as dinner and drinks. Vanessa was no problem. He had proved that. He didn't need any stumbling blocks in the way of his future. Justin Miles could qualify as a stumbling block; that is, if he didn't have something or someone to occupy his time.

That being the case, he hoped that the prince and his little princess would solve their dispute quickly. While Katherine might not agree with him, in Charles's opinion the longer Justin was preoccupied with his lady love, the better.

CHAPTER 16

Davia was so mad with Katherine that she could spit fire. What made her even angrier was that Justin appeared to be so calm about everything that had happened. Outside his mother's home, he had insisted that he drive her home, telling her that she was too emotional to drive safely. Resistant at first, she had finally given in, but instead of taking her home he took her to his house, where she raised hell.

Justin didn't argue with her. After she had calmed down, he ignored the silent treatment that she'd decided to give him. Then she watched in amazement as Justin had the gall to call her secretary and tell her to cancel the rest of Davia's appointments for the day. He called his office with the same directive. Leaving her to nurse her resentment, he disappeared into the kitchen. He reappeared carrying a tray laden with a teapot filled with her favorite tea, apple cinnamon, and huge chocolate chip cookies, her favorite snack.

The tea's aroma was enticing. As he placed the tray on the table before her, Davia continued her silent protest. As childish as her behavior might be, she didn't want to be soothed or pacified. She wanted to savor her anger, but Justin was making it difficult.

Her anger wasn't directed at him. How could it be? He had come to her defense against his own mother and had left Katherine's house to be by her side. Justin hadn't wavered in his support of her for one minute. He was proving to be every bit the man she thought him to be and she was glad that her instincts had proved right—so far. But years of mistrust of the opposite sex were so pervasive that the security of absolute certainty seemed foreign. After all, Katherine Miles *was* Justin's mother, and loyalty to friends and family was an intricate part of his character. How could a son go against his mother?

"I would never ask you to go against her."

Justin looked startled at the first words she had uttered since entering his home. He knew the meaning behind those words. He didn't question them or her as he settled on the sofa beside her, careful to keep distance between them.

Davia made eye contact with Justin. She expected him to react to her statement.

He didn't. Instead, he changed the subject entirely.

"So you're the *owner* of Small Sensations."

Davia was evasive. "What does that have to do with anything?"

"I'm just asking. Are you or aren't you?"

Davia thought she noted a hint of skepticism in his voice. She bristled.

"I certainly am." Her words left no room for doubt. "Leroy is out front because I want him to be. I own Small Sensations. I started sewing when I was a little girl, and when Stephanie came along, I designed and sewed all of her clothes. When I moved in with the Johnson family, I sewed for them and pretty soon neighbors from all over came to me asking me to make their kid's clothes. I'll have you know that I helped pay my way through college with part-time jobs and my sewing skills, and when I started the business I worked day and night, twenty-four seven, building Small Sensations. I sacrificed everything . . ." The defiance in Davia's voice wavered as she fought the emotions welling up inside of her. "Including Stephanie."

Taking her hand, Justin entwined their fingers. "I'm not questioning your ownership of Small Sensations. I'm trying to point out that someone intelligent and mature enough to accomplish something like that is displaying some very immature behavior right now."

Davia's eyes narrowed. "So what? Don't you think I have a right to be angry that your mother invaded my privacy? The woman had me investigated!" Her stance dared him to disagree.

Justin chose his words carefully. "You're right, and she was wrong. I'll deal with her about that later, but right now I'm concerned about you. I want you to know that I'm here for you. I always will be."

Davia could feel her anger dissipating. Why did he have to be so agreeable? Gradually her irritation was replaced by a deep-rooted sadness. She laid her head back on the sofa and sighed heavily. "Oh, God, I'm so tired."

"Then rest, sweetheart. Let it go and rest." His voice was as soothing as his advice was wise.

"You make it all sound so simple, but some things are easier said than done. Your mother is just one of the obstacles in our way."

"No, Davia." Justin tugged at her hand, drawing her closer to him. "She's not in *my* way at all. If I have to go around her, over her, or through her to keep you, I will. I love you, and that's the bottom line."

Davia closed her eyes against the intensity of his gaze. So *this* was love. Love was absolute.

She shook her head. "But there are still things that you don't know about me, that you couldn't possibly understand."

Justin settled her against the beat of his heart. "You keep telling me that, but it seems to me that it's up to you to help me understand."

Davia sighed in resignation. He was right. It was time to open yet another door to her past.

"Today wasn't the first time that I was told by someone's mother that I wasn't good enough for her son. I never thought that I would ever hear it again." She proceeded to tell him about her daughter's father and his family's rejection of her.

Justin was appalled by the insensitivity she described, and he was touched by the plight in which she has found herself. "So, Mark's family was the reason you moved to Atlanta and changed your name?" He was confused. Her story warranted further explanation, especially since she had informed him that the family was deceased.

Davia shook her head, and he waited for an explanation. There was none. As always, he didn't force the issue.

"I'm sorry about what happened to you. God knows you've been through a lot." He tilted her chin upward as his eyes swept her face. She looked exhausted. "Listen, sweetheart, you need a break. We both do, and I know where we can go to get it. I have a beach house on the Monterey Peninsula in California. I'd like to take you there."

"No, Justin, I . . ."

"Please, just listen. We've both been working hard these past few weeks. We need to be alone, together, without the distraction of our families or our work. We need this. Go with me, if only for a few days . . ."

"No, Justin." Davia got up from the sofa, moving away from his gentle persuasiveness.

"There are things we need to discuss . . ."

"Yes, but not now." She retreated further into the room. Turning her back to him she wrapped her arms around her body protectively. She knew that he was right. There was so much more to be said, but she couldn't, not now.

"Davia?"

The question in his voice begged for resolution, but it was a plea she ignored. She didn't want to think about anything right now. The day had been draining and she needed rest. She wanted to erase Katherine from her mind. She wanted to make everything and everyone disappear, but then there was . . .

Money! Her mind raced to remember if his name had been mentioned during Katherine's tirade. It hadn't been. Katherine must not know about him. Few people did.

She had to think. She had to plan her next move, but she was so tired. Right now, getting home to Gabby was what she needed. She turned to Justin.

"I'm going home."

Her words were a demand that held an unspoken *or else*. Justin noticed that her eyes had taken on a hard glaze. He knew that any opportunity for communication would not be occurring today.

He watched silently as she prepared to leave. He didn't have to worry about her being too upset to drive. From the determined look on her face she would have no problem getting home.

"Thanks for everything," Davia said as she headed for the door, but her progress was momentarily halted by his final words.

"You can't run forever, Davia. You have to stop running sometime."

She didn't reply as she left the house. What was there to say about truth?

❧

Charles poured another shot of vodka into his glass, swirled it around thoughtfully and took a sip. Katherine had been ranting since he arrived, and that had been over an hour ago. She sounded like a parrot repeating the same old song. He was tired of hearing about it. It seemed the crown prince had really messed up this time with the "little slut," and Katherine couldn't stop talking about it.

Retracing his steps across the room, he sat down in a wingback chair, crossed his legs nonchalantly, and stared absently into the glass of liquor. As usual he tuned her out while managing to look interested and involved. He kept his ear attuned to bits and pieces of what she was saying so that he could nod, smile, or grunt at the appropriate times. She was really upset today. It looked as though she was going to wear a hole in the very expensive carpeting as she paced from one end of the room to the other, venting. It wasn't until something she said that sounded vaguely familiar caught his attention that he began to tune in.

"Sorry, Katherine, but what was that last thing you said?"

Katherine's look skewered Charles. What in the world was she doing with this social-climbing gigolo? Her taste wasn't any better than her son's. "I *said* that the little tramp can't even get her name straight! Davia. Nay Nay. *She*nay. Who knows what?"

Oblivious to the rest of Katherine's babble, Charles stilled with his drink suspended in midair, halfway to his lips. *Nay Nay? Did Katherine say Nay Nay? No way. It couldn't be.*

He finished the rest of his drink in one gulp, glad that Katherine was too preoccupied to notice the slight tremor in his hand. Placing the glass on the table next to his chair, he let Katherine's ramblings become background as his mind traveled back in time.

Nay Nay was about eleven or twelve when he first saw her. She was a surprise package that he'd stumbled onto by accident. Her ripe young body was just developing, but held promises of the treasures to come. Those incandescent eyes behind long, coal black eyelashes were meant to turn a man on. She was an innocent. What could be better?

He found out later that she was one of the young lookouts who worked for Bobo, one of the more enterprising drug dealers on the block—a man who eventually worked for him. As the years passed and his power and influence increased, he watched her surreptitiously as she grew and developed until the time was right.

Eventually, that crackhead mother, sister, or whatever she was to the girl needed some quick cash. It was then that he made his move. Nay Nay was about fourteen by then and fine as hell. Every hard ankle on the block was waiting for a piece of that action, but he had claimed her. She was his. That was until she made the biggest mistake of her life, then disappeared. He had been ready to offer her the opportunity of her useless little life, but she ran away and in the process left behind a permanent reminder of her miserable existence. He had his boys looking for her for a while, but they hadn't been successful. Yeah, Nay Nay. Shanay . . . What was her last name?

"Johnson! Maxwell! Smith or Jones, for all I know! Who knows her last name?" Katherine ranted. "Only *she* knows for sure. All I'll ever recall is that my son stood here, in this house, siding with some ghetto tramp from some Chicago slum . . ."

Charles inhaled. *Chicago?*

"The little tramp had a baby at fifteen. Can you believe it?"

Nay Nay had a baby.

"But what else could be expected from someone like her?"

"Who's the father?" He hadn't meant to ask that. It just slipped, but he was curious, especially if it was the Nay Nay he knew.

Katherine looked at him as if she had forgotten he was in the room. "How would I know who the father is? I doubt if *she* even knows. She certainly didn't name one on the birth certificate."

The birth certificate? Katherine had been thorough.

Katherine dropped into the chair next to Charles, her energy expended. In despair she dropped her head in her hands, massaging her temples.

"How in God's name could this happen? Justin has always been so levelheaded. How could he do this? The woman is a grandmother!"

Charles head snapped around to look at her. "A grandmother? What is she? Twenty-seven? Twenty-eight?"

"She's thirty-four."

Thirty-four? Nay Nay would be about that age.

Katherine slumped in the chair and closed her eyes. "My son, my beautiful, intelligent son is sleeping with a thirty-four-year-old grandmother. She has completely brainwashed him. But she doesn't know me. I'll never give him up, not to her, not without a fight."

Charles leaned his head back against his chair, but his eyes remained open. He was seeing everything clearly—

very clearly. As unbelievable as it seemed, his past might have caught up with him, and in the form of a girl he hadn't thought about in years. Piecing together the bits of information he had gotten from Katherine, it looked as if this was the reality. He wished that he had been listening to her ranting these past few months; he would have more pieces to this puzzle. He would be listening from now on, that was for certain, because if this woman was who he thought she might be, everything he had planned for his future might be in jeopardy. He wasn't about to let that happen.

CHAPTER 17

Shutting off the ignition, Justin turned to look at Davia asleep in the passenger seat. She had attempted to cover the darkened rings under her eyes with makeup, but signs of fatigue were still there. It had been barely a week ago that she'd stood in his house and said that she was tired. He knew that she was referring to being weary of the many secrets she harbored, but he also aware that she was physically exhausted, and that eventually it would catch up with her. He had been right.

The day she collapsed, Justin had called her house for the umpteenth time in an attempt to reach her. Since her fight with Katherine, Davia had been avoiding his calls both in her office and at home. He was hurt by her attempt to shut him out of her life, but he persisted. He wasn't going to let her face her pain alone. Reba had answered his last call to her house. She was hysterical. She had come home from a night class and found Davia unconscious on the floor. The paramedics were at the house as they spoke.

Terror was the only word that he could think of to describe what he felt as he drove like a maniac through the streets of Atlanta trying to get to Davia. Reba said that he looked like a madman when he burst through the hospital doors. Later, she recalled with amusement that she thought the hospital personnel would throw Justin out bodily because he was so demanding, but he didn't care. Dr. Zackary Miles had been a member of the hospital staff for years, and Katherine was a member of the board of directors. Justin had used all of the clout that his name could muster to get the best care for Davia.

Tests revealed that she was suffering from exhaustion. Reba informed him that she hadn't eaten or slept properly for days. She had been totally focused on Gabby and work.

Armed with this information, the trip to the Monterey Peninsula was a decision that was taken out of Davia's hands. He made the arrangements overnight. When she was released from the hospital, Reba and CeCe forced her into Justin's car and he drove straight to the airport, ignoring Davia's protest.

She gave him the cold shoulder during the trip west, but Justin had talked and laughed the entire time. He was delighted to have her to himself. When the plane landed, a rental car was waiting at the airport. She had fallen asleep as they drove to his beach house.

Smiling at her reclining figure, he raised the passenger seat that he had lowered earlier to make her comfortable and caressed her hair. It felt like a lifetime since they had been together. He was looking forward to the next few days.

Shaking her shoulder gently, he called her name. She didn't respond. He shook her again, calling her name a little louder, eliciting a small moan of awakening consciousness. Her lips parted and a second moan escaped, sending jolts of awareness to his groin. Reining in his hormones, Justin got out of the car and walked to the passenger side. Opening the door he unbuckled her seat belt, swept her up into his arms and headed up the walk to the front door of his home.

Upstairs, he carefully placed her on a rattan lounger near the bed. She turned onto her side and curled into a fetal position. After covering her with a brightly colored afghan, he stood in the moonlight drifting through the patio doors and watched her sleep. She looked peaceful, free of the stress of a high-powered job and the strain of raising a child alone. She was so strong, so capable. The more he got to know her, the more his admiration grew. But really getting to know her was a challenge. Davia's life was filled with secrets that she kept securely locked away. He and CeCe had talked about this when they were at the hospital awaiting the word regarding Davia's health.

Reba had left a message for CeCe about Davia's collapse and she had made her own dramatic entrance at the hospital, accompanied by Clark. It took Justin, Reba and Clark to calm her down. After the doctor explained the results of Davia's test to them, Justin and CeCe had a chance to be alone in the waiting room. He had comforted the weeping woman, who kept apologizing for being so emotional.

"It's just that Davia is the closest thing to a sister that I have," she explained. "Now her health might be in danger. It's so unfair. I've known this woman for over ten years and she's gone through enough. She carries pain she won't talk about even to me. When her daughter's father . . ."

CeCe caught herself, afraid of betraying her friend's confidence. But Justin wasn't to be denied. He told her that he knew about Mark and proceeded to tell her the story Davia told him.

CeCe looked shocked. "She did tell you, didn't she?"

He nodded.

"I've got to admit that I'm amazed. She told me that she really cared about you, that she even loved you, but I never imagined—" She looked at him in a new light. "Davia doesn't trust easily. Life hasn't given her many reasons to trust. So she's given to both of us something that is very precious to her."

"Yes, I know."

"She needs help, Justin. She needs to get rid of all that pain. She needs to talk to a professional. I'll do all that I can to encourage her to do so, and I hope that I can count on you." He had assured her that she could.

Justin sighed. Davia was a proud woman and a very private one. It wouldn't be easy to convince her to seek help.

The sound of her mumbling incoherently as she awakened interrupted his thoughts. Slowly, she opened her sleep-laden eyes. Justin peered down at her.

"Hey, sweetheart, are you awake?" Her wooden nod wasn't fully convincing. He kept trying. "We're at the beach house. Can you get up and get in the bed by yourself?"

She nodded, stood, and, on wobbly legs, stumbled toward the bed. Justin steadied her.

"Are you sure you're okay?"

She nodded in the affirmative, weaving sleepily from side to side. Wordlessly, he turned the covers down, and then swept her up into his arms and placed her in the bed. Taking her shoes off, he placed them on the floor. When he looked up to begin the all-too-tempting chore of undressing her, he looked straight into her dark brown eyes. Silently, he answered the call of what he saw in their depth.

Undressing hurriedly, he joined her in bed and they made love repeatedly through the night and into the early-morning hours. It was if their hunger for each other could not be satisfied. She made love to him with the intensity of a woman exorcising demons. He made love to her with all of the tenderness that she deserved. As they lay spent in each other's arms, Justin held her close and made a solemn vow. No one would ever hurt Davia again. He would kill the next man who tried.

They were to spend seven days at Justin's Peninsula home. Seven days! In her whole life she had never spent that long doing absolutely nothing but enjoying herself. While she tried to tell herself that it was a waste of valuable time, secretly Davia was delighted. It would take some getting used to, but Justin and his beach house would make it easy.

His home was a contemporary structure of stone and glass and within walking distance of the Pacific Ocean. Lshaped, it contained seven spacious rooms, three of which were bedrooms, each with its own bath. The master suite had a magnificent view of the ocean.

"A friend of mine turned me on to this house," Justin explained as he gave her a tour. "You might have heard of him, Brandon Plaine?"

Davia's eyes widened. "The owner of Plaine Deal Media?"

Justin nodded. Davia was impressed. She had read about the media mogul. Years ago he had taken one bankrupt radio station and turned it into the masthead for an African-American-owned conglomerate that now boasted of newspapers, radio and television stations across the country. Like her, Brandon Plaine was an entrepreneur, a self-made person. She admired him.

"My company provides his with a lot of advertising revenue," she informed him.

"Then I'll call and let him know that we're here. You two should meet."

"I'd like that." Davia was thrilled by the possibility.

"Anyway, I was looking for something simple but elegant as a vacation getaway. I mentioned it to Brandon, and he knew of a friend of his who wanted to sell this house and build a new one. He and his wife have three kids and wanted a bigger place. He hooked me up with his friend, and I mentioned to the guy that my friend was an architect. Clark ended up designing their new house, and I bought their old one. Everybody walked away happy. It's a great place."

Davia had to agree.

On the second day of their stay, between walks on the beach and making love, they rested, enjoying the simple pleasure of being together without interruptions. Justin called Brandon, and he invited them to dine with his family on day three.

"I think you're going to like Brandon's wife, Sash," Justin informed her as they drove down the highway toward the Plaine house. "She's an attorney. She practices family law."

"Sounds interesting."

The Plaines lived in an exclusive, gated community. The houses were large and lavish and the landscapes lush.

"This is nice," Davia said appreciatively as they passed block after block of impressive homes. "The architecture is fantastic. Did Clark design Brandon's house, too?"

"No, he didn't." Justin turned onto a wide tree-lined street and slowed as they neared the house. "But Clark did design Darnell Cameron's house. She lives on the Peninsula, in Carmel."

"You're kidding!" Davia squealed, sounding as excited as a teenage groupie. "She's my favorite singer. Wait until I tell CeCe."

They pulled into a long driveway that led to a huge yellow stucco house with lots of windows. Each seemed ablaze in light. Justin stopped the car. "We're here."

Brandon and Sash Plaine greeted Justin affectionately; the three of them hadn't seen each other in quite a while. Davia was usually reserved when she first met strangers, but it didn't take long for her to warm up to the Plaines. The handsome couple was easygoing and without a hint of pretentiousness. The dreadlock-wearing Sash was especially down to earth. With her baby girl, Imani, affixed to her hip, she gave Davia a tour of the house. It contained plenty of nooks and crannies and lots of ceiling to floor windows. Yet despite its size the house remained warm and cozy. Sash informed her that she had painted the colorful murals in her children's rooms. Davia was impressed with her creative flair and complimented her on her good taste.

"Thank you." Sash flashed a pleased smile. "I did most of the decorating myself. It's not that it was decorated badly before. Brandon had hired the best when he moved in here, but it was not a home. I called it the 'mausoleum' when I first saw it. But I have to admit, initially I didn't see this place under the best of circumstances."

As they headed downstairs to join their husbands, Davia wondered about her last statement, and then the answer came to her. This was *the* Sash Plaine. Years ago, her abduction and eventual escape had made headlines. Davia had been in California on business when the story hit. Not only had Sash been kidnapped, but so had the Plaines' oldest child, Trent. Yet despite that past trauma, Sash seemed so together. Perhaps time had healed her wounds.

During dinner, Davia watched the family's interaction closely. The love and warmth that Brandon and Sash showed toward each other made it clear that they were in love. They doted on Imani and Trent, whose nickname was Sweet; the little boy lived up to his name. He was adorable, with a ready smile and good manners. He was the kind of child that anyone would want for a son.

The Plaine family reminded her of the Johnson brood, and she couldn't help but think about what she had missed when she was young. A gentle hand clasping hers beneath the table brought her back from thoughts of the past. She looked at Justin, who gave her a knowing smile—one that assured her that one day they, too, could have a family like this. Davia dropped her eyes as she wondered if that was really possible.

The drive home from the Plaines household was a quiet one as Davia thought about Sash Plaine and how she seemed to have accepted life so positively.

"Did you know about Brandon's wife having been abducted?" she asked quietly. She would have thought that her having met Sash tonight had been a setup, except how could it have been? Justin wasn't aware of the final secret that she harbored.

He didn't pretend to be ignorant of the subtext behind her question. "Yes, it was big news, especially here on the Peninsula. That's how she and Brandon met. I also know that the life that they live now is a result of her having sought therapy for the trauma that she experienced."

Davia looked at his strong profile as he concentrated on the road ahead. "How do you know that?"

"Brandon told me."

Sighing heavily, Davia turned to look out the window. "I don't see how she could do it, talk about herself to some stranger. I don't want to see some shrink. I just want to forget the past."

"But it doesn't seem like it wants to forget you." Justin continued to stare ahead. "I won't lie to you, sweetheart, I'd like you to get some help so that you can begin to deal with everything that has happened, but *you* have to make the decision to do that."

"Justin, I . . ."

"Just think about it." He glanced at her before returning his eyes to the road. "I know that it's hard. It's not something that black people do easily, but there's no shame in needing help, Davia. You've got a lot to be proud of in your life, and I'm proud of you."

Moved by his words, Davia fought the lump in her throat. She wondered how a woman like Katherine Miles could have raised a man with such character. Justin was someone very special.

For the next few days he continued to prove to her just how true those words were.

Justin pampered her shamelessly. He cooked all of their meals, made sure that she took her medication and saw to it that she got plenty of rest. Despite his being overbearing at times, Davia loved every minute that she spent with him. They did everything together. They went for long walks along the ocean, shopped in the abundance of stores and shops in the quaint village of Carmel, explored the Monterey Pier, rode bikes along the area's scenic bike trails and hiked in nearby parks.

They made endless love, creating romantic interludes in places that Davia hadn't thought possible. Justin dispelled all of the myths that she had formed about men. His love and devotion were complete, and it was instrumental in helping her take some important steps toward self-healing.

They talked a lot about life and love, and about Katherine and how she affected their relationship. It was Justin's opinion that it was fear that motivated his mother's actions. She was a woman who had lost the love of her life. She now feared that she would lose her husband's reincarnation, her son.

While that explanation of his mother's behavior seemed plausible, Davia wasn't ready to forgive the woman. It also seemed that as Justin had previously suggested, she wasn't ready to forgive herself. In talking with him, she had to admit that over the years she had shut down emotionally. She feared intense emotions. They had always brought such pain. In the past, when it came to men, pain and love had been synonymous to her, but now things were different. She loved Justin and he loved her. She knew what love was really about. Despite this, she still wasn't ready for the two of them to discuss all of the secrets that she still harbored. He didn't hide his disappointment, but he continued to be supportive.

"I don't want to push," he told her. "I'll wait until you're ready, but there's one thing I'd like you to remember. Truth is the best foundation on which to build any relationship. The truth will set us both free."

Davia gave a lot of thought to those words. That evening she called Sash Plaine and invited her out to lunch. They agreed to meet the next day.

Sash picked a quiet little bistro in Carmel in which to dine. It was tucked away on a cobblestone side street far from the onslaught of tourists that swarmed the picturesque community. The atmosphere was calm and relaxed. They dined on chicken salad sandwiches and coleslaw with large goblets of lemonade to wash it down. Conversation was light as Sash kept Davia entertained with stories about her colorful life. As a student, she had traveled throughout Europe and Africa, having lived in the latter country for quite a while. She was quirky and uninhibited, and the more they talked, the more Davia liked her. She could see the two of them becoming good friends. Lunch passed quickly and the women lingered, ordering cups of cappuccino, not wanting their time together to end.

"I haven't had a good sister-friend talk in a long time," said Sash, taking another sip of her frothy drink.

Davia nodded. "I know what you mean. I work so much that it seems that my best friend and I haven't gotten together in ages, and we work in the same building." She hadn't thought about it until now, but that was true and she felt a pang of regret for having allowed that to happen. "But I sure have enjoyed today. You're so easy to talk to."

"I'm glad, but it's too bad that we haven't discussed what you called me about." Sash gave her an innocent smile.

Taken aback by her honesty, Davia was speechless at first. This woman pulled no punches, but she wasn't sure that she could be as candid. Placing her cup down on the saucer carefully, she kept her voice steady. "What do you think I called to talk to you about?"

Sash's gaze didn't waver. "You want to know how I survived my past, specifically my abduction. You want to know how I moved on with my life. You'd like to know exactly what happened and whether there was more to it than was reported. But you know that it's none of your business, and you're too polite to ask."

Astonished at her amazing insight, Davia had to chuckle at her last comment. She raised her cup in mock salute. "Lady, you are something else."

"I know," Sash deadpanned. "That's why my husband adores me, and he should." She then proceeded to tell Davia what she wanted to know.

At the end of her story, Davia was in tears. "How did you get through all of that with your head and heart intact?" Sash seemed so together.

"I did it with the help of the man who loves me, and the counselor who listened to me. I couldn't have done it alone."

Davia nodded. She understood.

Sash gave her a mysterious smile. "I don't know your story, Davia, and I don't need to know it, but I do know this. For everything there is a season, and nothing happens without a reason."

Sash's words followed Davia home and haunted her over the next few days. *For everything there is a season, and nothing happens without a reason.*

This was her season. Their seventh and last day at the beach house turned out to be the time. It wasn't an auspicious occasion. She and Justin had finished dinner on the deck of his house and he was thumbing through the evening paper. Davia was looking beyond him, wondering at the beauty of the towering pine trees surrounding the property. She was reflecting on the many blessings that had been bestowed on her in her life when—as had become her habit—without fanfare she started talking.

"My name was Shanay Davia Wells before I changed it. His name was Money; at least that's what everybody called him." She grunted bitterly. "Can you believe it? This was a man who turned my life upside down, and I didn't even know his real name."

Justin's eyes slid up from the newspaper to focus on Davia. She was staring off toward the wooded area behind the house as if in a trance. Slowly, he lowered the paper, careful not to disturb her concentration. *What was she talking about? Who was Money?*

"I knew who he was from the beginning, though. All it took was one good look at him, and I knew. I was only twelve when I first saw him, and I hated him." Her voice was thick with loathing. She stopped talking and stared into the past.

Justin was afraid to move, afraid to breathe. This was her moment of exorcism. The silence seemed endless.

Every breeze through the trees seemed amplified. The distant call of the seagulls seemed louder. Then she resumed speaking.

"Money was the main man on the block. He was the dealer that the others sold for. He was cool and slick. Nobody ever saw him directly pushing drugs, but the people who worked for him jumped to attention when he came around.

"Every time he saw me, he had something to say. He was always offering me a little treat, as if I would take anything from him. I remembered when he came to our hotel room to be with Phyllis. I remembered when he . . ." Pausing, Davia reined in her emotions. Taking a sharp breath, she continued.

"I didn't trust him for a second." She spat, reveling in the depth of her disgust for the man she was describing. "Anyway, my cousin Phyllis was in debt to Money for some dope she couldn't pay for. I knew about it and it scared me, because I'd heard that he was vicious. What I didn't know was that Phyllis had come up with a plan to pay him back.

"One day, when I was on the block doing what I did back then, Phyllis came barreling down the street. She was carrying a shopping bag in one hand, and she grabbed my arm with the other one and told me to follow her. At first I thought that we were moving again. I wasn't sure why, I'd paid the rent, but with her nothing was stable. So, I followed her, no questions asked. We walked a little and turned down an alley, where a car was parked. I remember that it was white, the color for purity and innocence. But there was nothing pure or innocent about what happened.

"The windows of the car were tinted, and they came down slowly. Money was sitting in the backseat. I came to a dead stop when I realized that the car was waiting for us. I didn't want to get in there with him, but Phyllis slapped me and told me that I'd better get in. She said that Money was giving us a ride to someplace she had to go.

"She finally pushed me in beside him and got in on the other side. I was scared and confused about what was going on. My instincts told me that there was something wrong, but the fear lessened because she was with me. I told myself that nothing could happen with her there." She snorted. "What a fool I was. I actually trusted her. Why, I don't know. She never came through with anything. But when you're a child, you want to trust somebody.

"We drove until we reached a blue house. It wasn't a bad place, kind of nice, in fact. I remember wondering if this was our new place. If so, it was definitely a move up. I thought maybe she was with Money now, maybe that was the payment for the debt she owed him. I wasn't thrilled about the prospect of being there with him. You see, this was the man who had tried to attack me when I was twelve . . ."

"What?" Justin hadn't meant to interrupt, but her statement had provoked his reaction. She didn't falter.

"But what could I do?" Davia's chest heaved as pent-up emotions fought for release. She turned to him with glistening eyes. "We went inside into the living room. Phyllis set the shopping bag down, turned and walked away."

Tears began to stream down her face. Justin placed her hand in his and squeezed it, silently urging her to go on.

"For a minute, I stood there in shock. I couldn't believe that she'd left me there with him. But she had. The shopping bag held my clothes, everything I owned. She had sold me, Justin, just like a slave on an auction block, in exchange for her debt to Money. She had sold me to save her life. Money owned me. Or so he thought."

Her words were excruciating. Justin could hardly contain his anger. He moved to her side, picked her up from the chair and placed her in his lap. Pressing her tear-stained face to his chest, he stroked her hair.

The dam had burst. Davia couldn't stop talking.

"Money decided to show me who was the boss. He grabbed me, like he had tried to do all of those years before, but that was his first mistake. I wasn't a skinny twelve-year-old anymore. I was fourteen and stronger, and I knew what he meant to do to me. So I fought him, Justin. I fought him with everything I had in me."

"It's all right, baby. It's all right." Justin's voice was raw with emotion.

Davia was hyperventilating, but she kept talking. "I . . . I decided that I would die before I'd let him rape me. Mark's mother had called me a whore because of what happened with him. I . . . I . . . wasn't a whore, Justin. I'm not a whore."

"No, sweetheart, I know you're not."

"He was stronger than me, and it was hard. I was pregnant then, but I didn't know it. Money hit me. He got on top of me, but I still fought him. I . . . I swore that nobody would ever use me again. I thought quickly and stopped struggling. I told him I'd have sex with him. I—I—I just wanted him to get off of me, and let me c—c—catch my breath. He fell for it, and m . . . m moved enough for me to wiggle free. I pretended to take off my T-shirt, a—a— and that's when I grabbed a bottle, broke it and cut him. I cut him badly too! I tried to kill him. I wanted t—t—to cut his heart out! B—b—blood was everywhere and he was screaming at me, saying that he would kill me when he got his hands on me. He'd locked the door so I couldn't get out, s—so I threw a chair through the window before his men could break the door down, and I climbed out and I ran. I—I ran a—a—away." And she had been running ever since.

Davia couldn't stop crying. She cried and cried. She cried for her lost childhood and the loss of innocence. She cried for the little girl who had found more solace in a dark basement than in the light of day. She cried for the young teenager, pregnant and alone in the world, and for her precious daughter, who'd fought her own demons without her mother's support. She cried while Justin rocked her and soothed her until she cried herself to sleep.

After putting her to bed, Justin wanted to join her, but found that he couldn't. He was too wound up, too enraged. He prowled the house like a caged tiger. He wanted blood so badly he could taste it, and Davia had given him a name—Money. He prayed that wherever the man was that he was dead, because if he ever came face to face with him, Justin would show him no mercy.

CHAPTER 18

"The woman's a liar, Justin. Small Sensations is owned by a conglomerate called the W.J. Collective. I don't know why she would make that claim. It can be so easily disputed."

Justin smiled inwardly. The W in the collective stood for Wells and the J was for Johnson. But that wasn't for Katherine to know.

"Don't worry about that, Mother, just remember what I said. Whether you like Davia or not, she's in my life to stay, and you might as well accept it. I can't believe that you had the audacity to hire a private investigator."

"Well, I did, and I had a good reason."

"There's *no* good reason. I love you. You're my mother, but what you did was wrong and I don't like it. If a word of what you've found out about Davia leaves this house I'll never forgive you. I hope I make myself clear."

Katherine fell back onto the pillows propping her up in the bed. She had worried herself sick over Justin in these past two weeks. She hadn't heard a word from him after the confrontation with that horrid woman. It was Vanessa who had informed her that he had left for his house in California. She had further informed her that the Davia woman was with him. Katherine had taken to her bed that day.

Depression was like a dark cloud hovering over her. Now, after weeks of no communication, her son had come to her home to chastise her. To make matters worse, he had informed her that he was deeply in love with that woman and that he would reject his own mother for her, if necessary. It was all too much. Tears began to flow.

"I'm an old woman, Justin and . . ."

"You're sixty years old, healthy and vibrant," Justin retorted. "Please don't try the pity act with me. It won't work."

Katherine dabbed at her tears. "How can you be so cruel? Is this the result of raising you, loving you with everything in me and giving you the best that money can buy? You come here and treat me like *this*. What have I done to deserve such ungrateful children? Vanessa runs around here all but ignoring me, and you won't speak to me at all unless it's to fuss at me while I'm in my sickbed. What I did in finding out information about that woman was what any concerned mother would do."

"No, a concerned mother would let a grown man live his own life." Justin's eyes narrowed. "I meant what I said. Whatever you found out about Davia is not to leave this house."

Katherine's eyes fell to her hands as she smoothed the satin bedspread covering her lap. She hadn't said a word about what she had discovered about that woman to anyone, except to Charles, of course, and he didn't count. She had hoped to use the information as leverage to get the woman to leave her son alone, but that seemed to be moot at this point.

Katherine's demeanor raised alarm bells for Justin. "You haven't told anyone, have you, Mother?"

Katherine sighed in disgust. "Who is there to tell? Do you think I want my friends knowing the depths to which my son would stoop to find a woman?"

"That's it!" Justin rose from the chair beside his mother's bed. "I don't have to take this." He headed toward the bedroom door.

"No, Justin! I'm sorry," Katherine entreated, anxious about the deep anger she heard in his voice. She had to do something before she lost him forever. "I'm really sorry. I'll try not to say things like that again. It's just that . . . Son, I love you so much and I want the best that life has to give you."

Justin's face softened. "Davia is the best thing in my life. I love her more than anything in this world." Katherine winced but Justin continued. "She makes me happy, and if it takes me the rest of my life, I'll see to it that she's happy."

Katherine grimaced at the rapture on her son's face as he spoke about that woman. The Justin she knew was gone from her. That woman owned him.

Justin checked his watch. "I have to go. I have an appointment to get to." He kissed Katherine on the cheek. "I hope that we won't have to have this discussion again."

As he started to exit, he nearly tumbled over an unexpected obstacle in the doorway. Bianca stood at his feet looking up at her uncle. She was wearing pajamas and hugging her teddy bear tightly to her chest. He scooped her up into his arms.

"Hey, peanut!" He nuzzled her neck and gave her a loud smooch. Usually this brought a hail of giggles from her, but today she didn't respond. She lay listlessly in his arms, her usually bright eyes looking at him blankly. Justin's heart wrenched. It had been weeks since he had spent time with his niece. He had neglected her badly since meeting Davia. Actually, he had neglected his whole family. Guilt washed over him as he hugged her small body to his.

"What would you say if you and I go to the zoo this weekend, or maybe even to Stone Mountain? We could ride the train. Would you like that?"

Bianca shrugged and wiggled to get out of his arms. Justin set her back on the floor and watched as she padded across the room and climbed into her grandmother's bed. She looked so little and sad.

Katherine lifted the covers for the child to crawl under and hugged her beloved granddaughter to her. "We've *all* missed you, Justin. Your neglect of us has hurt."

Her words had their intended effect. Justin sighed and pinched the bridge of his nose. "Yes, I know, and I'm sorry." There were simply too many demands, and they were taking their toll.

Pausing, he gave it one more try. "Give yourself a chance to know her, Mother. She's a wonderful woman. She's strong, capable and resilient—one of the most courageous women I've ever met. She's a lot like you." With that, he turned and left the room.

Katherine steeled herself against her son's parting words. Neither his charm nor his compliments would sway her. That Maxwell woman had to go.

For Davia the trip to California had been life renewing. She returned to Atlanta free from the burdens of the past. A few days after returning home she shared the last of her long-harbored secrets with CeCe.

Davia had started out with an apology. "First, let me tell you how sorry I am that I've left you out of so much of my life over the years. You are the best friend that I've ever had. Outside of the Johnson family, no one has been there for me more or loved me longer than you. I wouldn't hurt you for the world. Yet, I didn't trust you with everything about my past and I know that I hurt you."

There could be no doubt about that. They had met years ago on a rainy, winter day in Atlanta. They both had been applying for the same waitress job. Each was down to her last $5, and both needed the job desperately, but neither got it. Instead, they had walked away with something more valuable—a friend.

Now she watched as CeCe sat in silence thinking about what she had been told. She could see her mind at work. From now on, there would be no more secrets between them.

"I'm so glad that I've finally told my story. I never thought that I could talk about the days before the

Johnson family. It hurt too much. But Justin has made me realize that keeping it buried inside has been hurting me more."

Her talk with CeCe was the final catharsis. She was free now to live her life.

Having formulated her thoughts, CeCe focused her attention on Davia. "Other than Justin and me, who else knows about all of this?"

"Mama Willa. She told Papa Josh."

"You didn't want them to adopt you because of what happened?"

Davia was in the bedroom of her friend's condo. She slipped from the bed on which they both had been sitting and walked to the window. Looking out into the moonlit night, she pondered CeCe's question.

"I didn't want them to adopt me because I feared for their lives." She turned back to face her. "Money had put a contract out on me because I tried to kill him."

"It's too bad that you didn't." CeCe's voice was granite.

The room was quiet as Davia rejoined her on the bed. CeCe looked at her pensively. There were tears welling in her eyes.

"You know something, Davia, you must have a guardian angel that has been working overtime in your life when it was most needed, because, girlfriend, you are truly blessed."

The comment caught Davia off guard. If she thought about her life and the dramatic twists and turns it had taken over the years, perhaps "blessed" wouldn't be the first word she would use. Yet there was Stephanie, the Johnson family, Gabby, Reba, CeCe, Leroy and now Justin—a collection of friends and family, each holding a special place in her heart. They had been there when she needed them, and each filled her life with miracles that she hadn't imagined were possible. Perhaps CeCe was right. Despite all that had happened to her, she *was* truly blessed.

Charles Cash had never been one to panic. He had built his reputation on his ability to maintain his composure under pressure. He wasn't about to change now. Having finally listened to what Katherine had been saying to him about the Maxwell woman, he had taken the information she provided and carefully sorted the facts. His final analysis had been conclusive. This woman who called herself Davia Maxwell was the scrappy kid he had known twenty years ago as Shanay. He had never known her last name.

How could he forget the girl? She was soft, luscious and ready for all that he could teach her, and she had also scarred him for life. Shanay had tried to kill him. He had ended up in the hospital fighting for his life. He still carried the gruesome scar she gave him across his stomach.

He had vowed revenge. He'd had his men looking for her for weeks. They were to kill her on sight, but she disappeared. Time passed and things changed. He had abandoned the search. He vaguely remembered that years later his man BoBo told him that he saw her somewhere. He did say something about her having a kid with her and that she panicked when she recognized him. Bobo was willing to find her and kill her and the kid, but lucky for her, the death of his father turned his interest elsewhere. Yes, it was true that he carried the scar that reminded him of Shanay, but the truth was that as the years passed, he could barely remember the girl.

That was then. This was now. He was a different man back then, with a different name and a different way of life. Then she was no threat to him, but this time it was different. He was the man he was born to be with the name given to him at birth. Now he had much more than pride to lose.

He hadn't officially met Shanay, aka Davia, and he didn't think that there had been an occasion when she would have gotten a good look at him. When she did, would she recognize him? It had been two decades. He had put on a little weight and his hair had turned grayer, but basically he looked the same. She certainly didn't. Her progression into womanhood had resulted in a fine package that had grown finer with time, but that aside, the woman could present a problem for him.

He was a man of substance, most gained by legitimate means. After his mother died he discovered that she had reversed his father's will. He was no longer the disinherited son. The money she left him wasn't a fortune by some standards, but it had been quite substantial. That and the funds that he had accumulated through his business dealings were enough to resume his life as Charles

Cash. He no longer had to live under an alias in a part of Chicago that he never would have set foot in, if his own father hadn't disowned him. He had been disinherited because of a simple misunderstanding about the housekeeper's little girl. However, his mother had rectified the situation concerning his inheritance, and he was able to rejoin the ranks of the social class into which he had been born. When he moved to Atlanta, it was with plans to further elevate his status. He was a well-to-do-man with plans to become even wealthier. Hobnobbing with Katherine and her friends was a major step toward achieving that goal.

His days under the name of Money were behind him. Bullets, dope or disease had claimed the riffraff that knew about his past. It was a certainty that it wouldn't be long before he married well. Such a union would increase both his social status and his bank account. The money was needed. He had expensive tastes, and bad investments were seriously threatening his lifestyle. Until now, there had been nothing in his way.

It had taken him nearly a lifetime to get to this point in his life. He wouldn't tolerate any obstacles, especially from a ghetto rat pretending to be a swan. Something had to be done about Davia Maxwell. He would kill her before he let her stand in his way.

CHAPTER 19

Everything was falling into place. Fears and doubts that Davia had carried throughout her life were fading with each passing day. The floodgates of truth were slowly opening, but they were opening, and for that she was grateful.

It still took a while for her to seek the counseling that Justin and CeCe suggested that she might need to sort out her feelings. As far as she was concerned, the very idea suggested that she might be unbalanced, but eventually she began to understand that talking with a professional meant that she was truly ready to shed the pain of the past.

Reba recommended one of her former professors who had recently opened her practice. Davia found her to be not only skilled, but warm and friendly. After her first session with the doctor, she left her office looking forward to the weekly appointments.

Stepping out of the elevator, Davia's steps felt lighter. The future looked brighter, especially the one she would have with Justin in her life.

Since returning from California, she and Justin had taken care to arrange their schedules so that they saw each other more often during the week. He had also vowed to spend more time with his niece. As for

Katherine, he had assured Davia that his mother would not be a problem. The information that she had gathered would not be used or repeated.

Davia wasn't as sure about Katherine as her son seemed to be. She had taken her own measures to neutralize her.

Hurrying from the building, Davia's face lit up at the sight of Justin sitting in his car at the curb waiting for her. They were going out to dinner to celebrate her first session with the doctor. He had called it her brand new day, and with each step that took her closer to him, her heartbeat increased. Her love for this man had taken on dimensions that she couldn't understand, so she simply accepted love's power and thanked God for His blessings.

Justin glanced up in time to see the wide smile on her face. He opened the car door and she slid in beside him. He gave her a peck on the lips.

"How did it go with the doctor?"

Davia nodded. "I like her. She's sharp."

"Do you think this can help you?" He sounded hopeful.

Davia sighed. "It couldn't hurt."

She was hopeful, too. She was tired of hurting . . . tired of running . . . tired of being afraid.

It had been fear that brought her to Atlanta after she and Stephanie had literally bumped into one of Money's cohorts at a mall. Years had passed, but he had recognized her and told her, gleefully, that Money was still looking for her and was going to kill her. More terrified for Stephanie's life than her own, she had left a note expressing her gratitude to the Johnsons and she fled. For the second time in her young life she became somebody else. In Chicago when she lived with the Johnsons, she had used the name Davia Johnson. In Atlanta she emerged as Davia Maxwell. Shanay Wells had died long ago. It was time to bury her for good.

Arriving at the restaurant, Davia excused herself and retreated to the powder room while Justin went to see about their table. Minutes later, she emerged and stepped into the restaurant foyer. She spotted Justin standing at a table next to the window. He was talking to someone. A closer look revealed that it was his mother, Katherine. Davia groaned. Of all the restaurants in Atlanta, Katherine had to pick this one in which to dine.

Davia barely noticed the man sitting opposite Katherine. Her gaze was fixed on Justin's animated mother. It was obvious that she was agitated. Davia could easily guess the reason why. The man at the table looked up to speak to the approaching waiter, and the movement caught Davia's attention. Her gaze shifted to him. She vaguely remembered seeing him before. Where was it?

He turned his head, giving her a better look at him. Obviously bored with the conversation between mother and son, his gaze began to wander aimlessly around the room.

Davia continued to stare. She knew that man from somewhere. His gaze stopped on her. Embarrassed at being caught staring, she started to turn back toward the entrance. She was leaving. She wasn't up to dining in the same restaurant as Katherine. Yet there was something about that man—

She turned once again to sneak another peek at him and found him boldly staring at her. Davia's eyes held his eyes. *Where? Where did she know him from?*

A fleeting picture of the charity ball flashed through her memory—a moment, a brief glimpse of someone. That was it! The ball! She'd seen him talking to Katherine. She remembered thinking that he reminded her of—

Raising a water goblet in mock salute, the man's hard eyes pierced Davia. He gave her a sardonic smile. She inhaled sharply. Her heart slammed against her chest.

No! No! It couldn't be!

She recognized him. She knew who he was. Charles saw it in her demeanor. Calmly, he took another sip of water. No matter, it was inevitable. He would have had a good laugh at the irony of the entire situation if he had been alone, but he wasn't. His attention drifted back to Katherine. She was upset and complaining bitterly to her son about something. Mother and son were speaking in whispered tones, making sure that he was excluded. No matter, he had business to attend to at the moment.

"Excuse me for a minute," he said, getting up from the table. Katherine waved him away absentmindedly. She didn't notice his expression darkened at her detached dismissal, nor did she notice his exit as she attended to the matter at hand.

"You can tell your little friend that I don't appreciate getting calls from some third-rate flunky in the White House," Katherine huffed, trying to maintain her decorum.

Justin was amused. Under different circumstances his mother would have taken an ad out on billboards letting everyone in Atlanta know that she had received a call from Burton Johnson, special assistant to the President of the United States. But this circumstance was different.

"You didn't receive the call, Mother, your spy did."

"He was not a spy, dear. He was a paid employee, a professional."

"He's an unemployed professional now." Justin couldn't keep the amusement out of his voice.

Davia had pulled out all of the ammunition in her arsenal against his mother. It looked as though Katherine had met her match this time, and she was at a loss as to what to do about it. Verbal attack was her only option.

Katherine scowled. "The man was threatened. If I'm not mistaken, intimidation *is* against the law."

"How was your 'employee' intimidated? From what I heard, all Burton wanted to know was why the man had been hired. Doesn't a brother have a right to ask about his sister's welfare?"

Katherine had called Justin that morning to complain that the private investigator she had hired to check on Davia had informed her of the call from Davia's foster brother. Actually, there had been two telephone calls made to the investigator. The first was from Bernard Johnson, an Illinois congressman. To further emphasize his twin brother's point, Burton had called Katherine's employee and had made his own inquiry. The detective had gotten the point. He quit.

"Burton and Bernard Johnson are *not* that woman's brothers, and you know it," Katherine sniffed. "Anyway, I know people in high places, too."

"In the White House?" Justin mused. "As influential as you might be here in Atlanta, Mother, your contacts don't reach the presidential office."

Katherine was fuming. She knew he was right, but she would never admit it.

"I'll tell you what, Mother. Davia and I are about to have dinner. Why don't you pull out the white flag and say hello to her? She should be joining me shortly." He looked toward the foyer, but didn't see her.

Katherine looked incredulous. "You must be kidding! I doubt if *Ms. Maxwell* and I have anything to say to each other." She followed his gaze. "And from what I can see, it looks as if the woman has abandoned you."

Outside the restaurant Davia leaned against the side of the building, fighting the nausea that had overcome her. Surely she had been mistaken about the man with Katherine. It couldn't possibly be Money! A woman like her would never be seen with a man like him. Besides, the man was heavier. His hair was gray. His face was lined. He had to be a look-alike. There could be no other explanation.

Having convinced herself that this was plausible, she regained her composure, straightened her shoulders and started around the building, determined to leave the vicinity immediately. She took two steps, bumped into a solid chest and plunged into a nightmare.

"So, Ms. Maxwell. We finally meet."

Stepping back, Davia gasped. His voice chilled her to the bone. It was Money. There was no doubt. She steeled herself to look at him, gaining courage and resolve as she did. *No fear. No fear.* She would show no fear.

Their eyes met. Neither pair wavered.

"Yes, we do meet." Davia's eyes hardened. "*Again.*"

A muscle in his cheek flickered, but he remained stoic. "Oh, have we met before?"

"If we haven't, how would you know me? So don't play with me, Money. I'm no longer a child."

Calmly, Charles took a sterling silver case out of his jacket and withdrew a cigarette. He took his time as he lit it, then took a long draw. "I'm afraid that you have me mixed up with someone else, Ms. Maxwell." He held out his hand. "I'm Charles Cash, a friend of Justin's mother. She pointed you out to me."

Davia ignored his gesture and stared him down. Chuckling, he withdrew his hand and took another draw on his cigarette.

"Katherine has told me *all* about you, Ms. Maxwell."

"Good, now you know who you're up against." Davia started backing out of the alley. She never planned on turning her back on this man again. Charles grabbed her roughly by her upper arm.

"Are you crazy? Get your hands off me." Angrily, she tried to wrestle from his grasp. His grip tightened.

"I just wanted to express my concern, *Ms.* Maxwell. You should be careful standing out here in alleyways alone." He gave her a crooked smile. "Anything can happen to you."

Davia snatched her arm away. "Take your best shot. But let me warn you that you had better not miss."

Backing away, she rounded the building. By the time she reached the restaurant entrance, Davia was livid. Justin was out front looking for her.

Relief washed across his face at the sight of her. "Where have you been? You had me worried." He noticed her angry demeanor. "Uh-oh. You saw my mother in the restaurant."

"Take me home." Her tone left no room for argument.

Charles watched as they drove away just as Katherine made an appearance outside the restaurant. He sauntered to her.

"Where have you been? I've been looking for you." Irritation and impatience laced her voice.

"I came out here for a smoke. I saw your son leave with his young lady. Did you get to settle your little matter with her?"

Katherine pointedly ignored his question. "We're leaving." She swept past him with her head high.

Following her, Charles chuckled. Poor Nay Nay. She would have major mother-in-law problems . . . if he let her live.

The drive home from the restaurant was a quiet one. Davia was seething. Money had threatened her. She had been running from this man since she was fourteen years old, and the lowlife was still threatening her life.

Leaning her head back against the headrest, she closed her eyes. As soon as she calmed down she would tell Justin about what occurred in the alley. Right now she was too wound up. It was hard to believe that this was happening.

Money was in Atlanta! The man who had haunted her nightmares most of her life had stepped out of them to taunt her. Well, was he in for a surprise! Her running days were over. She was no longer easy prey.

He had said that Katherine told him all about her. What did that mean? How much did he know? Did he know where she lived? Did he know about Gabby? Where she went to school?

At the thought of that possibility, fear tried to replace reasoning. She fought it, and with that effort came clarity.

A woman like Katherine would never become involved with someone like Money if she knew who and what he was. That being the case, Katherine must not know about Money's unsavory past. This would mean that Davia would be the only one who did know about the real Charles Cash.

Cash, was that a synonym for Money? Was Charles Cash his real name? How had he hooked up with Katherine? And why?

Davia's mind began racing. Whether Money was using an alias or not there was a reason that he was with Katherine. She definitely wasn't his type. She was too close to his age. So what was he doing? Romancing her? Swindling her? Using her to get to her friends so that he could push dope? However, one thing was for certain, Money didn't relish seeing her anymore than she did seeing him.

No, Money didn't want Shanay Wells to step out of his past and impede his present. She could ruin his plans. She could ruin *him*. Davia's excitement grew as she thought about the advantage his situation put her in. It also put her in a dangerous position, as his threat indicated, but she could handle that. He was the one who had better watch out. Calm began to replace anxiety as it occurred to her how the balance of power had shifted.

Davia opened her eyes, ready to share her revelation with Justin. She was surprised to find that she had arrived home. They were parked in her driveway. She looked up to find him looking at her with concern. With a gentle finger he wiped away a tear.

"What's really wrong, sweetheart? Why are you crying?"

Davia touched her face. There was moisture on her cheeks. She had been weeping and didn't know it. Were they tears of relief or of victory? She wasn't sure.

"What is it, baby? Was the session with the doctor more than you could handle?"

Justin laid his forehead against her forehead as a surge of anger infused him. When would her pain come to an end? "Never mind, you don't have to answer that, but I want you to know one thing. I swear to you, Davia, I swear on my father's grave, if I ever find the man who did this to you, I'll kill him."

Davia went cold. She remained silent as Justin took her lips in a kiss that sealed the promise of his fiery words

Later, from the window of her bedroom, she watched as he drove away. His fervent declaration to harm Money had frightened her. There was no doubt that Money deserved whatever he got, but she didn't want Justin harmed in any way. She would have to figure out how to handle telling him about Money and keep him from carrying out his threat. Meanwhile, she planned on doing some handling of Money herself.

Years ago she had been part of the streets that he had trolled. She had been a child then and hadn't known the rules of the game he was playing, so he had won. She was no longer a child. Neither was she Shanay Wells. She had become Davia Maxwell, a woman of substance and financial means. She meant to use all of the power that came with that name, and she would use it with a vengeance. She had handled Katherine, and she would handle the man who called himself Charles Cash. This time the playing field was different. This time Davia would win.

CHAPTER 20

Davia wasted no time gathering information on Charles "Money" Cash. Following Katherine's lead she hired a private investigator to discreetly find out about him and offered a large bonus if the investigator had the information in her hands within forty-eight hours. It proved to be the perfect incentive. He was hired on Thursday morning. The information was in her hands by the end of the workday on Friday.

The life that Charles led in Atlanta was an open book. She knew where he lived, worked, played, and even where and what he ate. She discovered that his name really was Charles Cash and that he was from a prominent Chicago family. That came as a surprise. What didn't come as a surprise was that he had taken great care to cover up his life of crime in the Windy City. There was nothing about his stint as the notorious Money in the report.

It did say that he had disappeared from the family fold for a period of twelve years. His whereabouts was no mystery to her. She knew the story all too well. Now he was in Atlanta unfolding a new chapter in his sordid life, but he had found an unexpected obstacle this time— Davia Maxwell.

After spending Friday night reading the investigator's report, she never wanted to hear Charles Cash's name again. Yet, it would come up soon in a way that she would not have imagined.

Saturday afternoon she and Justin took Gabby and Bianca to Stone Mountain Park on an outing. Reba had packed them a picnic lunch and the four of them spent the day exploring. Heading back home after a very long day, the two little girls fell asleep as soon as they were settled in the car. The adults were also exhausted, especially Davia.

"Now don't you fall asleep on me, too," Justin admonished Davia, squeezing her bare thigh as she nodded off. "If you don't stay awake and talk to me I might fall asleep at the wheel."

Davia sat up and shook her head to clear it. "Well, we don't want that." She yawned, then settled back to enjoy the jazz drifting from the CD player. She checked the backseat where the girls slept soundly. Their heads were touching. She smiled at the sight.

"They sure did enjoy themselves, although Bianca did seem a little reserved today. I thought you said that she's usually bubbly and full of life?"

Justin sighed. "I think she's still mad at me for being the neglectful uncle. I've told her that I'm sorry, and I've tried to make it up to her, but I think the little devil wants to bring me to my knees before she forgives me."

"I'm sure that she missed you, Justin. She's not used to sharing you."

He nodded. "That's true, and I'm not used to sharing her, either, but it looks like somebody else might have won a spot in my little pumpkin's heart."

Davia stretched the kinks out of her body. "Who would that be?"

"This guy named Charles Cash." Justin wasn't aware of the hint of resentment in his voice. "I think I might have mentioned him before, or maybe not."

Davia tried not to react as the alarm bells went off. Her pulse quickened. She was careful with her question. "What do you mean?"

"I mean that I'm jealous. Vanessa told me that for a while Bianca was quite taken with Cash. He was bringing her little gifts, riding her on his shoulders. All of the things I used to do."

Davia told herself to breathe normally. She forced air through her lungs. Justin noticed the subtle change.

"Are you okay?"

She nodded, afraid that her voice might give her away. He didn't look convinced, but much to her relief he didn't pursue it. Except for the music, the car's interior fell silent as Justin concentrated on the road ahead, leaving Davia to the myriad of thoughts tumbling through her head. They were frightening. She couldn't give voice to them at the moment; she could only consider them, and they were devastating.

She whispered a silent prayer that what she suspected was untrue. *Not this time! Not again!*

She berated herself for having waited to reveal Money for what he was. She would wait no longer. There was too much at stake. She only hoped that it wasn't too late.

When they arrived at her house, she could barely wait for Justin to stop the car before unbuckling her seat belt. She darted out of the car and rushed to the backseat.

"You take Gabby and I'll get Bianca. We're taking them both inside." Her words weren't a request but an order.

Justin looked surprised. "What? Bianca and I . . ."

"Bianca's staying here tonight." Taking the sleeping child into her arms, she hurried toward the house before Justin could question her. With heightened curiosity, he picked Gabby up and followed Davia.

Inside, she directed Justin to take Gabby upstairs to her bedroom. "It's the second room on the right. I'm taking Bianca to the family room." She ignored his confused look as she made her exit.

After settling Gabby in upstairs, Justin joined Davia. She had placed Bianca on one of the love seats and was pacing the room from one end to the other. He watched her for a moment, noting her state of agitation. His glance fell on his niece sleeping peacefully, then back to Davia. They were a study in contrast.

"All right, what is this about? Why do you want Bianca here tonight? Vanessa is out of town on a business trip, and Bianca is supposed to spend the weekend with me. I didn't clear anything else with her mother." Justin was getting an uneasy feeling as he watched Davia pace.

She stopped and turned to him. The look on her face was so filled with anguish that he crossed the room and held her at arm's length.

"What's going on?"

Davia looked him in the eye. "I'll tell you, but before I do, I want you to promise me something."

He hesitated. He didn't want to make a promise that he might not be able to keep.

"I want you to promise me . . . no, swear to me that you will sit down and listen to what I'm going to tell you and to think before you react. I don't want you to frighten Bianca."

He looked at his niece, then back at Davia. His anxiety increased. "I just want to know what's happening."

"No, not until you swear that you'll listen and try not to react."

Justin's mouth went dry. Fear gripped him. Whatever she had to tell him, it wasn't good, and it had something to do with Bianca. He nodded. "All right, I swear that I'll try my best."

Davia looked at him steadily. She could see the panic in his eyes and felt bad that she had put it there. She knew that he had made a vow that might be difficult to keep, but it was better than nothing. She beckoned. "Let's go to the kitchen."

He followed obediently. She motioned for him to sit down at the table in the nook. Taking a seat across from him, she took both of his hands in hers. Justin looked at their joined hands, then back at her. "What's wrong, Davia?"

She got straight to the point. "The other day in the restaurant, I did see your mother, and I saw the man sitting with her.'

"That was Charles Cash."

"He's also the man that I know as Money."

Justin uttered an expletive as he shot out of the chair. He didn't question her statement. She would know the man who tried to rape her anywhere. Justin was like a raging bull.

Davia grabbed his arm in an effort to restrain him. "Listen to me. Listen to me! This is important."

Snatching away from her, he headed toward the family room to Bianca, his fury mounting with each step. "If that animal touched her—"

Davia jumped in front of him so suddenly that he nearly tumbled over her. Grabbing her by the forearms, he steadied them both.

"Lower your voice," she whispered harshly. "You'll wake her up! Just stop and think."

"Think about what?" Justin hissed. "How I'm going to kill him? Because he's a dead man, that's for sure."

"I want to question Bianca."

"Oh, God!" Justin's cry was strangled. He stumbled backward, unable to comprehend the horror that might have occurred to his niece. "First you and now her! I know where he lives. I'm going over there!"

He stormed toward the entranceway. Davia hurried after him, trying to restrain him. Justin kept walking, dragging her unhindered.

"Maybe nothing happened." She prayed silently that her words were true. "Let me wake her up and talk to her. You go on back to the kitchen. Let me see what she says. It might be me being paranoid."

Justin stopped abruptly, grabbing at any straw she could give him. He ran his hand over his face in despair at the well of emotion threatening to overflow. "God, I hope you're right."

"Promise me you'll stay here. Don't leave the house. Bianca might need you." She looked at him apprehensively. "Will you stay?"

Justin was trembling with rage. His head was throbbing and breathing normally was impossible. Money! Charles Cash was Money! This monster had put his hands on Davia and now—

He nodded in agreement. He wouldn't go after Charles—*yet*. He headed back to the kitchen. Davia went into the family room.

Justin fell onto a stool, his legs unable to hold him any longer. He fought for calm. He had to think positively. Maybe Davia was right. Maybe nothing had happened to Bianca. She was too young. She was only four years old! If only he had been there. If he hadn't been selfish and inattentive, his niece wouldn't have turned to someone else.

For the next hour Justin sat in a trance, waiting for Davia to return from questioning Bianca. He couldn't go in there. He didn't want to hear what his precious niece had to say. He didn't want to see the unbearable pain on her little face that had been etched on Davia's. He prayed. *Please, God, don't let it have happened.* Silent tears fell.

Justin didn't move when Davia entered the room. Only the flicker of his eyes meeting hers indicated that he was still among the living. She went to him and cupped his cheek in the palm of her hand. His eyes searched her eyes. She delivered the news quietly.

"He hasn't raped her."

Closing his eyes, Justin expelled a grateful breath. "Thank God."

"*But . . .*"

Justin's eyes flew open.

"He did touch her inappropriately. She's scared of him."

"He's a dead man!" With eyes ablaze, he started to get off the stool. Davia managed to stop him.

"We've got him, Justin. All of these years I've wanted him to pay for what he did to me, and this is it. He's going down on child molestation charges."

Cursing, Justin leaped from his perch. "Are you kidding? Do you know what they give first-time offenders in child molestation cases? A slap on the wrist! After what he did to you, to Bianca and God knows who else, is that all you think he deserves?"

Davia's eyes hardened at the thought of what Money really deserved. "No. You know what I think ought to happen to him, and I'd be the first one in line to do it."

The malice in her voice sobered Justin as he remembered that the depth of his feelings toward Cash was nothing compared to Davia's. Subduing his own pain and anger he went to her. They stood holding each other, each absorbing the other's pain.

Dressed in pajamas and a robe, Reba entered the kitchen. "What in the world is all this shouting about? I could hear . . ." She stopped short as she observed them in their embrace. A grin replaced a stifled yawn. "Oh, excuse me. I see that the matter has been settled."

She started to turn and make a hasty retreat until she noticed the couple's demeanors.

"What's wrong?" Concern laced her voice.

Swiping at her tears, Davia drew away from Justin. "I'll fill you in later. Meanwhile, we're going to have an extra guest. Bianca is staying overnight. So go on back to bed. We're going to have our hands full in the morning."

Reba hesitated, her eyes shifting from Davia to Justin. He avoided her eyes as he turned and walked toward the family room. She returned her attention to Davia.

"Are you sure everything's all right?"

Davia nodded and tried to give Reba a reassuring smile. She failed.

With one last look toward where Justin had disappeared, Reba turned and left. Davia followed Justin into the family room. He was standing at the patio doors, looking out into the star-filled night. A sleeping Bianca was in his arms; her head was nestled in the crook of his neck. He was rocking her slowly, his face buried in her profusion of curls. His shoulders were stooped, heavy with grief.

As badly as she wanted to go to him Davia kept her distance, allowing him space. She could feel the turmoil of his conflicting emotions. Her fear was that he would act on them with violence. Somehow she had to reach him.

"Justin, I beg you. If you love me like you say you do, don't do anything rash. Don't confront Money. Just leave

Bianca here with us. You go home and get a good night's sleep. We need to talk to Vanessa when she gets back . . ."

"Vanessa!" Justin whirled to face her as breath seeped from his body. He spoke in a tortured whisper. "This is going to kill her."

Davia went to him, resting a comforting hand on his arm. "No, Justin, it won't kill her, but it will free Bianca, and that's what's important now."

As Justin drove along the highway, he fought to concentrate on traffic, but he couldn't. The anger he felt was embedded into his very being. He had promised Davia that he would go home and get a good night's sleep. Tomorrow Vanessa would return to town and they planned on telling her what had happened. After that the three of them would go to the authorities. It was a reasonable plan, and he tried to convince himself that Davia was right. He should let the law handle Cash. Yet it didn't seem to be enough. Every time he thought about that sleazy predator putting his filthy hands on Bianca, he wanted him dead. How had things come to this?

He thought about Katherine and Cash. His snobbish mother was so cautious about everyone she met. Why not this slime? Hadn't she had an inkling of the kind of character he was? Katherine Miles claimed that she wasn't easily fooled by people. She had been quick enough to condemn Davia, but this snake in a man's clothing she

had let slither right into her home! How had Cash managed to dupe her?

With every thought, every question, Justin's simmering
rage mounted. In one way or the other, Charles Cash had
violated every woman that Justin loved. He came to the
conclusion that there was no way that he could let him get
away with that. Cash had to pay. Promise or no promise,
Charles Cash was going down. Tonight!

Davia called Justin at home, but there was no answer.
Judging from when he had left her house, she knew that
he should be there by now. She called his cell phone.
Voice mail answered. It was then that she knew that he
had broken his promise. He had gone to confront
Money. Justin was out for blood.

It was fear and concern for Justin that had Davia
parked down the street from Charles Cash's condo at one
o'clock in the morning. Nestled in her jacket pocket was
a pearl-handled .22 she had purchased for the protection
of her household. It had been safely locked away since she
bought it and had never been used. But it would be used
tonight, if harm came to Justin.

As Money, Cash had been slick and streetwise.
Chances were that he still was. Justin wasn't. He had
never had to live by the game of survival. She had, and so
had Money. In his arena Justin would be outmatched.

Davia hadn't planned on seeking satisfaction from
Money through the barrel of a gun. She was willing to

use the law, even though Justin's words did haunt her. *Do you know what they give first-time offenders in child molestation cases? A slap on the wrist!* The inkling of doubt, that mistrust of the legal system honed from her past kept Davia wondering if he wasn't right. Whatever the case, the fight with Money was her fight, not Justin's. She should be the one to confront Money, not him, and she was armed for protection if it was needed.

The condos in which Money lived were individual townhouses built of recycled brick. Each townhouse had its own garage, and when Davia found Money's home, there blocking the driveway leading into his garage was a red Lexus sports car. It belonged to Justin.

Parking, she got out of her car. Her heart pounded wildly as she approached Money's place. She prayed silently that Justin hadn't acted on his emotions. Taking a deep breath, she climbed the stairs to Cash's front door with the hope that he hadn't harmed Justin, either. For a second she stood there, frozen in place. Behind the polished oak door was the man who had changed her life forever. He had violated her, threatened her, and affected her every waking hour. She hadn't come here to kill him, but if he had hurt Justin in any way, tonight Cash would take his last breath.

Davia closed her eyes, and Stephanie's face floated across her memory like morning mist. It was replaced by Gabby's face, then Bianca's. They were the faces of innocence. They were the faces of trust. Money was trust betrayed. His was the face of evil. She almost wished that Charles "Money" Cash would try to pull something. She would feel justified putting the man's madness to an end.

Opening her eyes, she slipped her hand into her pocket and withdrew the gun. Carefully, she released the safety, and then tucked the weapon back into place. Her finger curled around the trigger. She was ready for whatever was to happen. Ringing the doorbell, she waited.

CHAPTER 21

The door opened slowly. Davia took a steadying breath and exhaled all in one action as a face appeared in the doorway. But it wasn't the face of the man that she loathed. It belonged to the man that she loved.

"Justin!" Her relief was palpable as she removed her finger from the trigger.

He was stunned. "What are you doing here?"

Davia couldn't answer as tears of relief flowed. Unmoved, Justin grabbed her by her shoulders and shook her. His tone was harsh.

"You have to get out of here! I thought you were the police! You have to go before they come."

"The police?" Davia's eyes widened.

He ignored the alarm in her voice as he looked hurriedly up and down the dark, deserted street to see if they were being observed. He hustled Davia down the four stairs to the brick sidewalk. "Where's your car?"

She motioned toward where she had parked. Spotting it, Justin all but dragged her along the street as she tried to keep up with his rapid stride.

"W-what's w-wrong?" she stuttered breathlessly, trying in vain to escape his vise-like grip. "W-where's Money?"

"Don't worry about him." Justin pulled her along unceremoniously.

"What do you mean?" She tried to jerk away again. "What's wrong with you?" His demeanor was totally out of character.

He didn't answer as they reached her car. With one hand he opened the unlocked door and with his other one he made an attempt to force her into the vehicle. She resisted.

"No!" She continued to struggle against his hold. "Stop manhandling me! I'm not leaving here until you tell me what's going on!"

"Keep your voice down," he growled, but he released her arm.

Davia could see the anxiety on his face as his eyes swept the deserted street. Fear gripped her. Something *was* wrong. She spoke quietly this time, emphasizing each spoken word.

"Justin, where's Money?"

Their eyes met. "He's dead."

Davia's body went numb. A cold chill swept through her. She gripped his arm as if her life depended on it.

"Dead?" Her voice was hollow. *He couldn't be!*

"No! I don't believe it. I've got to see him!" Turning, she headed back down the street toward Money's house. Justin caught up with her in one swift motion, pulling her back toward him.

"Let me go!" She was angry, combative. She had to know that what he was telling her was true. Maybe it was a mistake. "You don't know him. Money is slick. He's pulling some sort of trick trying to trap you, trying to trap both of us. He's . . ."

"Stop it, Davia." He shook her roughly. "It's no trick. It's no trap. He's *dead*."

A dry sob caught in Justin's throat as he crushed her to his chest, stifling her horrified scream. With his mouth pressed against her ear, he whispered desperately, "If you love me as much as I love you, don't ask questions. Just leave here now."

She couldn't breathe. She shivered with shock. Reality had spun out of control. Money was dead. He was dead!

Justin forced her trembling body into the car. "Baby, you can't lose it now. Start the engine."

Shakily she retrieved her keys from her pocket. Somehow she managed to put the right key into the ignition and turn it.

"Drive away," he ordered, shutting the door firmly.

She did, watching him in the rearview mirror as he turned and hurried back to the townhouse. In the distance she heard sirens.

&

She drove blindly, on autopilot. She didn't get more than a couple of blocks before she had to pull over and empty the contents of her stomach. It seemed that whether he was dead or alive, Money made her physically ill.

As she sat with her back propped against her car, she tried to comprehend all that had happened. Money was dead. Those words didn't bring the morbid pleasure she would have expected under different circumstances.

Whatever had happened, Justin might be implicated. She had brought this trouble on him. If she hadn't told him about Charles Cash being Money, none of this would have happened. As she sat propped against her car, she gradually gained some sense of control. She had to know what was going on.

Gathering herself, she slipped back inside her car, made a U-turn, then backtracked, headed toward the street on which Money lived. This time her driving was steady, her manner resolute. She was determined to find out what had happened and how Justin was involved.

When Davia reached Money's neighborhood, the street was blocked off. Finding a parking place a block away, she parked and walked back. The lights from a half-dozen squad cars lit up the night. A small crowd, dressed in nightclothes, had gathered outside the yellow crime scene tape. One policeman guarded the closed townhouse door while two others were busily trying to keep people at bay.

"What's happened?" Davia asked as she approached a woman standing at the edge of the taped area.

"They carried a body out of that house over there." She pointed toward Money's place. "The man who lived there is dead."

"Oh, my goodness!" Davia didn't have to disguise the distress in her voice. "Does anybody know what happened?"

A man standing on the other side of the woman answered. "I overheard the police talking and it sounded like foul play. They took some guy out of the place and put him in a squad car."

"I know that I was walking my dog around midnight and there was a woman who left the house . . ."

The voice of the female standing next to her faded into the background as Davia's heart nearly stopped! Justin! The police had arrested Justin! She needed to get to him. She needed to find out where he had been taken. She was turning to leave when the voice of the woman talking to her penetrated her consciousness.

"I wonder if she might have been involved, too?"

Davia looked at her bewildered. "She who?"

"The woman who I said was here earlier when I was walking my dog. I'd better tell the police."

Fear gripped Davia. She was talking about her. Would she be arrested, too? As the woman tried to get the attention of an officer nearby and her neighbors lamented the increase in crime, Davia discreetly removed herself from the throng and headed back to her car. She had to talk to Justin, and she had to do so soon.

Justin wasn't sure whether the police believed his story or not, but he was too tired to care. He told them that he and Cash had gotten into a verbal argument over some borrowed money. The man had turned away angrily, tripped over a rug, fallen, hit his head and died. That was his story and he stuck to it. He had been in the interrogation room at the police station since 2 a.m.; it was now ten in the morning, and he was exhausted. His attorney, Anthony Sharp, an old classmate and fraternity brother, was at the station waiting when he arrived. Justin had called him as soon as he knew that he was going to be taken in for questioning.

Released under his own recognizance, he was told that further questioning would be in order. He hadn't been surprised that the authorities let him leave. The Miles family had political clout in Atlanta. Booking Justin Miles without ironclad proof of his guilt could prove disastrous for somebody's career. As unfair as it might be, that was the reality, and right now he was grateful for the inequity.

Wearily, Justin trudged through his house, discarding clothing as he moved toward his bedroom. When he got to the spiral staircase, his legs collapsed from under him. He sank to the bottom step. Lately, whenever he climbed this staircase, all he could think of was the pleasure that he had shared with Davia on this twisted piece of metal.

Davia. When he'd opened Cash's door and had seen her standing there, panic had been his only emotion. What had possessed her to come to that man's house?

She had begged him not to go there, and in hindsight he wished that he had listened. If he had followed her advice, maybe things would have turned out differently. He sighed heavily.

The death of any human being was difficult, but at least Davia no longer had to concern herself with Charles Cash. He was in hell where he belonged. No one could connect him to her. Not even Katherine knew the connection between the two of them. Justin was sure of that. Davia was finally free.

She had been calling his cell phone and texting him. He'd give anything to have her in his arms at this moment. He needed her, but it was best that she wasn't here. There was too much to explain, and right now he couldn't think clearly. He needed rest. He would call her later.

Rising, Justin dragged himself up the stairs. With a shower and a few hours of sleep, maybe things would begin to look better. There were matters he had to tend to. They were ones that he dreaded, but ones that were necessary. Breaking the news to Katherine about the death of Charles Cash was the first thing on his list.

At the police station he had discovered that the beat reporter for the *Atlanta Constitution* hadn't gotten wind of Cash's death or Justin's involvement—yet. That was good, but it wouldn't last. He wanted to break the news to his mother personally before she heard it from other sources.

Glancing at the clock on the dresser, he was surprised to see that it was almost noon. His mother would be home from church soon. He planned on being at her house when she returned.

When Davia arrived home in the early hours of the morning, everyone at her house was still asleep. Instead of joining them, she called information and got the telephone number of the Atlanta Police Department, and then she called every station and substation in the city.

She was relieved to discover that there was no record of Justin having been booked for a crime. Her calls to him on his cell and land phones and her text messages to him had all gone unanswered. Exhausted, she had fallen asleep at the kitchen counter with the telephone in her hand.

By the time she climbed the stairs, took a shower and changed her clothes, it was noon, and she was about to pick up the telephone to call him again when it rang. She glanced at caller ID and picked it up instantly.

"Justin!"

"Hi, sweetheart, how are you doing?"

Relief shook her. "Oh, baby, talk to me. Tell me what happened. Where are you? I was just about to call."

"I've been at the police station, but they released me. Now I'm in my car headed over to my mother's house. I've got to break the news to her about Cash."

"Please tell me what happened." She tried to keep her voice even. Calm was needed at the moment.

"We had a verbal fight, Cash tripped, hit his head on a marble coffee table and died."

Davia sucked in her breath. That was it, cut and dried. Money lived. Money died.

She felt nothing for him, but she did feel for Justin. He was not a violent man. How horrible this must be for him.

"I want to be with you, Justin, by your side, whatever happens."

"And I need you by me, baby. God knows I do, but I want you to keep a low profile right now. That's the best thing you can do for me. How's Bianca?"

"I peeked in on her and Gabby when I got home. She was sleeping peacefully. The two of them are happily playing now."

"Good, she deserves all of the happiness that she can get, and so do you." Justin was silent for a moment. "You'll never have to worry again, sweetheart. Your days of running are over." He paused, letting the enormity of that reality sink in. "I'll call you back later and we'll talk more. Remember that I love you. Everything is going to be all right." With that he broke the connection.

Davia held the telephone to her cheek for a second. Would everything really be okay? She had never had a man outside the Johnson family who had been there for her as Justin had. She had never had faith or trust in any man until him. With him she had gained something she never thought that she would have—peace of mind. He had been there for her through all of her drama and had never wavered. It was time to reciprocate. It was her turn to be there for him.

CHAPTER 22

As much as Justin regretted having to tell his mother about the death of Charles Cash, he would have given his life to have spared her the double blow of telling her about Bianca. The look on her face was one he would never forget.

"Bianca! Our baby? He . . . He . . ." Her gray-blue eyes met his, searching for some falsehood in the words that he had spoken. She saw none.

Pale and shaken, she buried her head in her hands and sobbed. Sitting on the sofa beside her, Justin took her in his arms and let her expel her anguish. It took a while.

Having absorbed the shock of the news her son had brought to her, Katherine wiped the tears from her eyes, waved the brandy away that he offered and exhaled. She was back in control.

"Son, I want you to understand that my grief is not for Charles, but for our baby, and for the fact that I let that monster into my home. I hope he rots in hell!"

Justin nodded, relieved at the revelation and agreeing with the latter declaration. "I don't think that there's any doubt about that."

"What we must do now is get you out of this situation and help Bianca all that we can."

"And what about Vanessa?"

"Oh, my Lord!" Katherine gasped. "She'll be home today from her buying trip. This news about Bianca will destroy her." Katherine rose and began to pace. "How can we tell her? She's so fragile."

"It might be that she's a lot stronger than you think, but we'll have to be there for her."

"Of course we will, but you don't know Vanessa. She's weak. She always has been. But that's not important right now. You are."

Justin frowned. He hated it when his mother dismissed his sister. "Listen, Mother, Vanessa will need your support now more than ever."

Katherine was barely listening as she laid out her plans for her son. "I know who we'll get to defend you if it comes to that. I'll call Lazarus Dorman . . ."

"He's on the Georgia Supreme Court, he doesn't practice law anymore. Anyway, I called Anthony. He's my attorney."

"Oh, no." She stopped and looked at him disapprovingly. "Not him. He went to some nondescript law school up north. You'll need better representation than that."

"Anthony is my lawyer, and that's the end of that discussion."

Katherine looked at her son in exasperation. "Please, Justin, not this time. Don't fight every decision that I make. This is too important. This could mean your life." She began to tear. "I couldn't bear it if anything . . ."

"Here's everybody!"

Startled, Justin and Katherine turned simultaneously, equally surprised at the sound of Vanessa's voice. A second later she breezed into the living room, luggage in hand.

"Look who I found outside."

Two pairs of eyes shifted to the figure behind her. It was Davia. Justin and Katherine both froze.

"How dare you come into my house," Katherine hissed.

Unfazed by the arctic greeting, Davia had eyes only for Justin as he rose and walked across the room to her. Neither of them noticed his mother's glare as he and Davia found consolation in each other's arms.

"Sweetheart, you shouldn't have come." Justin's words were a contradiction to the kisses he rained from her hairline down to her lips. He needed this. He needed her, and Davia needed him.

"I couldn't stay away." She caressed his goatee lovingly. "I had to see for myself that you were okay."

"Well, he's fine." Katherine's frosty voice interrupted their reunion. "And I'll be frank with you, *Ms. Maxwell.* It's obvious by your presence that my son has confided in you before confiding in me. But at this moment we are discussing a *family* matter, and I'd like for you to leave my home."

Justin turned to his mother, placing his arm around Davia protectively. "If she goes, I go."

Katherine recoiled as if she had been struck. Her eyes were ablaze as they shifted from a determined Justin to Davia, who heaved a troubled sigh.

She wasn't up to another fight with Katherine, but if she wanted one, she was willing to give it to her. The tension in the room was stifling. Vanessa chose to retreat.

"I'm going upstairs to see Bianca," she announced, fingering the strap on her luggage nervously. She started out of the room.

Davia started to speak up and inform her that Bianca was at her house, but Katherine's strident voice stopped her.

"No, Vanessa. Stay here. Justin and I need to talk to you." Pointedly, she glanced at Davia. "*Alone.*"

"Let her go," said Justin. "We can talk later." His voice and manner softened as he addressed his sister. "Go on upstairs, hon. Get some rest."

Katherine looked at him in amazement. "No! She stays right here. What has to be said can't wait. I'll talk to her if you won't. Since you think that this matter is of so little importance, you and your little lady friend can go do whatever it is you have to do."

Ignoring Katherine, Davia took in Vanessa's appearance. The woman looked as if she was about to pass out. She was nervous and jumpy. Her eyes were red and her color didn't look good. Justin had said that she had taken a business trip. Perhaps it had been a difficult one. Unfortunately, what Vanessa was coming home to might be the most difficult thing she would ever have to face. As a mother Davia knew the pain that the revelation about Bianca would bring, and her heart went out to her. It was Justin's gentle squeeze on her shoulder that refocused her attention.

"Sweetheart, have a seat, please." He nodded toward a chair and then moved toward his sister as he addressed Katherine. "Vanessa looks as though she needs her rest."

Katherine was livid. "This is my house, and I don't want this woman here, Justin."

"We'll be leaving as soon as I help Vanessa upstairs." He slid her bag from her shoulder.

"Come on, sis."

"No!" Katherine was emphatic. "She must be told what has happened, and it must be *now*. Your life may depend on it!"

Vanessa's eyes flew to Justin. "Your life? What is she talking about?"

"It can wait until later," Justin said gruffly as he tried to hustle his sister out of the room.

Vanessa resisted, turning questioning eyes on Katherine. "Mother?"

"Charles Cash is dead, Vanessa. The police think your brother might have caused his death."

"What?" Vanessa's hands flew to her mouth as she stifled a scream.

"Mother!" Justin stormed at Katherine. The overnight bag crashed to the floor. A trembling Vanessa took refuge in a nearby chair. Davia rose in an attempt to see to her, but Katherine waved her away as she went to her daughter.

"Why did you do that?" An angry Justin crossed the room to pour a glass of brandy for his sister. "I told you that I'd handle this."

"I don't care," Katherine retorted, patting Vanessa's back solicitously. "This is a family crisis and we must deal with every aspect of it immediately." She looked at Davia. "And without *her* being involved."

Justin returned to Vanessa's side with a snifter of brandy. "Here, drink this." He then turned a cold eye to his mother. "If it wasn't for Davia, who knows what would have happened to Bi . . ." He glanced at Vanessa, who looked back at him with alarm.

"Bianca! I have to go up to her." Her voice rose hysterically as she tried to get out of her seat.

"She's not upstairs." Katherine informed her. "Justin left her with Clark."

"Clark?" Vanessa's puzzled eyes shifted to Justin.

"She's safe," he reassured her.

Vanessa spun toward her brother. "I thought that you were going to bring her home from her house." She indicated Davia.

Davia shot Justin a questioning glance. Katherine also caught her daughter's words. She was incensed.

"When you said that you left Bianca with a close friend, I thought that you meant Clark. I can't believe you did this. You're dragged to jail like a common criminal, and you go to her first. You took my grandchild to *her*?" Katherine whirled on Davia. "I want you out of here! Out!"

Wrapping her arms around herself protectively, a hysterical Vanessa wailed. "Mother, please! Enough is enough. I just want Bianca. My baby needs me!" She began sobbing.

Davia sat quietly watching the drama unfolding before her—Katherine's jealous vindictiveness, Vanessa's emotional distress, and Justin, the devoted son and brother, trying to put Band-Aids on everyone's wounds.

To the outside world the Miles family appeared to have it all—wealth, social status and respect. Yet, this was a family with challenges far beyond those it presently faced. She wondered if they possessed the love and strength that it would take to endure what lay ahead for them. Only time would tell. As for now, there was something wrong here, and it was becoming increasingly clear to her what it might be. Years of survival had honed instincts that revealed truths that others might miss. She hadn't missed a thing.

Davia rose and went to Justin, who had hunkered down before his sister. Gently, she touched his shoulder.

"Justin, let's go. Let's take Vanessa to her daughter. They need to be with each other now."

Justin turned to Davia, detecting something different in her tone and manner. His gray-green eyes met her dark brown ones. They held and he realized that she knew.

The silent exchange confirmed Davia's suspicion. It also warned her that this was a man who would protect and stand by his sister, no matter the cost. But the price he might have to pay for his love and loyalty to his family might be too high. So Davia took the decision out of his hands.

She turned to his sister. "Vanessa? How did you know that Bianca was at my house? Justin never mentioned to me that he had spoken to you."

For a brief moment panic passed over Vanessa's fine features. She glanced quickly at her brother, then back at Davia, but it was Katherine who did the talking.

"What has that got to do with anything? The question is what is my granddaughter doing at your house instead of being here at home where she belongs?"

"Stop it, Mother!" Justin demanded. "We owe Davia too much for you to give her this attitude of yours."

"I don't owe her a thing," Katherine said. She turned to Vanessa. "I'm sorry, dear, but I'm afraid there's something your brother and I need to tell you . . ."

"You don't need to tell her about Bianca, Mrs. Miles," Davia interrupted. "Does she, Vanessa?"

"Don't say a word," warned Justin. "You're out of place, Davia."

"Humph, you're right about that," Katherine agreed.

"I'm telling you to keep out of this, Davia," Justin said harshly.

Davia looked at him, taken aback. He had never talked to her so sternly. The adage "blood is thicker than water" crossed her mind. Perhaps it was best to suppress her suspicions and walk away. But if she did that, Justin could pay the price for her silence. She ignored his warning.

"Vanessa, I was at Charles Cash's townhouse at one o'clock this morning . . ."

"Davia!" Justin's warning took on threatening tones. Meanwhile, Katherine looked at her, bewildered.

"How did you know where he lived?" She turned to Justin. "Was she with you?"

Justin ignored her as he focused on Davia. "Don't go any farther."

She did. "I was afraid that Justin might go to his house and confront Mon . . . Cash. And as I suspected, he was there. He told me that Cash was dead, then he sent me away, but I went back . . ."

"What?" Justin roared.

Davia remained unfazed. "The authorities had taken Justin to the police station by the time I returned, but there were still neighbors milling around. And while you and Justin were talking, I was sitting over there thinking about that night and how I caught snatches of conversation among the bystanders."

"It's time for you to go." There was an unspoken plea in Justin's voice.

His words went unheeded as Davia continued. "I remembered hearing one woman saying something about walking her dog around midnight and seeing a woman leaving Cash's townhouse. I know that was way before I got there."

Her eyes strayed to Justin who, for a moment, looked stricken by her statement, but he quickly recovered. "So the woman was mistaken. That had nothing to do with this."

Davia addressed his sister, who sat as still as stone. "Vanessa knows that it has everything to do with it."

"You're wrong. She doesn't know anything. So leave this *alone*, Davia." There was a chill in Justin's voice that threatened finality. She could lose him if she continued, but she could lose him if she didn't. He had been there for her, no matter what. She could do no less for him.

Katherine was confused by the direction the conversation was taking, but was delighted at her son's displeasure with her nemesis.

"Young lady, I have no idea what you're talking about, and I'm sure my daughter doesn't, either. My son has asked that you stay out of our family's business and leave. So get out. I'll get Henry to follow you to your house so Bianca can be brought home where she belongs."

Davia ignored everyone but Vanessa. "Your brother loves you. If nobody else in the world was ever there for you, he has been. That's the kind of man he is. You know that he'll do anything for you. *Anything!* And you know what I mean."

"Get out, Davia!" Fury was in Justin's every word as he stormed across the room to the entrance and pointed the way for her.

Folding her arms across her chest, Katherine looked at her triumphantly. Blood *was* thicker than water.

Davia was shaken by the depth of Justin's anger. She was used to seeing fire and desire in the depths of his eyes, not the pain and rage now reflected there.

Justin could hardly breathe, he was so angry. How could the woman he loved do this to him? She was making him choose between her and his sister. Why did she have to force his hand? He had proven his loyalty to her, defied his mother to be with her. There was little he wouldn't do to be by her side. Where was her loyalty? How could she betray him like this? Silently, his eyes beseeched her to go away and let things be as they were.

Davia looked at Justin's rigid stance and wondered if this would be the end for them. Would the death of Charles Cash be the catalyst to end what even his mother could not destroy? Was Money reaching from the grave to snatch this bit of happiness from her? It was her call. All she had to do was ignore the truth, turn and walk out of the door. The world wouldn't stop revolving, and things might be right again. It *was* her call, and she took it.

She turned back to his sister. "Don't let him go down for this, Vanessa. You love him too much to let him do this. Save him." Davia could hear the breath leave Justin's body.

"What is this woman talking about?" Katherine asked her daughter. Her son had sunk into a chair and covered his face in despair. "Exactly what are you supposed to save Justin from?"

Vanessa's shoulders sagged as she looked at Davia with red-rimmed eyes. "Prison."

"Vanessa!" Justin shot from his chair and charged across the room to his sister. "Think of Bianca."

"I am thinking of her. That's why it's over, Justin."

Katherine looked completely befuddled. "Will somebody tell me what's going on?"

Vanessa looked past her mother as she spoke, her eyes devoid of emotion as she took a shuddering breath. "I killed Charles Cash."

"No you didn't!" Justin's voice cracked as he knelt down beside his sister. Davia placed a comforting hand on his shoulder. He shook it off.

Katherine backed away from her children as she looked at Vanessa in disbelief.

"What are you saying? Are you insane? How could you kill Charles? You've been in Dallas for two days."

"I came back last night. I was upstairs at Cash's house when Justin came to see him . . ." She turned to look at her mother. "Upstairs in Charles's bed."

Katherine gave a sardonic cackle. "Do you expect me to believe that?"

"I figured that you wouldn't, but it's true. We've been lovers for about a month."

Katherine's hand fluttered to her throat as she looked at her child as if she didn't know who she was. "How could you, Vanessa? Why would you do such a thing?"

A bitter laugh escaped from deep within Vanessa. "Because you thought I couldn't and wouldn't, and I had to prove to myself that not only I could, but I would."

Speechless, Katherine dropped into a nearby chair, reeling from the venom lacing her daughter's words.

"But for once, Mother, this isn't about you. It's about that S.O.B. and how he got what was coming to him." Vanessa looked through Katherine, as her mind took her back to the townhouse of Charles Cash.

"I recognized Justin's voice right away. I could tell that he was angry . . ."

As his sister spoke, Justin's thoughts drifted back to last night and the events as they had unfolded—

He had been livid when he arrived at Charles Cash's home. It was obvious that Charles was surprised to see him—surprised because he knew what Justin's presence at his home must mean. Davia had shared their secret. He was sure that Charles hadn't expected that to happen. He probably figured that she would want to continue to hide her past from the aristocratic Miles family, but he had figured wrong. More than likely Charles had berated himself for having made that mistake.

Charles had played it cool. He showed no outward signs that Justin's anger had fazed him. He feigned ignorance regarding the accusations that had been flung at him about his past under the name Money.

"I have no idea what you're talking about, Justin," he had said as he turned from him and poured a scotch and soda. Turning back to face him, he sipped slowly as he stared Justin down. Then he said, "You know something, Justin. You come here to my home, my castle, my place of solitude like some pampered prince, ranting and raving about things you know nothing about. You're a boy playing a man's game, and if you think that I'm going to let some harlot, who your mother hates anyway, discredit me, you have another think coming. I don't know what your little girlfriend might have told you, but it's that little slut's word against mine."

Incensed, Justin had gotten in his face. "You sick, filthy monster. You may have gotten away with molesting children in the past, but those days are over. If you put your filthy hands on my niece again, I swear to you I'll kill you!"

Charles's cool demeanor slipped for a fraction of a second. Justin knew that he had never expected Bianca to talk, and while Katherine might not have believed Davia, she certainly would believe her own granddaughter. Justin could see on the man's face that he knew that any support that he expected to get from Katherine was over. Still, he tried to bluff.

Charles had sneered, "I don't know where you get your information, but I'd suggest that you don't repeat what you've said if you don't want to be hit with a lawsuit for slander."

Justin couldn't contain himself any longer as he lunged for the much smaller man. He grabbed him by the collar and slammed him against a wall. The glass in Charles's hand tumbled to the thick carpeting.

"You listen to me, you scumbag! My niece said that you molested her, and her word is all I need." With a vicious push Justin had shoved Charles away from him. His hands felt soiled by the contact.

Charles had straightened the collar of his black silk robe with a shrug. "Then the kid's a liar, too."

Once again he turned his back to Justin and started back across the room toward the bar. It was then that Vanessa had appeared out of nowhere. She leaped on Charles's back, beating him with her fist unmercifully and screaming like a banshee.

"My baby! My baby! You touched my baby." She had been out of control.

Caught off guard, Charles had tried to shake her off. Turning toward Justin, Charles managed to dislodge Vanessa from his body, but as he backed away from her, he stumbled over a Persian rug and lost his footing. He tumbled backward.

Justin refocused his attention on his sister as she told her side of the story to Katherine and Davia. Vanessa's voice harbored unshed tears.

"Charles hit his head on the coffee table. There was this sound, like a melon splitting open. I looked down and he was lying on his back, in a pool of blood. He was dead, and I wasn't sorry."

Davia sighed. And so the life of Charles "Money" Cash had come to an end. She doubted if there was anyone in this room who would shed a tear. However, she had to swallow the lump in her throat after witnessing Vanessa's pain. She felt little triumph in having elicited her confession, but it had been necessary.

"And Justin told you not to worry, and he made you leave." Davia had no doubt about that scenario. "He said that he would take care of everything, just like he always does."

Vanessa looked up into the face of the brother whom she adored. "You know him well, but I didn't know that he would take the blame. I can't let that happen. I *won't* let that happen."

Katherine was devastated. Uncharacteristically, she started to cry. Her face was drenched with tears as she rose and went to her daughter.

"Oh, Vanessa, you didn't mean to kill him. We can get you out of this." With a shaky hand she started to caress her daughter's cheek. Vanessa pulled away. Katherine let her hand drop to her side.

Davia found herself feeling sorry for the woman. Despite everything, she was still a mother who loved her children. Unfortunately, she loved one more than the other, and the consequences might be ones that Katherine might have to live with for quite some time.

Davia turned her attention to Justin. The look that he was giving her was scathing. His voice was like stone.

"You couldn't leave it alone, could you? I asked one thing of you, but you couldn't do it. It had to be your way. So all right, you got what you wanted. You won. Now you can get out! We'll send someone for Bianca."

If he had taken a knife and carved the words he spoke onto her heart it could not have hurt more. Davia looked at the three of them huddled together; despite everything, they presented a united front. There was no place in their lives for a girl from the ghetto who was born with the name Shanay Wells. Without a word Davia turned and left the Miles household. Justin didn't try to stop her.

CHAPTER 23

It had been two months since the death of Charles Cash. His death had been ruled an accident. According to the official report, Justin Miles had been making an early-morning call on the man regarding some business when Cash tripped on an area rug, hit his head on a table and died.

No sympathy was wasted on the deceased, especially when it was discovered that he had swindled many of his investment clients out of money and worse. Reporters dug deeper and uncovered his sordid past. He was labeled for what he was—a pimp, a drug dealer and a thief. Rumors from his past hinted that he had been ejected from his prominent family after an argument with his father regarding some unidentified misdeed.

Katherine Miles was referred to briefly by the press, identifying her as Justin's mother, but the names of her daughter and granddaughter were never mentioned. The story made headlines for a while, but soon faded to be replaced by something else.

Davia should have been relieved that everything had worked out well, but she had felt only pain since she and Justin had parted. She walked, talked, smiled, and even laughed as if life were normal. It was all too familiar, too much like the past.

At one time in her life she had been a fragile seedling, but she had blossomed. She had survived. That's what she was, a survivor.

Sequestered in her Buckhead office, submerged in work, Davia didn't get a chance to respond to the knock on her office door before CeCe barged in. Without a word of greeting, she walked across the room and flopped down in one of the chairs in front of her desk.

Since the day that Justin and she parted, Davia had tried to avoid her friend. She wanted to suffer in silence, but CeCe wouldn't let her. Eventually, she had caught up with Davia and had been giving her hell about her standoff with Justin. Davia chose to ignore her tirades, but the woman was persistent.

While CeCe sat across the desk glaring at her, Davia continued typing on her computer. She could sit there all day if she wanted to; Davia wasn't going to acknowledge her. All CeCe wanted was to force her to talk about Justin, and she refused to do that. What was there to say? He had rejected her, and that was that.

The silence in the room continued. One minute passed . . . two minutes, the longest length of time that CeCe had ever been quiet. But, as expected, it didn't last.

"Clark said that Justin is miserable, impossible to get along with, and missing you like a man misses a limb."

Davia kept typing.

"Doggone it, Davia, why do you have to be so stubborn? The man loves you to death. What did he do that was so terrible? Stick by his family? So shoot him for being loyal, but don't make him suffer like this. Call him."

"He hasn't called me." Her eyes never left the monitor.

"Maybe he's afraid to. Maybe he thinks that you'll reject him. He knows that you were trying to help him and that he hurt you and that he was wrong."

"Yes, he was."

"So why can't you forgive him?"

Sighing, she typed another line into her computer before giving CeCe her full attention. "I haven't heard from Justin. He hasn't called me. Did he send you here to talk to me?"

"No, he didn't, but Clark and I love you both and we want to see you two happy again. So what will it take? Do you want Justin to get down on his knees and beg for your forgiveness? He'll probably do it."

"Justin has proved himself to be too much of a man to beg, and I wouldn't want him to." Davia massaged her temples in an attempt to relieve the building tension. "Listen, I know that you and Clark mean well, but I want you to leave this alone. I've been fighting battles all of my life and finally I'm at peace. Justin helped bring me that peace, and I'm not going through any more changes. He told me to go away, and I did."

"So this is your revenge?"

"No, CeCe, this isn't about revenge, this is about love. I did what I did for Justin because I love him and he sent me away. I won't be caught up in the Miles whirlwind. I'm not going to battle his family for his love and loyalty. If he wants me, if he wants us to be together, then our relationship has to become a priority and on an equal footing. I won't be dismissed because I won't bow to his commands. So, if you're playing the part of messenger, you can go back and tell him that."

She turned back to the computer to finish her work.

In Justin's office, Clark sat across the desk from his friend and watched him thoughtfully. He appeared to be concentrating on putting the finishing touches on a report, but Clark knew better. He knew for a fact that his man had not been in full control of his mental faculties since he sent Davia Maxwell away. The man hadn't been functioning well at all.

Normally, Clark wouldn't have interfered in his best friend's love life. Neither of them had ever stepped over that line. But despite Justin's denials, his pain was acute and Clark ached for his best friend.

Today's visit to Justin's office was an effort to help him rectify that pain. They were going out to dinner and follow that by a night out on the town, but Clark knew that this evening was only a temporary diversion. It would take much more than this to mend a broken heart.

With a frustrated sigh, Justin abandoned his attempt to complete the document in front of him. "That's enough for tonight. I'm ready to get out of here."

He placed the papers he had been working on in a manila folder and tossed it aside. Clark watched as Justin pushed the sleeves down on his once-crisp dress shirt and absently buttoned each cuff. He had carelessly discarded his tie earlier. Opening a desk drawer he retrieved it and placed the wrinkled bit of silk around his neck, making no attempt to knot it. He let it dangle without further thought.

Clark's eyes narrowed at Justin's disheveled appearance. Not only had he let himself go, but he had lost weight and there were bags under his eyes. He wasn't eating or sleeping well, either, and both of them knew the reason why.

"Uh, I take it that you're going home to change before we go out tonight," Clark said pointedly, making no effort to disguise his displeasure at what he saw.

Justin looked down at his wrinkled clothing, then back up at Clark. He shrugged.

"No, I hadn't planned to." He got up and crossed the room to where he had tossed his suit jacket on the sofa when he arrived at his office that morning.

Clark snorted. "If you think you're going anyplace with me, you'd better think twice. I've got a reputation to maintain."

Justin glanced over his shoulder at his friend, resplendent in his tailored suit and handcrafted Italian shoes. Clark took pride in his personal appearance, just as Justin had before he stopped caring. For the past few months, nothing had mattered anymore.

Picking up the rumpled suit coat, he put it on and grunted, "Suit yourself. I don't care if we go or not." Justin headed toward the office door.

"Then it's probably for the best that we don't. We might run into Davia anyway." Clark swung out of his chair easily, pretending not to notice Justin's misstep at the mention of Davia's name.

Justin frowned. When would it stop? When would his heart stop aching at the mention of her name? It was over. He had told her to get out of his life, and she was gone. But he couldn't keep himself from asking, "What do you mean, 'run into Davia?' She doesn't go out."

Casually, Clark walked past Justin and opened the office door. "Hey, man, all I know is what CeCe tells me."

Justin followed Clark out into his secretary's empty office. It was after eight in the evening, late by most standards, but early for Justin. Lately, he had been working sixteen-hour days. He knew the reason why. It was the same one that made him ask Clark the next question.

"So she's starting to go out, huh?"

"What do you expect? She's a beautiful woman. Men love to be in her company."

They were in the hallway at the elevators. At least Clark was; Justin had come to a dead stop.

"What do you mean? Is she dating someone already?" Justin hated the sound of desperation he heard in his voice, but he couldn't help it. The thought of his baby with somebody else wasn't sitting right with him. "Who?" he bellowed as his angry stride brought him face to face with Clark.

Clark hid a smile as he stepped into the elevator. Justin was right on his heels.

Clark pushed the button that sent them downward. "What do you care? You tossed her away like an old dishrag and haven't spoken to her since."

Justin flinched at the harsh assessment. "She could have called me," he countered, knowing that his defense was weak.

Leaning against the wall, Clark looked at him and chuckled. "You sound like some junior high school kid. What's that about? You were the one who told her to get out of your life . . ."

"Not my life man, just—" Justin fell back against the back wall of the elevator. *Just what?* He loved Davia Maxwell more than he loved his own life. Without her, he was a dead man walking.

Clark looked at Justin's defeated stance and knew that his man's begging time was near. "Man, go to the woman and tell her you're sorry and that you were wrong."

"I wasn't wrong," Justin huffed defensively. "There was nothing I wouldn't do for Davia. *Nothing!* And I never asked one thing from her, except her loyalty. I just wanted her to help me protect Vanessa, not destroy what little relationship there was between my mother and sister. And what did Davia do? She . . ."

"Did what she had to do to save you." A guilty silence met Clark's words. "That sounds like a lot of loyalty to me. Don't let foolish pride stand between you and the woman you love. Davia loves you! You fought this long and this hard to keep from being under your mother's thumb. You wanted to live your life the way you wanted to live it, and with whom you wanted. Now here you are falling right into Katherine's trap. You're walking away from the best thing that ever happened to you, and she loves it because now she's got you back again, all to her-self. Man, you need to quit it."

There was no denying his friend's words. Katherine was beside herself with delight at the turn of events in his relationship with Davia. Meanwhile, he was miserable.

The elevator doors opened and the men stepped into the lobby, empty except for the two guards sitting at their station. The men nodded their greetings as Justin and Clark headed out the front door and into the crisp night air. Justin sighed as he came to an abrupt stop outside the building's entrance.

"I love her so much, Clark. I can't take this."

Clark placed a comforting hand on Justin's shoulder. "So why are you telling me? I'm not the one who needs to hear it."

The friends proceeded to their cars in silence. Clark's point had been made.

It was ten o'clock that evening by the time Justin drove up to Davia's house. He was dressed in a fresh suit, shirt and tie. Slipping out of his car, he marched toward the front door like a man on a mission. He rang the doorbell and prayed that her face would be the first one that he would see. His prayer was answered. Davia opened the door.

She had been expecting a package delivery and was shocked to see him. Her first thought was to close the door in his face, but Justin didn't give her time to do so. He pleaded his case immediately.

"It's been two months, three days, six hours and . . ." he glanced at his watch, ". . . fifty-one minutes since I asked you to leave my mother's house. Right here, right now, I'm asking you to forgive me. I was an angry fool who made the mistake of his life." Justin's eyes and voice softened as he reveled in the feeling of being near her again. He reached out to run a finger down her cheek. She took a step back, avoiding his touch. His heart sank.

"Come in." Davia's directive was unemotional, but her heart was thumping wildly.

Justin's hope was renewed. He followed her through the house and into the family room. She motioned for him to take a seat, then sat on the love seat opposite him. For a few seconds she said nothing as she drank in the sight of him.

"I missed you, Justin, and I'd be lying if I said that I wasn't glad to see you."

"I'm happy to hear that, because I missed you, too."

"*But*, there are issues that need to be settled between us."

He gave a troubled sigh, "Yes, there are."

"You hurt me, Justin. You hurt me badly, and after you promised me that your love would never hurt."

The words that she flung back at him tore at his soul. Tears stung his eyes. "I know, baby. I know. All I can say is that I'm sorry, and I know that's not enough. But I want to be back in your life, and I swear to you that what I did to you will never happen again."

"How do I know that? How do I know that the next time you don't get your way that you won't turn on me, disrespect me? There's no way that I'm going to take that from you."

"And you shouldn't take it from me or anyone else."

The room was silent for a moment as they studied one another, each filled with torrents of emotions that they could barely contain. The air was thick with need and desire.

Davia broke the silence. "I guess you're happy. You won in the end. You got what you wanted. You took the spotlight off of Vanessa and she was left out of it."

He moved from his seat to sit next to Davia. They'd had enough distance between them.

"I never thought of what I did as a game to win or lose, Davia. Cash's death *was* an accident. That's a fact. I didn't have a feeling of triumph when it was ruled as that, because a man was still dead. But do I regret that my sister didn't have to go through the trauma of being a suspect? No. And I won't apologize for that. She had gone through enough, and I don't regret anything that I did for her.

"But let me tell you what I do regret." Reaching out, he took Davia's hand in his and she didn't draw away. "I do regret what I said to you and what I did to you. I regret how I callously disregarded your love and your fear for me, and I regret treating you as badly as my mother has done. I know that I'm a better man than that, and I'm ashamed."

Davia agreed. "You're right on both accounts. I didn't deserve that."

"No, you didn't. Will you ever be able to forgive me?"

She was candid. "My love for you hasn't lessened, Justin, but my trust in you has been shaken."

Justin winced. "Then I regret that most of all, because I worked so hard to earn it." He swallowed the hurt that her words had caused. "I'm not perfect, Davia. If you thought that I was, then we were was in trouble from the start. It's worth everything to me to try and repair what we had together. I'm willing to work overtime if I have to. So I'm asking you, please forgive me and let me back into your heart."

"Like I said, you never left it," Davia assured him softly. "And I know that I'm far from perfect, too." Justin had dealt with all of those imperfections and helped her to find the strength to move forward. Together they had laid the foundation for a relationship that was a bit shaky at the present, but with time it could be strengthened and turned into a powerful force. "I'll tell you what. I'll clear my calendar for tomorrow if you'll do the same. We can spend the entire day together. We'll turn off every device that might distract us, and we'll talk."

For the first time since he had arrived at Davia's house, a smile crossed Justin's face. "I'll do that, and we'll listen to each other as well. With all of the secrets behind us, and the future ahead of us, there should be a lot to say."

Justin ran a finger slowly down her cheek, then tilted her chin upward so that he could look into her eyes. They held the invitation that he was seeking, and with that he gave into the urge that he had been fighting since he arrived. As he feasted on lips that he had sorely missed, he let his tongue linger in the areas that he had come to know intimately and explored those newly discovered.

Davia let him explore all that he wanted. How she had missed him. When they parted she gave him a warm smile.

"We'll take this thing slow and see how it works, and if it does, maybe one day I might make you a grandfather."

Justin grinned. "I'm looking forward to the experience. Who knows? This grandfather thing could turn out to be a whole lot of fun."

EPILOGUE

Two years and three months after the marriage of Davia and Justin Miles, little Fredrick David Justin Miles was born. Known as Davie, he and Gabby became the center of attention for the Miles family household

Davie's Aunt Vanessa and his cousin, Bianca, were frequent visitors to the Miles household, along with Mama Willa, Papa Josh, and a vast assortment of Johnson aunts, uncles and cousins from all over the country. The Justin Miles family welcomed them all.

Conspicuously absent from Davie's life was his grandmother, Katherine. She didn't attend his parents' small wedding. Justin had tried to keep in contact, but the relationship between mother and son had grown increasingly strained. It was a telephone call from Vanessa announcing the arrival of Katherine's first grandson that informed her of his birth. Justin sent her a picture of his curly-haired son, but it was returned unopened. She heard nothing further from her son.

It was a lazy Saturday afternoon, nine months after Davie's birth, when the doorbell to the Miles home rang. With her squirming son in her arms and Gabby close on her heels, Davia padded to the door in bare feet and bathrobe. She looked less than her best. Opening the door, she expected to see CeCe. The sight of Katherine standing in the doorway was quite a surprise.

A curious Gabby stepped forward. They had been expecting her Aunt CeCe and her husband, Uncle Clark. "Who's that, Grommy?"

Katherine looked from the beautiful little girl to the beautiful baby in Davia's arms.

Her stoic demeanor wavered. Staring back at her was a tiny replica of her beloved Zachary, with a chocolate brown complexion and a pair of startling gray-green eyes.

An exasperated Justin rounded the corner and entered the foyer. "Come on in here, you two. We've been . . ." He came to a sudden stop at the sight of Katherine. "Mother!"

Moving closer to his family, he placed his arms protectively around Davia. Gabby looked from Justin to the lady standing in the doorway. The lady looked as though she was about to cry.

"Who are you?" Gabby inquired.

Katherine looked from her son to the family standing before her. It was a gorgeous family, a strong family, comprised of a myriad of complexions. It was a new generation of Mileses.

She looked down at the little girl. "I'm his mother." She indicated Justin, "And if you're Gabby, I'm . . . your great-grandmother." She looked up at her son and daughter-in-law. "That is, if you want me to be."

Davia and Justin exchanged looks and then turned back to Katherine. The older woman stood tall, with her shoulders squared and her head unbowed. She would accept their rejection with dignity. Katherine Miles wasn't one to bend. Yet, her eyes pleaded for forgiveness. She had made a mistake and had paid dearly. Her relationship with her daughter was practically nonexistent, and she had completely alienated her son. Loneliness and regret had been poor substitutes for stubborn pride.

Neither Davia nor Justin questioned what had made this indomitable matriarch change her mind about their union. She was a proud woman, and they both knew that it had taken courage for her to come to their home. The Miles home was a happy one. It was a place that welcomed all who brought harmony. So, they opened their door and allowed Katherine Miles to step into a new beginning.

THE END

2010 Mass Market Titles

January

Show Me The Sun
Miriam Shumba
ISBN: 978-158571-405-6
$6.99

Promises of Forever
Celya Bowers
ISBN: 978-1-58571-380-6
$6.99

February

Love Out Of Order
Nicole Green
ISBN: 978-1-58571-381-3
$6.99

Unclear and Present Danger
Michele Cameron
ISBN: 978-158571-408-7
$6.99

March

Stolen Jewels
Michele Sudler
ISBN: 978-158571-409-4
$6.99

Not Quite Right
Tammy Williams
ISBN: 978-158571-410-0
$6.99

April

Oak Bluffs
Joan Early
ISBN: 978-1-58571-379-0
$6.99

Crossing The Line
Bernice Layton
ISBN: 978-158571-412-4
$6.99

How To Kill Your Husband
Keith Walker
ISBN: 978-158571-421-6
$6.99

May

The Business of Love
Cheris F. Hodges
ISBN: 978-158571-373-8
$6.99

Wayward Dreams
Gail McFarland
ISBN: 978-158571-422-3
$6.99

June

The Doctor's Wife
Mildred Riley
ISBN: 978-158571-424-7
$6.99

Mixed Reality
Chamein Canton
ISBN: 978-158571-423-0
$6.99

2010 Mass Market Titles (continued)
July

Blue Interlude
Keisha Mennefee
ISBN: 978-158571-378-3
$6.99

Always You
Crystal Hubbard
ISBN: 978-158571-371-4
$6.99

Unbeweavable
Katrina Spencer
ISBN: 978-158571-426-1
$6.99

August

Small Sensations
Crystal V. Rhodes
ISBN: 978-158571-376-9
$6.99

Let's Get It On
Dyanne Davis
ISBN: 978-158571-416-2
$6.99

September

Unconditional
A.C. Arthur
ISBN: 978-158571-413-1
$6.99

Swan
Africa Fine
ISBN: 978-158571-377-6
$6.99$6.99

October

Friends in Need
Joan Early
ISBN:978-1-58571-428-5
$6.99

Against the Wind
Gwynne Forster
ISBN:978-158571-429-2
$6.99

That Which Has Horns
Miriam Shumba
ISBN:978-1-58571-430-8
$6.99

November

A Good Dude
Keith Walker
ISBN:978-1-58571-431-5
$6.99

Reye's Gold
Ruthie Robinson
ISBN:978-1-58571-432-2
$6.99

December

Still Waters...
Crystal V. Rhodes
ISBN:978-1-58571-433-9
$6.99

Burn
Crystal Hubbard
ISBN: 978-1-58571-406-3
$6.99

Other Genesis Press, Inc. Titles

Other Genesis Press, Inc. Titles (continued)

Blood Seduction	J.M. Jeffries	$9.95
Bodyguard	Andrea Jackson	$9.95
Boss of Me	Diana Nyad	$8.95
Bound by Love	Beverly Clark	$8.95
Breeze	Robin Hampton Allen	$10.95
Broken	Dar Tomlinson	$24.95
By Design	Barbara Keaton	$8.95
Cajun Heat	Charlene Berry	$8.95
Careless Whispers	Rochelle Alers	$8.95
Cats & Other Tales	Marilyn Wagner	$8.95
Caught in a Trap	Andre Michelle	$8.95
Caught Up in the Rapture	Lisa G. Riley	$9.95
Cautious Heart	Cheris F. Hodges	$8.95
Chances	Pamela Leigh Starr	$8.95
Checks and Balances	Elaine Sims	$6.99
Cherish the Flame	Beverly Clark	$8.95
Choices	Tammy Williams	$6.99
Class Reunion	Irma Jenkins/	$12.95
	John Brown	
Code Name: Diva	J.M. Jeffries	$9.95
Conquering Dr. Wexler's	Kimberley White	$9.95
Heart		
Corporate Seduction	A.C. Arthur	$9.95
Crossing Paths,	Dorothy Elizabeth Love	$9.95
Tempting Memories		
Crush	Crystal Hubbard	$9.95
Cypress Whisperings	Phyllis Hamilton	$8.95
Dark Embrace	Crystal Wilson Harris	$8.95
Dark Storm Rising	Chinelu Moore	$10.95
Daughter of the Wind	Joan Xian	$8.95
Dawn's Harbor	Kymberly Hunt	$6.99
Deadly Sacrifice	Jack Kean	$22.95
Designer Passion	Dar Tomlinson	$8.95
	Diana Richeaux	
Do Over	Celya Bowers	$9.95
Dream Keeper	Gail McFarland	$6.99
Dream Runner	Gail McFarland	$6.99
Dreamtective	Liz Swados	$5.95
Ebony Angel	Deatri King-Bey	$9.95
Ebony Butterfly II	Delilah Dawson	$14.95
Echoes of Yesterday	Beverly Clark	$9.95
Eden's Garden	Elizabeth Rose	$8.95

Other Genesis Press, Inc. Titles (continued)

Eve's Prescription	Edwina Martin Arnold	$8.95
Everlastin' Love	Gay G. Gunn	$8.95
Everlasting Moments	Dorothy Elizabeth Love	$8.95
Everything and More	Sinclair Lebeau	$8.95
Everything But Love	Natalie Dunbar	$8.95
Falling	Natalie Dunbar	$9.95
Fate	Pamela Leigh Starr	$8.95
Finding Isabella	A.J. Garrotto	$8.95
Fireflies	Joan Early	$6.99
Fixin' Tyrone	Keith Walker	$6.99
Forbidden Quest	Dar Tomlinson	$10.95
Forever Love	Wanda Y. Thomas	$8.95
From the Ashes	Kathleen Suzanne Jeanne Sumerix	$8.95
Frost On My Window	Angela Weaver	$6.99
Gentle Yearning	Rochelle Alers	$10.95
Glory of Love	Sinclair LeBeau	$10.95
Go Gentle Into That Good Night	Malcom Boyd	$12.95
Goldengroove	Mary Beth Craft	$16.95
Groove, Bang, and Jive	Steve Cannon	$8.99
Hand in Glove	Andrea Jackson	$9.95
Hard to Love	Kimberley White	$9.95
Hart & Soul	Angie Daniels	$8.95
Heart of the Phoenix	A.C. Arthur	$9.95
Heartbeat	Stephanie Bedwell-Grime	$8.95
Hearts Remember	M. Loui Quezada	$8.95
Hidden Memories	Robin Allen	$10.95
Higher Ground	Leah Latimer	$19.95
Hitler, the War, and the Pope	Ronald Rychiak	$26.95
How to Write a Romance	Kathryn Falk	$18.95
I Married a Reclining Chair	Lisa M. Fuhs	$8.95
I'll Be Your Shelter	Giselle Carmichael	$8.95
I'll Paint a Sun	A.J. Garrotto	$9.95
Icie	Pamela Leigh Starr	$8.95
If I Were Your Woman	LaConnie Taylor-Jones	$6.99
Illusions	Pamela Leigh Starr	$8.95
Indigo After Dark Vol. I	Nia Dixon/Angelique	$10.95
Indigo After Dark Vol. II	Dolores Bundy/ Cole Riley	$10.95
Indigo After Dark Vol. III	Montana Blue/ Coco Morena	$10.95

Other Genesis Press, Inc. Titles (continued)

Other Genesis Press, Inc. Titles (continued)

Naked Soul	Gwynne Forster	$8.95
Never Say Never	Michele Cameron	$6.99
Next to Last Chance	Louisa Dixon	$24.95
No Apologies	Seressia Glass	$8.95
No Commitment Required	Seressia Glass	$8.95
No Regrets	Mildred E. Riley	$8.95
Not His Type	Chamein Canton	$6.99
Nowhere to Run	Gay G. Gunn	$10.95
O Bed! O Breakfast!	Rob Kuehnle	$14.95
Object of His Desire	A.C. Arthur	$8.95
Office Policy	A.C. Arthur	$9.95
Once in a Blue Moon	Dorianne Cole	$9.95
One Day at a Time	Bella McFarland	$8.95
One of These Days	Michele Sudler	$9.95
Outside Chance	Louisa Dixon	$24.95
Passion	T.T. Henderson	$10.95
Passion's Blood	Cherif Fortin	$22.95
Passion's Furies	AlTonya Washington	$6.99
Passion's Journey	Wanda Y. Thomas	$8.95
Past Promises	Jahmel West	$8.95
Path of Fire	T.T. Henderson	$8.95
Path of Thorns	Annetta P. Lee	$9.95
Peace Be Still	Colette Haywood	$12.95
Picture Perfect	Reon Carter	$8.95
Playing for Keeps	Stephanie Salinas	$8.95
Pride & Joi	Gay G. Gunn	$8.95
Promises Made	Bernice Layton	$6.99
Promises to Keep	Alicia Wiggins	$8.95
Quiet Storm	Donna Hill	$10.95
Reckless Surrender	Rochelle Alers	$6.95
Red Polka Dot in a World Full of Plaid	Varian Johnson	$12.95
Red Sky	Renee Alexis	$6.99
Reluctant Captive	Joyce Jackson	$8.95
Rendezvous With Fate	Jeanne Sumerix	$8.95
Revelations	Cheris F. Hodges	$8.95
Rivers of the Soul	Leslie Esdaile	$8.95
Rocky Mountain Romance	Kathleen Suzanne	$8.95
Rooms of the Heart	Donna Hill	$8.95
Rough on Rats and Tough on Cats	Chris Parker	$12.95
Save Me	Africa Fine	$6.99

Other Genesis Press, Inc. Titles (continued)

Other Genesis Press, Inc. Titles (continued)

Order Form

Mail to: Genesis Press, Inc.
P.O. Box 101
Columbus, MS 39703

Name _____
Address _____
City/State _____ Zip _____
Telephone _____

Ship to (if different from above)
Name _____
Address _____
City/State _____ Zip _____
Telephone _____

Credit Card Information
Credit Card # _____ ☐ Visa ☐ Mastercard
Expiration Date (mm/yy) _____ ☐ AmEx ☐ Discover

Qty.	Author	Title	Price	Total

Use this order form, or call 1-888-INDIGO-1

Total for books	_____

Shipping and handling:
  $5 first two books,
  $1 each additional book
	_____

Total S & H	_____
Total amount enclosed	_____

Mississippi residents add 7% sales tax

Visit www.genesis-press.com for latest releases and excerpts.